"Great," she muttered one more time.

Because Hazel would make do until something better came along. Beggars, as they said, couldn't be choosers.

A few minutes later, Wylie appeared wearing jeans and a green scrub shirt and carrying a balled-up bundle of clothes. He'd lost his ball cap and his black hair was a hot mess, sticking every which way.

Hazel had the strongest urge to smooth it back into place.

So inappropriate.

Wylie caught her staring and frowned. "You don't look happy."

She waved a hand in front of her face. "This is my tired-from-driving-all-day face." And then she blinked a few times, trying to reset her attitude before smiling as broadly as she could. "Better?"

He muttered something that sounded like *"Sour sweet tart."* And then he ran a hand through his black hair, not making the situation up top any better. "This is a busy practice and I...I need this to work."

"I intend to make you proud." And leave town as fast as possible when her time was through, if not sooner.

Her future, after all, lay elsewhere.

Dear Reader,

They say that life is a journey. If that's true, my personal journey has been anything but a straight line. And yet I always meet people who believe they can get from Point A to Point B without any obstacles, sidetracks or interruptions.

Journeys are what I was thinking about when I created Dr. Wylie Newland. He's ready to settle down and start having kids. And this small town veterinarian believes finding a lifelong partner will be straightforward. He's hired a matchmaker and taken on a veterinary resident so he has more free time to date. Enter Dr. Hazel Hughes, his resident. She's smart and attractive, with a dream of finding a more permanent position at an experimental animal-surgery center in England. Falling in love isn't in her life plan. But hearts have a way of complicating matters, making Wylie and Hazel's journey an entertaining one.

I hope you enjoy Wylie and Hazel's love story and come to love the cowboys and cowgirls of The Cowboy Academy series as much as I do.

Happy reading!

Melinda

COUNTRY FAIR COWBOY

MELINDA CURTIS

HEARTWARMING

If you purchased this book without a cover you should be aware that this book is stolen property. It was reported as "unsold and destroyed" to the publisher, and neither the author nor the publisher has received any payment for this "stripped book."

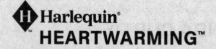

ISBN-13: 978-1-335-46007-3

Country Fair Cowboy

Copyright © 2025 by Melinda Wooten

All rights reserved. No part of this book may be used or reproduced in any manner whatsoever without written permission.

Without limiting the author's and publisher's exclusive rights, any unauthorized use of this publication to train generative artificial intelligence (AI) technologies is expressly prohibited.

This is a work of fiction. Names, characters, places and incidents are either the product of the author's imagination or are used fictitiously. Any resemblance to actual persons, living or dead, businesses, companies, events or locales is entirely coincidental.

For questions and comments about the quality of this book, please contact us at CustomerService@Harlequin.com.

TM and ® are trademarks of Harlequin Enterprises ULC.

Harlequin Enterprises ULC
22 Adelaide St. West, 41st Floor
Toronto, Ontario M5H 4E3, Canada
www.Harlequin.com

Printed in U.S.A.

Award-winning USA TODAY bestselling author **Melinda Curtis**, when not writing romance, can be found working on a fixer-upper she and her husband purchased in Oregon's Willamette Valley. Although this is the third home they've lived in and renovated (in three different states), it's not a job for the faint of heart. But it's been a good metaphor for book writing, as sometimes you have to tear things down to the bare bones to find the core beauty and potential. In between—and during—renovations, Melinda has written over forty books for Harlequin, including her Heartwarming book *Dandelion Wishes*, which is now a TV movie, *Love in Harmony Valley*, starring Amber Marshall.

Brenda Novak says *Season of Change* "found a place on my keeper shelf."

Books by Melinda Curtis

Harlequin Heartwarming

The Cowboy Academy

A Cowboy Worth Waiting For
A Cowboy's Fourth of July
A Cowboy Christmas Carol
A Cowboy for the Twins
The Rodeo Star's Reunion
Cowboy Santa
The Cowboy's Wedding Proposal

The Blackwell Belles

A Cowboy Never Forgets

Visit the Author Profile page
at Harlequin.com for more titles.

To those who fall in love at the wrong place,
in the wrong time and with the wrong person.
I hope you navigate your way to a happily-ever-after.

PROLOGUE

"Nicely done, Dr. Hughes."

"Thank you." Dr. Hazel Hughes knotted the last suture on the palomino mare's back and let loose a smile. "Dr. Reed, you're the cheese that makes my macaroni special."

On the surgical platform on the other side of the horse, Dr. Reed sighed.

Not everyone appreciated Hazel's upbeat bedside manner.

As her mentor professor, the brilliant, yet stoic, Dr. Reed was a blessing to Hazel even if she sometimes tried his patience. He'd taught her how to perform many advanced and experimental procedures, including this relatively new one—*interspinous ligament desmotomy*, the delicate removal of bony protrusions on a horse's spine. Those abnormal growths made it painful to carry a saddle, much less a rider.

Hazel removed her surgical gloves and mask, then gave the mare a pat on her golden-colored neck. "Sunshine, I couldn't ask for a better patient.

Of course, it's easy to be good when you have the best surgical team." Hazel made a hand heart, holding it over her chest and keeping it there for the staff to see that she appreciated them.

"Dr. Hughes, what have I told you about surgery theater decorum?" Dr. Reed may have been cheese to Hazel's macaroni, but he always encouraged her to cook at a lower heat. "We have a professional standard to uphold at this university."

Especially for the first-year veterinary students in the viewing theater, the ones now making hand hearts to the surgical team.

"Message received, Dr. Reed." Yet, Hazel couldn't stop smiling. When she left the university in three months, she was hopeful her upbeat slant on professional demeanor would be part of her legacy here. The stress of veterinary school, or life for that matter, needed a relief valve. Hazel's valve had taken the form of her sunny, if sometimes cheeky, disposition.

"Isn't today Match Day?" Tony, the vet tech, asked. He placed a bandage over Sunshine's stitches. "Kudos to you, Dr. Hughes. You seem really chill."

Smile falling, Hazel managed to nod. It was the third Monday in March. She'd been able to forget the date during surgery. But now…

Match Day. The one day that veterinary students across the country both looked forward to and dreaded. The day when veterinary students were matched with their residency assignments.

Placement wasn't just a matter of writing a stellar résumé, providing outstanding referrals, or nailing that all-important interview. Veterinary students also had to submit rankings of their preferred assignments from among those clinics and hospitals that showed interest. While those same institutions, in turn, submitted rankings of applicants they preferred.

And then all that ranking information went into a little black box that used an algorithm to spit out residency assignments, inside and outside the United States.

Hazel had her heart set on a prestigious surgery center in Newmarket, England. But so did hundreds of other candidates. And they were only accepting three residents.

Nerves about Match Day returned by way of unsteady knees, replacing the natural high from a successful procedure.

Hazel descended the surgical platform, taking careful hold of the guardrail.

Did I do enough to land the overseas residency? Am I in the top three?

Hazel knew she was in their consideration set because she'd been asked to interview. She hadn't wanted to apply anywhere else, but Dr. Reed had advised her not to put all her eggs in one basket. He'd convinced her to apply to a few other surgery centers, plus a small clinic run by one of his former protégés in Oklahoma.

Hazel had raised her brows at that last request.
Surgical protégés lived in Kentucky, California, or New York. Not Oklahoma.

But by that time last fall, she'd just wanted to make her mentor professor happy and focus on December finals.

Hazel walked with Dr. Reed to the sink to wash up, barely keeping herself from bolting to the locker room for her phone to find out where she'd been placed...or *if* she'd been placed. But Dr. Reed's professional standards, not to mention her nerve-weakened knees, kept her from doing so.

"I hope you'll be happy wherever you land," Dr. Reed said evenly. He was a tall man of few words. And when he chose to speak, Hazel always listened. "You're a skilled veterinarian with your entire career ahead of you."

The way he's talking...
Newmarket didn't choose me.
But...

Hazel's chest felt like it was caving inward, cinched by ever-tightening bands of stress that made her feel small.

He couldn't know if I got it or not.

The board only notified candidates and their new bosses of placements, not professors.

"It's almost prophetic," Dr. Reed continued as if unaware of her inner turmoil. "You'd be surprised at how many students come here with a concrete dream regarding a specialty only to find their journey takes them in a different direction on Match Day." He moved aside from the sink, using paper towels to dry his hands.

Oh, this was a message, all right. A bad one.

Hazel swallowed thickly. "These students... They... They settle?"

"That's very glass half-empty." Dr. Reed's tone gave nothing away. It was his words that were demoralizing. "It's more like a horizon they hadn't seen before finally comes into view and things fall into place."

"Are we talking in specifics or hypotheticals?" Hazel moved to the sink, filling her palms with antibacterial soap and lathering up, trying to ignore the ominous pressure in her chest that foretold of failure.

Smile and focus on the mundane.

The cold water on her hands. The silky soap slipping between her fingers. The rhythm of proper handwashing—across around, across around the other side.

"I was disappointed on Match Day," Dr. Reed admitted, with what might have been sorrow in his eyes. "I set my heart on the best equine surgery center in Kentucky and I didn't get it."

And he's brilliant.

Hazel's heart leaped into her throat, sticking there like a mis-swallowed vitamin.

The water gushed over her soapy hands but she clasped them together rather than rubbing them clean. "You… You say that like you know where I've been matched."

Like you know I'm not going to Newmarket, England.

Behind them, the palomino mare shifted, shod hooves stamping on concrete.

Immediately, the staff sought to soothe her.

"Could someone…" Hazel turned, reaching for a pleasant smile and a kind voice, perhaps not succeeding at either. She tried again. "Could someone administer another dose of local anesthetic, please?" And then Hazel quickly finished washing and drying her hands, all while Dr. Reed watched her.

Unnerving, that.

Can he see I'm nervous?

"Maybe we should talk about Match Day further," Hazel said evenly, smiling only a little.

Dr. Reed nodded. "And in private."

More confused than ever, Hazel followed Dr. Reed out of the surgery theater and down the hall toward his office, which was in the opposite direction of the lockers and her phone.

Is he saying I'm not good enough to be an elite surgeon?

Hazel had always known what she wanted to do with her life—heal animals. She'd been raised by a doctor and a veterinarian, after all. Both general practitioners. But she'd set her sights on being a veterinary surgeon. And those jobs... They were few and far between, requiring the best of schools, the best of students, the best of residencies.

Maybe I'm not the best. Maybe Newmarket recognized that. Maybe they didn't like my unusual educational path—me taking a gap year, my studies of alternative veterinary medicine, the vet school transfer. Maybe they didn't like...me.

Dr. Reed continued his silent, straightforward march.

Behind him, Hazel fell into an inner doom spiral.

Maybe I've done something to be washed out of the program altogether. Maybe Dr. Reed found out I performed postsurgical acupuncture on a stallion last month. Maybe the dean found out I used his parking space while he was on his honeymoon last week.

Dr. Reed ushered Hazel into his office and closed the door behind them, gesturing for her to sit. She'd seen happier expressions on funeral ushers.

Feeling faint, Hazel sank into a chair.

Dr. Reed sat behind his big oak desk, still looking somber. "I know this is unorthodox but... I heard from the clinic you've been matched with earlier today."

"At least... At least, I was matched." Some vet students weren't assigned on the first day. Hazel kept a smile on her face, trying to swallow the lump still wedged in her throat. "What's wrong? Something must be or we wouldn't be having this conversation."

"It's not all bad. You've been matched with my protégé's clinic in Oklahoma."

Not Newmarket, England?

Clearly, Dr. Reed had no idea what Hazel's version of bad was. For Hazel, this was devastating. Oklahoma was death to a surgery career.

Her mentor cleared his throat. "I know this is disappointing but…"

Blood roared in her ears.

Hazel didn't hear anything else Dr. Reed had to say.

CHAPTER ONE

It was a hot and dusty Monday afternoon in June when Hazel pulled her horse trailer into the cracked asphalt parking lot at the Clementine Veterinary Clinic.

Hazel took one look at her new digs in Clementine, Oklahoma, and considered heading back the way she'd come.

It's just like Mom's clinic outside of Bakersfield—a dead end.

The two-story building was a dingy white beneath a coating of dust. The windows dull and dirty. The clinic's plastic sign hanging over the door was cracked. An outdated gray sedan with a dented rear bumper was parked in a handicapped spot. There was a small red SUV parked near the door and a big, black truck parked further back.

Overall, it had an air of neglect and despair, as if it was one bad week away from calling it quits.

This can't be where I'm meant to be.

Hazel parked her rig and entered the clinic, triggering a bell over the door. Not an electric bell. A real one. Very old-school.

"Have a seat, Laramie," a brusque female voice called from somewhere down the hallway.

"I'm not a client," Hazel mumbled, glancing around the waiting room.

A church pew bench sat beneath the front window. A small table with pamphlets touting pet insurance policies had been set up near the check-in desk. Bulletin boards flanked either side of the entry. One seemed reserved for pet announcements—lost, found, up for sale, or adoption. The other featured photographs of patients—from sheep to German shepherds, from Labradors to llamas, from horses to hamsters.

Hamsters? What's next? Goldfish?

Hazel continued her inspection, moving to a wall with framed memorabilia.

A small photograph of a cowboy astride a tall bay caught her eye. That man looked like the descendant of cowboys who'd crisscrossed the West—broad shoulders, strong chin, clothes seemingly dust-covered. He was chasing down a steer, a lariat circling over his head, his face partially obscured by his hat brim. Another photo featured a long row of mounted cowboys, young and fresh-faced beneath a sign arching over a dirt-and-gravel road—*Done Roamin' Ranch*. The largest frames held a diploma and a veterinary medicine license for Dr. Wylie Newland, a.k.a. Dr. Reed's protégé and Hazel's new boss, a man she'd only seen once in a dimly-lit video interview. A man who hadn't resembled a cowboy of any sort.

The floor was a scuffed, discouraging gray linoleum. A sign on the check-in desk announced it had been three days since a pet had pooped in the lobby. The record was seven.

"The record would be longer if there was grass out front," Hazel muttered. Everyone, excluding so-called protégés in Oklahoma, should know that nervous animals need a moment outside before an exam.

Hazel sank deeper into dejection.

She came around the check-in desk and took a seat behind the counter.

The view wasn't much better from there.

Appointments were recorded on a paper calendar—*paper?*—the same way they'd been in the dark ages before computers. The beige telephone only had one line and no hold button. A dusty message recorder connected to the phone had a blinking light indicating unanswered messages. Patient folders were stacked on both sides of the desk proper, framing a blotter covered in flowery doodles and jotted notes.

I've stepped into a time machine.

The surgery facilities were bound to be disappointing.

Hazel scrubbed her hands over her face.

"You're not Laramie." A short, elderly woman

with white hair and an expression as wrinkled as a bulldog glared at Hazel. She was dressed to sit in her backyard—oversize gray T-shirt touting a decades-old county fair, khaki shorts, orthopedic sandals. "And you're sitting in my seat."

Behind the clinic's guard dog, a teenage girl held a small carrier with a tiny orange kitten.

Hazel stood, giving them an obligatory smile. "Hi, I'm Dr. Hughes."

"I don't care if you're Doctor Dolittle. You don't sit in my seat!" The heat of the bulldog's glare intensified.

So much for a warm welcome.

Hazel moved out from behind the counter. "Where is Dr. Newland?"

"Out on a call." The battle-ax took her seat behind the counter. Her short white hair was thin on top. What she was missing in follicles, she made up for in grouchiness. "Name's Maisey. This here is Lulu."

"Hi, Lulu." Hazel smiled at the teen.

"I'm Nancy." The teen smirked, but it was a commiserative kind of smirk. "Lulu is my kitten."

"We identify clients we treat, not their humans," Maisey explained, in a superior tone. "Might do things a bit differently than they do at your fancy university."

"I can see that." If the old woman was trying to put Hazel in her place, she'd have to try harder. Hazel was used to professors who didn't give an ounce of respect until their students earned it. But she was also used to winning them over with her knowledge and never-ending positivity.

A man entered the clinic. Tall. Muscular. Older than Hazel but not old, per se. Face a set of hard angles that made his green eyes glitter. Black hair mostly covered by a ratty baseball cap with a tractor logo. He wore a green T-shirt and blue jeans, both bloodstained. His muck boots looked like they'd seen the inside of a deep and muddy paddock.

This couldn't be her new boss. During their video interview, that man had worn a cheap suit and tie. On screen, he'd looked washed out and closer to forty than this man.

Hazel's gaze flickered toward the photograph of the roping cowboy on the wall and then back to this newcomer. The Dr. Newland she'd met online hadn't looked like he was the proud, strong descendent of the cowboys who'd crisscrossed the West. But this man... This man did.

He closed the door behind him, stare connecting with Hazel's as if she was the only person in the room who mattered.

Oh, my. Oh-my-oh-my-oh-my.

Hazel's heart beat faster, her mouth went dry, and her mind went blank. She felt like the time she'd been sixteen and Tommy Verdugo—high school senior, homecoming king, and star quarterback—

had noticed she was alive. She'd been frozen silent then. She was frozen silent now.

"Dr. Hughes, I presume. We expected you yesterday." The man came forward, large hand extended. "I'm Dr. Wylie Newland. Nice to meet you in person. You can call me Wylie." His hand encompassed hers. Strong. Calloused. Shocking.

He'd hold me breathlessly close. He'd kiss with devastating command.

Hazel yanked her hand back from his and shoved unexpected attraction to a dark corner of her mind as she tried to channel the professional tone Dr. Reed lived by. "Yes. I'm Dr. Hughes. A flat tire delayed me. Didn't you get my message? I left one on your answering machine." When Wylie and Maisey exchanged knowing glances, Hazel hurried to add, "I'm Hazel to my friends and colleagues."

"She's trouble," Maisey snapped before turning her attention to Nancy and the orange kitten. "We take cash or check. Plastic may be convenient to you but not to me."

Nancy handed Maisey a wad of bills without looking surprised.

But Hazel... Hazel was stunned. Her jaw dropped. "We don't accept—"

"Let me show you around, Hazel." Wylie didn't wait for Hazel to agree. He headed toward the back of the clinic, walking down a hallway lined with windows facing the parking lot.

Despite Wylie's exasperating interruption, a reel of him riding on horseback and twirling a lasso kept playing on repeat in her brain.

Stop it.

This man and this place weren't for her. Hazel had put the word out that she was still looking for a surgery center position. There was always a chance that a resident would be unhappy where they'd been assigned and she could go elsewhere.

"Since the last time we talked in any depth was your interview in November," Wylie was saying, "I'll give you a quick tour. I run an expanding operation with two exam rooms and a mobile unit for ranch calls." He gestured toward the open exam rooms as they passed. Nothing extraordinary about them. Then he opened a third door that revealed the heart of the clinic—a large room lined with cupboards, their counters filled with scientific equipment. "You'll find my lab is fully equipped."

How a practice was stocked and managed said a lot more about the veterinarian who owned it than his heart-pounding presence. The bulldog and her antique methods said one thing. And this room… This room said another.

I'm in love.

With Wylie's lab.

A refrigerator and a locked case full of medicine flanked a closed door on one end. A hallway branched off the room with animal cages attached to the wall. The kennel ended at a doorway marked

Exit. There were no windows but the overhead lights made it as bright as a sunny day. And those lights glimmered on shiny, scientific equipment. Lots and lots of apparatuses that drew her forward.

"Now, this is what I'm talking about." Hazel was itching to explore the content in the cupboards, if only to see what other medical goodies lay in their depths. One particular piece caught her eye. "Is that a portable ultrasound?"

"I may be a rural vet but I don't use antique tools." Wylie gave her a careful smile. "The cages over there have our day surgery patients."

Handwritten index cards were clipped to the two occupied cages. A yellow Labrador puppy and a fluffy gray cat stared at them with the sleepy eyes of the recently sedated.

"You performed surgery this morning?" Hazel didn't even try to hide her enthusiasm.

He nodded, smile growing. "Nothing fancy. Neutering and tooth extraction. Our surgery room for small animals is through here." Wylie opened the door between the refrigerator and medicine cabinet.

Hazel slipped past him into the small animal surgery, taking stock. The room smelled like it had been cleaned top-to-bottom with a bucket of disinfectant. *Good.* It was well-lit and surprisingly well-outfitted—a large operating table, anesthesia cart, vital signs monitor, surgical microscope, X-ray machine, plus a variety of equipment stored on shelves. *Even better.* "I bet it's not a burden to perform surgery in here."

And wasn't that a relief?

"You seem surprised," Wylie said slowly. "Didn't Dr. Reed tell you that I enjoy surgery and perform a variety of procedures?"

"No." She turned to face Wylie, once again struck by his good looks. "I assumed..."

Expression hardening, Wylie crossed his arms over his chest. "You assumed that since this is a rural practice that we focus on inoculations and neutering, sending more complicated procedures to larger practices."

"Well... Yes." Hazel shrugged. There was no point in lying. "I grew up in a practice just like this."

"Did you? Well, my business is split fifty-fifty between large and small animals and serves clients in a fifty-mile radius." Wylie's aloof stare would have done Dr. Reed proud. "There's an area in back for standing livestock surgeries, plus paddocks for recovery. I've done everything from ACL procedures to cancer operations to laparoscopic surgeries. About 40-percent of my caseload involves surgery. And do you know why it's so high?" Wylie lost his detachment. He was practically breathing fire—green eyes flashing, deep voice rising.

And I'm here for it.

Or Hazel would have been had Wylie not been her boss.

"Because out *here*," Wylie continued, in an impassioned tone, "farmers and ranchers will do anything to keep operating costs low. They inoculate their own stock. They treat minor abrasions and infections themselves. And when they do call me? It's only when they haven't encountered that illness before, or the animal is too unruly for them to manage safely, or whatever is wrong is too serious, and beyond their skill level to treat." The hard look Wylie gave Hazel implied he wouldn't be surprised if it was beyond hers.

"I'm sorry." Hazel backpedaled, the persistent, internal purr of attraction silenced by his disdain. "I'll own my ignorance on your small-town clinic." And her disrespect. "Just so you know, I had my heart set on a residency at a full-time, experimental surgery hospital. But I'm sure I have a lot to learn from you and your diversity of patient cases." Hazel backpedaled right into a healthy serving of humble pie. And then she topped her apology off with a peacemaking smile.

Wylie was just as much a hard sell as Dr. Reed had been. He stared at her in silence, expression still oozing disdain.

"Can we start this conversation one more time? I'll go first." Hazel cleared her throat and then proceeded as if he'd agreed to a do-over. "Dr. Newland, you have a progressive setup here, one that I admire. I'd heard small-town practices are changing for the better and you've proven that point.

I'm so happy to be your resident." And then Hazel smiled. She smiled hard.

And she imagined she'd be smiling with unbreakable intensity until her quest to win Dr. Wylie Newland over succeeded. Professionally, that is.

"You'll get plenty of opportunities to conduct surgery here," Wylie grudgingly assured Hazel. "Especially since I know of your interest."

"Thank you. I'm grateful for the opportunity." But if they talked like this any longer, it was going to get awkward. Hazel turned to something she'd been hesitating to bring up. "I brought a horse with me. One I'm rehabbing. Budge is a rescue and I'd like to keep him close. Is there a boarding stable somewhere nearby?"

"No. Folks around here who own horses also have enough land to keep them on." Wylie sounded relieved that the subject had changed. "If he's still in need of critical care, you can put him in a paddock out back. If not, you can keep him at my place."

"The paddock here will suit us." Hazel didn't want to intrude on Wylie's goodwill, not to mention she didn't want to spend more time in the magnetic glow of his presence at his home.

"Let me show you where you'll be staying." Wylie led her back into the main hallway overlooking the parking lot. Then he opened a door with a sign designating it Private, revealing a flight of steps. "The upstairs apartment runs the length of the clinic. You'll share it with Maisey."

"Great." So much for thinking free rent was a consolation prize to Newmarket. "Maisey is a gem."

Wylie paused mid-step, glancing back at Hazel with those green eyes that seemed to see everything negative about her. "Maisey may have a few rough edges but she's a good vet tech and she's been here since my father opened the clinic. She's earned her place here."

And I haven't earned mine.

"I didn't mean..." Hazel stopped. Apologized. Put on that you-can't-upset-me smile while making a mental note about Wylie's boundaries and hot buttons. "I'm not normally sarcastic."

"Time will be the judge of that." She hadn't won him over.

Yikes. Hazel regrouped. "Under normal circumstances, some might call me too positive." Like Dr. Reed. "When I was a kid, my dad used to joke that I could find the humor in a broken pencil, even if it was pointless."

Ba-da-bah.

"Dad jokes. Hmm." Wylie's disapproving expression cracked. Seemingly placated, he continued upstairs. "Sorry about the shattered dream of being a full-time surgeon."

"I like to think of it as a delayed, not a shattered,

dream." She had to keep holding out hope, or she'd lose what little good humor she had left.

Wylie reached the second-floor landing and turned to look down on her. "I hope you brought appropriate attire because..." He tugged on his stained T-shirt. "I'd hate you to ruin those fancy clothes of yours."

"I wear scrub tops, if that's what you mean." Nor were her white tank top and tan breeches fancy.

Regardless, Wylie nodded and moved out of her way.

Hazel reached the top of the stairs and took in her residency accommodations.

The second story was an open floor plan with hardwood floors. A galley kitchen was next to a small dining area that flowed toward a living room. Everything was outdated. The white microwave operated on a dial rather than a digital keyboard. The living room furniture was an uninspiring army green with cushions that sagged. A beige landline phone with a long, twisted cord hung on a wall, while a decades-old television—an oblong box, not a flat-screen model—sat on a sturdy TV stand. The window coverings were thin, slatted blinds, all closed, making the space feel unwelcoming.

Kind of like Maisey.

"It's...*great*." Hazel searched very hard for something else positive to say. "My grandparents used to have a phone like this." She took hold of the tangled cord and gave it a twirl, like a lasso spinning just above the floor. "Gives me a feeling of nostalgia."

"Me, too," Wylie said gruffly. He pivoted, pointing out four closed doors near the top of the stairs. "Maisey's room. Bathroom. Coat closet. Your room."

Hazel opened the door to her bedroom. It was surprisingly large and contained a full-size bed, a wide dresser, and a small desk beneath a south-facing window. The blinds had been pulled up, making it feel more welcoming.

Something moved in the corner, something on a dog bed and beneath a bunched-up, fuzzy gray blanket bathed in sunlight from the window. A small, pointed nose and tiny pair of bulbous eyes moved to the edge of the blanket and peeked at Hazel. A soft grumble filled the air.

"Fluffy," Wylie said in a voice just as displeased. *"No."*

Fluffy retracted her head back like a turtle, disappearing completely beneath the gray blanket.

"I bet Fluffy's a character." Just like Maisey. "I'm sure we'll get along great."

Fluffy growled her disagreement.

Hazel came to stand next to Wylie.

"I'll have Maisey move Fluffy's dog bed into her bedroom." He stared across the living room toward a door on the far side of the apartment.

"What's over there?" Hazel asked.

"My father's office. He used it when he was

alive. If you'll excuse me, I keep a change of clothes in here." Wylie opened what turned out to be a small closet, grabbed some items, and then disappeared into the bathroom.

He's going to change his clothes now? In there?

Hazel scurried back into her bedroom, trying not to imagine her boss's muscular, bare chest.

Fluffy groused but didn't show herself.

"Great. This place is...*great*." Hazel inspected the narrow closet on the other side of the bed from the unhappy dog. "Great," she repeated.

Or it would have been great if not for the part about sharing an apartment with the ray of diluted sunshine that was Maisey and her equally unfriendly canine. Or if she hadn't been attracted to her boss and he didn't make a habit of changing in her bathroom.

"Great," she muttered one more time.

Because Hazel would make do until something better came along. Beggars, as they said, couldn't be choosers.

A few minutes later, Wylie appeared wearing clean jeans, a wrinkled green scrub shirt, and carrying a balled-up bundle of dirty clothes. He'd lost his ball cap and his black hair was a hot mess, sticking every which way.

Hazel had the strongest urge to smooth it back into place.

So inappropriate.

Wylie caught her staring and frowned. "You don't look happy."

She waved a hand in front of her face. "This is my tired-from-driving-all-day face." And then she blinked a few times, trying to reset her attitude before smiling as broadly as she could. "Better?"

He muttered something that sounded like, *"Not normally sarcastic?"* And then he ran a hand through his black hair, not making the situation up top any better. "This is a busy practice and I… I need this to work."

"I intend to make you proud." And leave town as fast as possible when her time was through, if not sooner.

Her future, after all, lay elsewhere.

Thomas Reed sent me a princess.

After showing Hazel where the paddocks were, Wylie went to the front desk to retrieve the file for Austin Dodger's breeding stallion. He needed to fill out the details of the stud's injury and treatment in the chart. Earlier today, a cat had spooked the stallion. The stud had bolted into a barbed wire fence, creating a series of nasty lacerations that had required stitches, antibiotics, and a mild sedative.

But instead of heading to the lab to do his work, Wylie stopped at the last window in the hallway facing the parking lot while Hazel walked toward her rig.

Why did I tell her that's Dad's office upstairs?

He never went into his father's old office, not even to change clothes. It was just...a room no one entered anymore. It must have been her reference to dad jokes.

Outside, Hazel opened the back of her horse trailer.

On the surface, Hazel looked like the kind of woman Wylie wanted to date. She was pretty. Her waves of strawberry blond hair fell over her shoulders in a kaleidoscope of red, orange, and yellow hues. And her eyes... They shone with intelligence and were a distinct shade of gray that reminded him of the purple-slate color of winter dusk.

I can't believe I'm analyzing my employee's appearance.

Wylie rubbed his furrowed brow.

Dr. Reed is wrong. This isn't going to work.

Hazel was too elegant. Too filled with ambition. Too...too...

Too much like Tabitha.

Wylie rubbed his brow harder. Hazel was nothing like his ex-fiancée.

Hazel presented herself like a dressage rider—tan riding breeches tucked into her spotless muck boots, white tank top clinging to intriguing curves. All she needed was a helmet, English riding boots, and a close-fitting riding jacket and she'd be ready to enter the dressage competition ring. This was ranching and rodeo territory. His clients were going to take one look at her and...

Not treat Hazel like an experienced vet. They'd second-guess her decisions. They'd call Wylie for reassurance that Hazel knew what she was doing. They might even reject her services. Instead of freeing up his schedule, Hazel might be creating more demands on him and his time.

Wylie sighed. This was a complication he hadn't anticipated.

He knew Hazel was smart, top of her class. When he'd interviewed her back in November, she'd impressed him with her knowledge and sweet, mellow demeanor. She'd answered his questions succinctly, getting right to the point. And she'd had her hair pulled back and worn a suit jacket, looking like the consummate professional Dr. Reed preferred to take under his wing. Wylie had expected a studious nerd who would sink into the woodwork.

Wrong!

Of course, back when he'd interviewed Hazel, Wylie had been awake for three solid days, busy handling one calving emergency after another. Worn out, he'd dutifully stuffed himself into the one dress shirt, tie, and suit jacket he owned minutes before the video call and worked hard to keep himself from yawning. If he'd been on his game, he might have noticed that Hazel was all wrong for his practice.

Now, his resident slowly backed a raw-boned chestnut out of her one-horse trailer. The gelding's ribs were showing and he walked on his heel bulbs because his hooves were overgrown in front. His slow, wooden gait resembled that of an unsteady equine Frankenstein. Most folks would look at a horse like that and put him down.

But not Hazel.

Wylie's respect for her rose several notches. Humans who rescued abused animals were good people. But being a good person didn't necessarily mean she was the right veterinarian to work for him.

Wylie needed someone who could satisfy his clients right away. Because this was the summer that he was going to find a soul mate. Someone to share his life with. Not that he had anyone specific in mind. But he had an image in his head of the kind of woman he'd fall in love with and he'd hired Ronnie Keller, the local matchmaker, to make sure this was the last summer he spent alone.

Hazel led the chestnut slowly toward the paddocks. She talked to the horse nearly nonstop, gesturing with her hands and smiling, as if the gelding were a close confidant.

Wylie leaned forward, trying to hear what Hazel was saying. But she was talking too softly to eavesdrop and then they disappeared around the corner. Disappointed, he turned toward the lab.

I should make sure she has everything she needs back there.

Wylie frowned. Hazel would know her way

around a paddock, including how to open a gate and fill a watering trough. Fawning over her wasn't going to free up his time.

Wylie entered the lab and set the stallion's folder on the counter where he usually filled out his case notes. But his attention wasn't on his last patient. He was curious about Hazel and the chestnut gelding.

A soft whine from the indoor kennels had him moving to check on his surgery patients. This morning, he'd neutered Chipper, a yellow Labrador. The well-behaved pup rested his paw on the wire door, as if asking to be released.

"Your family will be here soon, Chipper." Wylie stroked his velvety paw before checking the card on the kennel where Maisey had written the puppy's vitals while he'd been gone. "Looks like you can go home with a cone of pride." Not shame. There was no shame in being neutered.

Several cages away, the gray cat panted in her kennel.

Wylie opened her door and reached in to gently pluck her skin to check for dehydration.

Gracie bit him for his troubles. Or rather, gummed him, almost immediately flinching back as if the action hurt her more than him.

"I suppose I deserve that, Gracie." He'd extracted ten of the feline's diseased teeth this morning, including her fang-like canines up front. He closed the door and returned a few minutes later with a small syringe filled with water. He eased the tip of the syringe into her mouth and slowly encouraged her to drink. "There's water in your cage for a reason, girl."

When Wylie was through getting water in her, he gave the cat a gentle scratch behind the ears. Just tending to the animals made him feel more grounded, less rattled by the confounding presence of Dr. Hazel Hughes.

The door to the outside facilities opened and Hazel entered, just as Maisey poked her head into the lab from the hallway. "Laramie is in room one. Should I get *her* to do the exam?"

Wylie was caught in between the two women. He looked from one to the other.

Hazel walked past Wylie at the cat cage. "If by *her*, you mean me, Miss Maisey, I'm right here. Ready to work." She wore that easygoing smile Wylie was becoming familiar with.

Tabitha's smile had never been easygoing.

Wylie rolled his shoulders back and tried to return Hazel's smile in kind. "Why don't you take the lead on this one, Hazel? It's a good way to get familiar with the practice."

"Great." That seemed to be Hazel's most frequently used word. "Where's Laramie's chart, Miss Maisey? What's the reason for the visit? Did you take his vitals?"

Maisey wasn't swayed by Hazel's smile. She looked down her nose at their newest staff member and said, "When Dr. Newland told you to take the lead, he meant from start to finish."

"Maisey," Wylie warned, suddenly recalling how uncooperative she'd been when he and Tabitha had first taken over the practice after his father's death.

"What a great idea, Miss Maisey." Hazel smiled as if Maisey's bad mood couldn't touch her. "We need to learn to trust one another. And being able to cover for a team member start-to-finish is a great way to establish that faith. Thank you." Hazel left the room with measured steps, her optimism firmly in place.

Wylie gave his vet tech a long-suffering look. "Do we have to make this difficult?"

"You can't just open the practice to any Tom, Dick, or Hazel." Maisey snorted, straightening her gray T-shirt. "If this city slicker can't prove herself, you'll be thanking me for running her off."

"Oh, she'll prove herself and…" Wylie didn't know how to complete that sentence. He frowned. "If anything, Hazel is overqualified for this practice."

He and Maisey stared at each other in silence, probably thinking the same thing: *Like Tabitha was overqualified for this practice.*

Wylie left the lab, putting bittersweet thoughts of his former fiancée out of his mind.

Ahead of him, Hazel stood in the hallway as if collecting her thoughts. Then she opened the door to exam room one, that determined smile stuck on her face.

"Hi. I'm Dr. Hughes." She paused in the doorway, as if rattled. But only for a moment. And then, Hazel entered the exam room and shut the door behind her.

Leaving Wylie, who couldn't remember why Laramie had an appointment, standing outside in the hallway, hesitating to go in after her.

HAZEL STOOD JUST inside exam room one, complaints about territorial vet techs and good-looking, brooding bosses fleeing her head.

A little girl of about seven or eight with white-blond pigtails and a tear-stained face sat in the visitor's chair. She held a very large gray tabby in her lap.

One of the cat's ears was inflamed and tattered. The top of his head was an engorged pus-depository. And one of his eyes was nearly swollen shut.

A wisp of a woman with the same white-blond hair as the little girl pushed away from the wall she'd been leaning on. Her straw cowboy hat sat atop a brown purse on the floor next to the visitor's chair. "Hello. I'm Izzy and this is my daughter, Della-Mae."

"I'm sorry to have kept you waiting." Hazel used her softest voice, the one she reserved for skittish animals and very young, very scared animal owners. "I can see right away that Laramie's been in a fight." Hazel kneeled down in front of the little girl and carefully extended her hand toward the tomcat, who was purring up a storm. When she wasn't hissed at, scratched, or bitten, Hazel stroked the cat's dull, greasy fur. "He's got a good purr-motor, doesn't he?"

"He purrs all the time," Della-Mae said in a young, loyal tone of voice. "Especially during snuggles."

"Some cats purr both when they're happy and when they're sad," Hazel told her.

Wylie entered the room with a nod to Laramie's two-legged family. Then he went to the small counter and retrieved a stethoscope, possibly recognizing that Hazel hadn't unpacked hers yet.

"Thank you, Dr. Newland." Hazel was all about appearing to be one of the proverbial team and she was rewarded with a small smile from Wylie for her efforts.

Wylie should smile more often, just not while I'm in the midst of an exam.

Hazel eased her fingers deeper into Laramie's thick, gray fur, searching for other wounds. He was hot, most likely feverish, and had several scars, most likely from previous altercations. "When did he get in this fight?"

"We're not sure," Izzy said, a bit sheepishly. "He's been missing for a few days."

"Cats sometimes want to lick their wounds in

private." Hazel checked the feline's paws next, more to continue their introduction than for medical purposes. Her patient continued to purr. "A few days, though… That explains the swelling and infection."

Wylie moved to the farthest corner of the room, ceding her control of the exam, which was nice. Hazel imagined if Maisey was here, she'd be kibitzing every conclusion and comment Hazel made.

"Is Laramie gonna die?" Della-Mae asked in a trembly voice.

Hazel stopped her tactile inspection and looked the little girl squarely in the eye. "I don't think this is Laramie's first fight, is it?"

"No, ma'am," Della-Mae said solemnly. "Mama says he's not very good at staying out of trouble."

"Cats with a habit of finding trouble also have very strong survival instincts." Hazel stood, hoping this was true in Laramie's case, if only so little Della-Mae wouldn't be heartbroken later. "Let's get him up on the table so I can do a thorough exam. May I?" She held out her hands and waited for Laramie's little guardian to give her approval before taking that purring bundle of hurt. "Since I'm sure you've been here before, Della-Mae, I don't need to tell you how important it is that you stand right by Laramie and help reassure him while he's on the table."

Little Della-Mae leaped out of her chair and

rushed to assist Hazel, cowboy boots ringing on the floor.

Hazel put on the stethoscope and began to take the cat's vitals.

"Is Dr. Hughes buying into your practice, Wylie?" Izzy asked as if Hazel wasn't in the room.

"No. She's my resident."

Wylie and Izzy moved on to make small talk about a Fourth of July party someone was putting on.

"I told Chandler, and now I'm telling you, Wylie," Izzy said without chastising. "Your foster parents aren't as spry as they used to be. They need help, even at the county fair. *Especially* at the county fair since it comes early this year—before the Fourth of July. The ranch staff is stretched thin this rodeo season."

"I hear you," Wylie said softly.

Wylie had foster parents? That was odd considering he'd mentioned this used to be his father's clinic.

The cat got twitchy about having his temperature taken. Hazel recentered, concentrating on the details of her patient's condition rather than the particulars of her boss's life.

A few minutes later, Hazel had jotted Laramie's vitals on the back of a heartworm prevention brochure, had finished her exam, and was ready to present her diagnosis and treatment plan on a level that even a third grader, like Della-Mae, could understand. "Laramie's got a fever. That's his body's way of fighting infection, as is this milky fluid seeping out here." Hazel gently framed the cat's head, indicating the swollen wounds on the top and side. "The infection comes from cat claws, which are notoriously dirty. Not to mention, a lot of bad bacteria in a cat's mouth is transferred when they bite another animal."

Della-Mae and her mother nodded solemnly. Wylie was silent behind her.

So far, so good.

"I'd like to clean and drain Laramie's wounds, plus begin a round of antibiotics." Hazel refused to look back at Wylie for confirmation. He'd given her the patient and she was going to deal with his condition her way. "The swelling on top of his head is what concerns me most. I'll insert a tube beneath Laramie's skin to help it drain and flush the infection. I'd like to start treatment right away and keep him overnight. If he's well enough, he can go home tomorrow."

"Yay!" Della-Mae brightened, her smile a ray of much-needed sunshine. "Do you hear that, Laramie? You're gonna come home tomorrow."

Laramie kept right on purring.

"If he's well enough," Hazel repeated gently. She turned to Izzy. "I'll work up an estimate before you decide on treatment."

Izzy waved her off. "We'll do it regardless. Laramie's a member of the family."

"Just like Papa Chandler, Sam, Rusty, and Biff," Della-Mae piped up, still grinning.

"Laramie must be very special to you." Just as the cat was to Hazel. She was excited to be jumping right into something that required a scalpel. "Do you have a dog kennel you can keep Laramie in when he comes home? He shouldn't exert himself by jumping onto furniture. And he should stay inside until we remove the tube. That should take about seven to ten days."

"We have a portable dog kennel." Izzy nodded, scrunching her nose. "But a week or more of an outdoor cat stuck in a cage? Fun times. Can't it be less?" She turned to Wylie expectantly.

Wylie, not Hazel, whose nose was now bent out of shape.

"We'll see," Wylie said, not looking at Hazel.

"We'll know more tomorrow morning." Hazel was smiling but not on the inside. "If you're interested in natural supplements for improved healing, I can give you a few recommendations."

Izzy's brow furrowed. "You mean like herbs and such?"

"Yes." Hazel gently rubbed Laramie behind his ears. "There are healing synergies to be found with a combination of Western and Eastern medicines."

"We'll talk about that more later," Wylie said gruffly, although to no one specifically. He ruffled the little girl's white-blond hair. "Della-Mae, why don't you say goodbye to Laramie? And then

Dr. Hughes will bring him back to get his treatment started."

Which was Maisey's job. *Hello*...

"Start to finish," Hazel muttered under her breath, waiting as Izzy and Della-Mae showered the cat with affection. And then she carried a still-purring Laramie back to the kennel and put him in a cage at the very end, far away from the overly-friendly puppy and still groggy cat. Until she was ready to perform the procedure, Laramie needed peace and quiet.

I need it, too. And it's only my first day!

Maisey entered the lab with one hand behind her back. "I'll need you to fill out Laramie's chart."

"Funny thing about Laramie's chart." Hazel smirked at the uncooperative vet tech. "It wasn't in the exam room."

"It must still be at the front desk." Maisey's smile was as sharp as a surgical blade, one that slid smoothly into Hazel's back.

She's the one driving this rig.

"You need to fill out an estimate sheet for service." The old woman brought her hand from behind her back, revealing a piece of paper with grids on it that she set on the lab counter. "Check the boxes on the procedures you think Laramie will need and I'll type up the anticipated fees for Izzy to sign."

"I'll get right on that, Miss Maisey," Hazel promised, taking a firm hold of this power struggle and tugging back. "That is, if you bring me Laramie's file."

"Like I said, it's probably sitting on my desk if you want it." Maisey had her nose in the air, implying Hazel could come and get it herself.

Game on, sister.

"I took notes on one of the brochures in the exam room." Hazel's smile was so stiff it was at risk of cracking. "You can just put that in the file."

"That's not the way we do things here." Maisey opened the lab door as if to leave, and then paused, hard smile growing. "By the way, Dexter is in exam room two."

Hazel rolled her eyes. "And Dexter is…"

"By the looks of him, the other half of that cat fight Laramie was in. I'm thinking Dexter is the reigning champ." Maisey triumphantly left the room as if she'd won the skirmish.

And she probably had.

Hazel bent to Laramie's level, looking the beaten feline in the eyes. "You're probably used to the shenanigans of this place, fella. Got any tips for me?"

The cat just kept on purring.

CHAPTER TWO

"SHE'S TROUBLE," MAISEY REPEATED to Wylie at five o'clock. She stared out the front windows toward Hazel, who was unloading suitcases from her truck. "Trouble, I tell you. Brewing like a summer thunderstorm."

Gazing at Hazel, Wylie felt that, too. Trouble. But he'd always enjoyed those booming, prairie thunderstorms. They made him feel alive. "Swallow your pride, Maisey."

And tuck away your interest in your resident, Wylie.

"Hazel did fine this afternoon," he continued, mention of herbal remedies aside. Hazel would be considered a snake oil salesman if she pressed natural remedies too often. "You have to hand it to her. She was efficient in treating those cats." All without complaint despite Maisey throwing obstacles in her path.

Hazel rolled with the punches and kept saying, *"Great,"* while flashing what Wylie was coming to think of as her you-can't-get-to-me smile.

Wylie faced Maisey. "I've got to go. Why don't you help Hazel unload? It'll make her feel welcome."

"And aggravate my sciatica?" Maisey shook her head. "Besides, she's a wagon headed elsewhere. No need to make her feel at home."

His vet tech might just as well have declared war on his resident.

Wylie had no idea who held the advantage here. Nor did he have any desire to witness their skirmishes. "I'm off the clock. There's somewhere I need to be. If anything comes in, put Hazel on it."

"Oh, I will," Maisey assured him, not without a worrying amount of pleasure in her expression.

"Here are the mobile clinic keys in case Hazel needs them." Wylie removed the fob from his pocket and dropped it on a hook on the underside of the check-in counter. Normally, he drove the mobile clinic everywhere, just in case he was needed to make a house call in the middle of the night. He was relieved to be rid of the responsibility and looking forward to some down time.

"Speak of the devil…" Maisey nodded toward Hazel, who was nearing the front door.

She dragged two large, wheeled suitcases behind her.

Wylie held the door open wide enough for Hazel to pass through. "I've got to run. I'll see you in the morning."

"Great." Hazel's smile never wavered.

Wylie drove home in his black truck for the first time in what felt like forever, mind wandering.

He passed through Clementine proper with its hundred year-old brick buildings. Betty's Bakery. The Buffalo Diner. Brown's Brewery in what was once the town jail, back in the era of the wild west. Now that Wylie had a competent resident on staff, he could afford to relax in such places. Have a beer with friends and catch up without worrying he'd be called away.

I can dream, can't I?

He drove out of town on a narrow two-lane highway. Houses went from being built close to the road to being set further and further back. Barbed wire fencing marked ranch boundaries, filled with cattle, horses or sheep. He passed by the Rowland Ranch with its mixture of sheep and alpaca. And then, he pulled onto the gravel driveway at his place.

"Home, sweet home," Wylie murmured, taking in his rambling ranch house with its white walls and green shutters. There was a small barn in back next to a three-acre pasture. It was a good size property for a family who didn't earn their living ranching.

All I need is the family. Actually, what I need, is a date.

Wylie entered his house, struck by the thought of touchable, strawberry blond hair. He showered. Put on cologne for once, as well as what he considered his Saturday night clothes—yoked, blue buttoned shirt, newer blue jeans, rodeo champion belt buckle, brown felt cowboy hat, and silver-tipped, black cowboy boots. He thought about gray eyes the color of winter dusk and smiles that implied she'd weathered storms, not just caused them. And then, he thought about Hazel's desire to be a specialty surgeon, like Tabitha, whom he hadn't seen or spoken to in years.

His ex-fiancée had been too much on his mind today.

He and Tabitha had gone to university together, fancying themselves a power couple ready to take on the veterinary world. They were good enough and lucky enough to land surgical residencies—Tabitha in Kentucky, Wylie in California. After they finished their residencies, they'd planned to open a surgery center of their own in Texas, which they'd researched and found was an underserved area. They'd moved to Houston, found a great location, and went in search of financing.

But before their loan paperwork was processed, Wylie's dad had died unexpectedly. That time had been a blur of mixed emotions. He and Tabitha returned to Clementine. She'd wanted to sell the clinic and use the money to get their new life started in Houston. But Wylie… He'd realized something was missing from his life—connections. His found family was here. With Tabitha, the clinic, and the people and community who'd shaped him, he'd realized this was home.

Unfortunately, Tabitha hadn't seen what Clementine had to offer.

That's why Hazel reminds me of Tabitha. She doesn't want to be here either.

Shaking off the past and its association with his new employee, Wylie drove back into town and parked at the Buffalo Diner. He got out, settled his brown cowboy hat more firmly on his head and went inside.

The Buffalo Diner had a retro vibe with its long row of counter seats, worn booths, and scarred white Formica tables. It was run by the steely Coronet Blankenship, who claimed her pecan pie was the best this side of the Mississippi. She was on duty tonight, buzzing around with her usual brisk efficiency.

"Wylie!" Ronnie Keller waved to him from a booth by the window. Ronnie had long, dark hair, dark eyes, and a knack for finding folks true love. She was also very pregnant. "Have a seat. I ordered you a coffee because I can't have any." Ronnie laughed effusively, patting her large, round belly. "But I'm still energized by the smell."

"It's the little things we love that keep us going, isn't it?" Wylie sat down across from her and placed a folded sheet of paper on the table. "To save time, I made a list of qualities I'd like my life partner to have."

"We don't have to talk business right away." Grinning, Ronnie ignored the list he'd spent hours mulling over. "I hear you have an associate on staff this summer."

"News travels fast." Wylie tapped the list, not thinking about Hazel. "Dr. Hughes is going to spend her twelve-month residency with me."

"Like a regular doctor would at a hospital?" Ronnie nodded, still smiling, still ignoring Wylie's list. "Are you judging stock at the county fair this year?"

"Always." Wylie sipped his black coffee and wondered how long he had to make polite conversation before they could get down to brass tacks—the required traits and characteristics of his future soul mate.

"Do you still own that fine-looking bay?" Ronnie seemed intent upon trying to make small talk. "The one you used to compete with?"

Wylie nodded, not much of a small talker. "About that list…"

"We'll get to that." Ronnie's air of effusiveness didn't dim. "Still planning to vacation on Padre Island this summer?"

"Yep."

"Okay. This was helpful." Ronnie tapped something into her phone.

"Helpful?" Wylie frowned. "In what way? You haven't even read my checklist."

"No need." Ronnie chuckled. "I've known you

nigh on forever. You think you want someone bright and easygoing, attractive but not high-maintenance. A cowgirl, if possible, open to having kids soon because you're in your mid-thirties."

"Thirty-six." Still frowning, Wylie took his list and shoved it into his pocket, fully intending to toss it in the trash at home. "That's quite a party trick."

Ronnie laughed, louder this time. "The trick is knowing that every cowboy who hires me thinks they want the same thing." She leaned in closer, inviting him to do the same. "But the truth isn't that simple."

"No. This time, it is." Wylie sat back, bumping his hat brim upward with his knuckles. "This is what I want. Simple. Easy. No complications." His life was complicated enough. Exhausting, if truth be told.

An image of Hazel talking to her horse drifted into his head. He had no idea why. She wasn't uncomplicated. Quite the opposite, in fact.

Wylie rubbed his forehead before drawing his hat brim down low and giving Ronnie a stern look. "I know what I want."

"Do you? Simple and easy means no spark. No thrill. No personality." Ronnie eased back in the booth, placing the flat of her hand on her round belly and pressing down, as if that kid in there was giving her grief. "I can introduce you to quite a few women who check your particular boxes but I can also guarantee you won't fall in love with any of them. Love is harder to come by the older you get."

The older you get...

Wylie frowned. "Wow. And here I thought I'd hired you to cheer me on."

"You hired me to cut to the chase *and* cheer you on." Ronnie shifted in her seat, arched her back, and blew out a long breath. "So, here's me cutting to the chase. You're not a big talker, might even live too much in your head, brooding over the past *and* the future, if I had to guess. And that's probably why you go with the flow most times. You're a creature of habit. You volunteer to help the community. And you're a kindhearted, pragmatic man whose business is growing." She shifted in her seat once more before continuing. "If I got anything wrong, let me know."

"I'm sounding a bit dull," Wylie admitted, not that he could think of anything exciting to add to her list of his attributes. "Do women want quiet, successful, reliable men who are low-maintenance?"

"Around here?" Ronnie shook her head. "They want James Bond in a cowboy hat. Wealthy, sexy, and a bit dangerous."

"You're saying they don't know what they want either." It was Wylie's turn to laugh. "That makes me feel better." If only a little.

Ronnie nodded. "Which is why you need to leave the driving to me. We don't want to attract the wrong candidates and waste your time." She tapped rapidly into her phone. "I invited you to the speed dating session tonight just to get your feet wet. You haven't dated in a long time. There'll be ten women and ten men attending. I want you to ask someone out for coffee tomorrow morning. Say ten o'clock? Are you free then?"

"Yes..." Hazel could cover his appointments. "But... Who should I ask out?"

Ronnie glanced up from her phone to give him a stern look. "Obviously, the woman who makes you want to get to know her better. And if there's more than one, ask out more than one."

Again, the image of Hazel leading her horse toward the paddocks came to mind.

Wylie frowned.

"I sense your hesitation to follow my recommendations." Ronnie tossed her long, dark hair over her shoulder and beamed at Wylie. "Trust me. You'll learn a lot from this exercise. And look there... Some of the women are arriving."

Wylie turned. But for some reason, all he saw was the image of strawberry blond hair and unusual gray eyes.

What was happening?

He blinked and refocused. Sure enough, a gaggle of cowgirls in going-out clothes approached the diner door.

He'd never had a woman stick in his thoughts the way Hazel did, not even Tabitha. It knocked him off-balance.

And if Ronnie the matchmaker knew that, he was afraid what she'd recommend next—that the right woman was right under his nose.

"Is this more of your baggage?" Maisey, the elderly vet tech, stood at the closed paddock gate, a disapproving look on her wrinkled face and a hairless little dog in her arms.

"This is Budge," Hazel said crisply, putting a reassuring hand on her horse's shoulder. "He's not baggage."

"More work for me, no doubt," Maisey continued to grouse. "I can see his ribs. What's he got? Worms? And those hooves…"

"Miss Maisey." Since Hazel was giving Budge a treatment, she returned her attention to keeping him still, rubbing the gelding behind his coppery ears. "I rescued Budge a month ago. He's on his road to recovery. I'll take care of him. He's none of your concern."

"Dietary restrictions?" Maisey asked, not missing a beat. She'd be a good vet tech if she wasn't such a sourpuss. She put the pink, hairless dog on the ground.

Small, pointy nose. Tiny, bulging eyes. Thin frame, short legs, whip tail.

Fluffy?

The dog stared at Hazel and growled.

Yes, it's Fluffy, she decided, giving Maisey props for her irony when naming her pet.

"I said, does Budge have dietary restrictions?" Maisey repeated testily, shooing Fluffy off with the instruction, *"Don't go far."*

The little dog moved with the slow, belabored steps of an animal with severe arthritis or nerve pain.

I could help Fluffy.

Although Hazel suspected Maisey wouldn't approve of acupuncture.

Hazel set her urge to ease the dog's discomfort aside. "No dietary restrictions, Maisey. Budge has tolerated everything well, so far." She continued to scratch the gelding behind his ears, earning a nose rub on her chest. "His biggest issue is—"

"Somebody couldn't afford to feed him or have his hooves trimmed on the regular." Maisey silently opened the gate and entered the paddock. She reached into a pocket of her khaki shorts and produced an oat cube, holding it out with a flat hand. "Seen it before. How long did he go without a blacksmith? Six months? A year?"

"Closer to a year." Poor Budge had suffered in the past. There was nothing Hazel could do about that but make his life a joy in the future.

"What are you..." Maisey gasped, moving closer. "Are those needles sticking out of him? Are you using that horse as a pin cushion?"

"No." Hazel held on to her patience as well as a brittle smile. Barely. "I'm giving Budge an acupuncture treatment to encourage circulation in his legs. It'll ease his pain and promote healing."

"It's barbaric." Maisey's face rumpled into those bulldog folds. Her hand closed around the cube she'd offered to Budge. "I should report you to—"

"I'm licensed to administer acupuncture treatments to animals." Hazel hesitated, gaze drifting toward the little, hairless dog. And then she did something foolish. She gestured toward Fluffy and said, "Acupuncture could help Fluffy feel better."

Maisey stiffened, expression hardening. "You won't experiment on *my* dog."

"Acupuncture isn't an experimental treatment." But Hazel knew her words fell on deaf ears.

Budge ambled over to inspect Maisey. Extending his nose toward her in his own version of how-do-you-do, sniffing her short white hair and stiff shoulders before Maisey's expression softened and she gave him the oat cube.

"Is there a place in town you'd recommend for dinner?" Hazel stayed in the middle of the paddock, afraid if she joined the pair that Maisey would spook and return to her normal, crotchety self. "I'm too tired to cook."

Not to mention, Hazel was too hungry to cook. She'd skipped lunch and had worked all afternoon. Her stomach growled, much as it had been these last few minutes.

"You could try the Buckboard if you fancy a beer and a conversation with your meal. Lots of single cowboys there." Maisey gave Budge a second oat cube. "Might be quieter over at the Buffalo Diner."

"I could use some quiet." A few minutes spent slouched in a booth while scrolling through social media on her phone and seeing how her friends were doing at their residencies. A few minutes of envy before she devoured a plate of comfort food.

"I'll get you the number of our best local blacksmith to treat your fella," Maisey said, seemingly having forgotten her dislike of Hazel and her methods.

Fluffy tottered over to Maisey's side, growling at Hazel when their eyes met as if picking up the slack where prickly Maisey had left off.

In one swift movement, Maisey scooped up Fluffy and tucked her into the crook of her arm before turning away. "You'll do well here, Budge. Unlike our new needle-poking intern, I'd wager." She marched off, flung open the door that led into the kennels, and let it slam shut behind her.

"I'm a *resident*." Hazel stared at Budge, who held his head high and ears cocked forward, as if waiting for Maisey to reappear. "She won you over that easily?" Hazel sighed.

Her cell phone rang. It was her mother, calling to check in.

Guilt set in, refusing to go away. Despite that, Hazel spent several minutes being cheerful about the people and cases at the Clementine Veterinary Clinic.

Hazel knew she was letting her mother down. Mom lived alone in their hometown of Taft, less than an hour west of Bakersfield. Dad had divorced her twenty years ago and moved to Los Angeles. Of their three kids, Mom had pinned her hopes on Hazel taking over her veterinary practice.

When her phone call was done, Hazel removed Budge's acupuncture needles and praised him for being a good boy. Then she went to shower and change into a yellow sundress, sandals, and a delicate cowboy hat with a peacock-feathered hatband. With her phone-wallet in her dress pocket, she hurried downstairs, planning to go through the back door. But she heard something in the front of the clinic and veered that way instead.

Maisey sat at the lobby desk doing a crossword in one of those big, large-print puzzle books.

"Are we still open?" Hazel checked the time. It was after six.

"No. But I was taking a break before doing the filing." Maisey double-underlined the clue for eight across, which was blank in the puzzle. "It takes a lot of commitment to run a small business."

"Does it, now." Hazel leaned over the desk to peer at the clue Maisey was stuck on. *"Curmudgeon."*

The old woman raised her head, fire in her eyes. "What did you call me?"

"That's eight across." Hazel bolted out the door, a big smile on her face. She was so distracted by her victory that she almost ran into a girl of about twelve who was carrying a small piglet in her arms.

The girl gasped, startled. The piglet wheezed as if struggling for breath. It couldn't have been more than a few weeks old.

A harried-looking cowgirl slung her purse to her shoulder as she reached Hazel. "Is the clinic still open?"

"Yes. I'm Dr. Hughes." Hazel immediately transitioned from triumph to triage mode. She eased the piglet from the girl's arms into her own. "Who have we got here?"

"That's Fiona." The girl bit her lip. She had braces and acne and the most endearing sense of worry for her baby pig. "I came home from riding this afternoon and Fiona wasn't breathing right. That's why we're here."

Hazel took note of the piglet's droopy, watery eyes, felt the struggle the young pig made to draw a breath, and ignored her own rumbling, empty stomach. She opened the clinic door and walked toward the exam rooms in the back. "Come on in."

"Who's this?" Maisey demanded, closing her puzzle book.

"Fiona." Hazel kept walking.

"Does Fiona have an appointment?" Maisey demanded in that drill sergeant voice of hers.

"No." Hazel doubled back to the check-in counter. "She doesn't need one. It's an emergency. Come with me, Fiona's family." Hazel smiled reassuringly at them and led the way to an exam room. Once there, she rested Fiona on the large, gleaming table and gestured for her human mama to steady her. "What's your name?"

"Piper." The teen had an abundance of thick, brown hair. "I'm raising pigmy piglets for the county fair this year but Fiona is a runt and special."

"I'm Allison, Piper's mom." The cowgirl with the purse sank into the visitor's chair, giving a pointed look at Hazel's dress. "Who are you again? I'm sorry. We were expecting Wylie...*er*... Dr. Newland."

Hazel reintroduced herself. "Today is my first day and I was just heading out to grab dinner." She took the piglet's vitals, jotting the readings down on the back of a heartworm pamphlet again since Maisey wasn't kind enough to bring her a chart to fill out. She was probably stuck on a seven-letter word for "one who shirks their duty." Answer being: *Slacker*.

"You're a vet?" Piper was in awe. Or doubt. It was hard to tell since most of Hazel's attention was on her patient. "You don't look like Dr. Newland. He's always got stains on his clothes and he hardly ever smiles."

"I'll let you in on a little secret." Hazel worked hard to keep her tone chipper because it seemed like she'd been defending her veterinary honor all afternoon. "Where I come from, veterinarians smile and joke and change out of their dirty clothes in between patients." Because surgery was sanitary business. But still…

"Wow." Piper seemed in awe, which made Hazel feel better.

"Fiona has a respiratory infection." Hazel went over the piglet's symptoms with them, explaining how Fiona's lungs crackled when she tried to fill them with air. "I want to put her on an antibiotic right away. It's liquid and you'll administer it orally through a dropper. I'll be right back with it."

Hazel left them and entered the lab. Since she'd retrieved some things there earlier, she had no trouble finding the antibiotic and a small, plastic-wrapped syringe to administer it. When she returned to the exam room, she wasn't surprised to find Maisey there, looking persnickety, as usual.

Persnickety? There's a word I never thought I'd use.

Hazel gave the piglet a dose of the antibiotic. Then she spoke to Allison and Piper. "Once my marvelous assistant, Miss Maisey, types up your dosing and care instructions and rings you up, you may take Fiona home. If you aren't comfortable with that, you can leave her here. If you do take her home, keep her in a room with a humidifier tonight. Dust will exacerbate her condition. Any questions?"

Piper and Allison both looked toward Maisey, not the doctor in the room.

Ugh.

Hazel rubbed her temple, wishing she could rub her wounded pride back to its original, confident form.

"Don't you worry, folks." Maisey thrust her traitorous nose in the air. "I'll confirm everything with Dr. Newland before we go any farther."

Hazel drew a slow, deep breath, seeking a space where persnickety characters couldn't upset her.

Despite that breath, a hot burst of anger rushed through Hazel's veins. She almost lost her smile. Almost.

I won't let this experience get to me.

Hazel turned and washed up in the sink, taking a moment to compose herself. "It's always wise to get a second opinion." She dried her hands with a paper towel, then faced her patients, setting her cowboy hat at a jaunty angle.

Perhaps sensing the power struggle in the room, Piper and Allison looked at a loss as to what to do.

Hazel's stomach growled. "Well, I'll be having dinner at the Buffalo Diner if you need anything else."

"I just knew she was uppity," Maisey said as Hazel walked out.

CHAPTER THREE

WYLIE WAS HAVING second thoughts about speed dating and the dates hadn't even begun.

Tables in the middle of the Buffalo Diner had been set up in a row with ten chairs on either side. Cowboys milled about nervously near the counter seats, staring at their boots. Cowgirls huddled in two groups on the window side of the tables, casting speculative glances toward the men. Ronnie was reviewing colorful index cards at the booth where she and Wylie had met earlier.

"First time?" Fletcher asked. He was a former Done Roamin' Ranch foster, the same as Wylie. He worked there now as a ranch hand and didn't look like he'd had time after his shift to clean up. He had a streak of dirt down one leg of his jeans.

"Yep, first-timer at speed dating." Wylie felt embarrassed admitting that. "You?"

"Same." Fletcher took off his straw cowboy hat and removed a wooden matchstick from the inner hatband. He stuck it in his mouth and plopped his hat back on his head. "Everybody in our foster family is settling down and finding love. I figured it was time to do the same."

"I'm on that page, too." Wylie nodded. "It's as good a reason as any to get serious about finding love."

"Yep." Fletcher chomped so hard on the matchstick that it broke. Half of it fell to the floor.

Wylie and Fletcher stared at the red, sulfur-tipped remains.

"Nervous?" Wylie asked his foster brother.

"Yep." Fletcher picked up the broken tip and stuck both halves into his jeans pocket.

"Ronnie caught me in the feed store." Calvin Cowser joined their conversation. He worked at a dairy farm near Friar's Creek, the town closest to Clementine, and had gone to school with Wylie. "I was almost a no-show. Still have my doubts. Kind of feels like I'm being put in a window display for women to inspect."

Accurate.

Wylie nodded. "What changed your mind?"

"Ronnie told me Evie Grace was making her peach tartlets for every participant." Calvin's expression turned dreamy. "You know, Evie wins the county fair baking competition most years."

"She hasn't won in two years," Fletcher pointed out. "It's been that old Burns fella."

"All I'm saying is that she's a good baker." Calvin patted his stomach. "I've decided baking is the way to my heart."

Wylie wasn't sure what would win his heart. But luckily, he had no time to dwell on that. His cell phone chimed with an email. It was long, detailed, and from Maisey. He'd given her a tablet years ago, hoping it would reduce her fear of technology. But the only thing she used it for was sending him emails. She didn't have a cell phone and didn't text. This lengthy missive asked him to confirm Hazel's diagnosis of a respiratory infection for a piglet.

And so it begins.

He emailed back his support of Hazel with a succinct: Agree with Dr. Hughes. Proceed with treatment.

"All right, everyone. Please take your assigned seats," Ronnie announced just as Hazel entered the Buffalo Diner with a swish of her yellow sundress skirt.

All eyes turned toward the newcomer.

Hazel glanced behind her as if checking to see if someone was about to follow her in.

No one was behind her.

Wylie was willing to bet that the speed dating cowboys were taking in that striking combination of strawberry blond hair, unusual gray eyes, and the fit of her pretty yellow sundress. Because that's what Wylie was doing. At least, until he reminded himself that she wasn't marriage material. At least, not for anyone with roots in Clementine.

Hazel waved uneasily at no one and everyone,

and then took the closest counter seat and hid behind a large, laminated menu.

"Speed dating is about to begin," Ronnie said with her usual enthusiasm.

Hazel peeked over her menu, gaze finding his.

And suddenly, Wylie wanted to hide, too. From embarrassment. He could feel the heat of it crawling up his neck.

Great way to impress my new employee.

Hazel's menu rose but he had the distinct impression that she was smiling behind it. And not that grin-and-bear-it smile either.

The heat of embarrassment increased.

"Anyway..." Ronnie herded the speed daters toward their chairs and handed out the index cards she'd been working on. "You each have two cards with conversation prompts. One of those cards is specific to you. Don't trade. You'll have four minutes to get to know one another and then the men will rotate chairs. Any questions?"

There were none.

Wylie sat down across from a pretty brunette who looked as nervous as he felt.

"Okay." Ronnie clapped her hands. "On your marks. Get set. *Date!*"

"Hi, I'm Mandy." The brunette hunched over her index card. "I'm a dental hygienist from Friar's Creek. Born and raised there. I like women's soccer, soft-serve ice cream, and taking long, slow walks on hot sandy beaches." She laughed nervously, staring up at Wylie with an open smile. "That last one is a lie. I've always wanted to say that to somebody. My prompt is to tell you what my favorite Saturday night would be. And... It's at home with a good book, preferably romance. Preferably historical." She cast Wylie a nervous glance. "Your turn."

"Right." Wylie stared at his first card. It had the same generic questions Mandy had answered. "I'm a veterinarian. I've lived in Clementine all my life." *Boring.* "I don't watch much sports or... really...much of anything." *Really boring.* "My favorite dessert is anything chocolate. Maybe mud pie. My mom used to make that at Easter." *Don't talk about her!* She'd abandoned him and Dad. "And as for Saturday nights... If I'm not out on a call, I might fall asleep watching whatever is on TV." *Super boring.*

Wylie tried to smile. He imagined he wasn't doing any better at speed dating than Mandy was.

Is it too late to bail?

"Right." Mandy wasn't impressed. She flipped to the next index card and read, "The last movie that made me laugh was..." Mandy's nervous smile turned into a more judgmental frown. "I don't watch movies. I read books."

Okay. Mandy is sounding about equal to me on the boring scale.

Boring equaled simple, right? And her being a book reader meant she was intelligent, right?

And she seemed very straightforward, meaning not high-maintenance, right? Which meant that she checked Wylie's boxes. And although there was no spark, that could come with time...right?

Should I ask her to coffee?

Behind Wylie, at the counter, Hazel ordered a double cheeseburger with a side of mashed potatoes and applesauce.

He bit back a chuckle.

Hazel eats like she's twelve.

Wylie smiled, pretending to study the conversation prompts on his card but imagining what Hazel had been like as a kid. Intelligent, friendly, not high-maintenance. She'd probably been the most popular babysitter in her neighborhood.

"What was the last movie that made you laugh?" Mandy asked, bringing him out of his reverie.

Wylie's smile fell. "I'm drawing a blank."

"How's the pecan pie?" Hazel asked Coronet, her waitress.

Several speed dating participants answered, mostly the cowboys.

"It's the best in Oklahoma."

"Not to be missed."

"A must-have."

"Worth every calorie." That came from Mandy.

"My peach pie is better," Evie said, although she practically flinched when diner owner Coronet gave her a look of comeuppance. "But yeah,

Coronet's pecan pie is the best pecan pie this side of the Mississippi, just like the menu says."

"Nice save," Mandy whispered to Evie, who sat next to her.

"Time!" Ronnie instructed the cowboys to say goodbye to their first date and rotate to the right. She waited until everyone was situated to say, "On your marks. Get set. *Date!*" And then Ronnie went over to talk to Hazel.

Wylie couldn't hear what was said between Ronnie and Hazel. Was Ronnie trying to sell Hazel on her matchmaking services? Tell her something about the pecan pie? Asking her where she'd bought that pretty cowboy hat?

"Hi, I'm Evie." Across the table from Wylie, a familiar blonde cowgirl gave Wylie a calculated expression. "I was born and raised here, as you very well know." They'd gone to school around the same time, although not in the same grade. "I love rodeo and late morning horseback rides after a night of dancing at the Buckboard." The town's local honky-tonk. "I can answer yours for you, Wylie." And she proceeded to do just that. "Clementine resident. Workaholic. The kind of man who asks a woman on one date and then never contacts her again."

Oh, the sarcasm.

Wylie frowned.

But... I deserve that.

"Yeah." Wylie rubbed a hand behind his neck,

watching Hazel out of the corner of his eye. "Sorry. Summers are one of my busiest times of year." And the date they'd gone on had been lackluster and forgotten in the flurry of work. Then, when Evie brought her cat to the clinic a few months later and she hadn't been gracious about his oversight, he hadn't wanted to pursue anything with her. Bitter and begrudging weren't on his wish list for a wife. "It wasn't personal."

Evie gave him an arch look. "You could have at least texted to say work was impossible."

"That's the thing about being a workaholic. Anytime you aren't working, you're sleeping." His excuse made him sound even more boring. What on earth did he have to offer a woman other than a nice income and a nice little ranchette?

Ronnie moved a laughing Hazel to the far end of the counter next to the wall.

Wylie wondered what they were laughing about and why Ronnie thought putting Hazel in a corner would make her less of a distraction. She was like a hothouse lily in a field of wildflowers, exotic and not to be overlooked.

"I bought a new pair of boots for our date." Evie pursed her lips. "I haven't worn them since."

"You haven't worn them? Not ever again?" Wylie was taken aback. "Why? Because they don't fit well?"

"No." Evie huffed. She was always upset about something. "I was waiting for you to ask me out to wear them again." Evie inspected the tips of her blond hair as if looking for split ends. "I had this idea in my head that they were my lucky boots. The ones I'd wear for the man I'd fall in love with. After all, you admired them when I wore them the first time."

Wylie didn't remember what her boots looked like or if he'd been impressed with them or simply searching for something nice to say. But one thing he did know. Evie wasn't someone he'd consider as marital material. "I think you should wear those boots for someone else."

"Is it time yet?" Evie called to Ronnie in a cold voice. And since it wasn't, she proceeded to glare at Wylie in silence for the rest of their session.

Meanwhile, Hazel was busy scrolling through her phone and occasionally laughing to herself. He imagined she was a cute kitten video fan. On the rare occasion when he opened social media, he found amusement in cute kitten videos.

Boring!

"Time! Rotate. Here's a bonus question for everyone." Ronnie passed out red, heart-shaped pieces of paper with writing on them.

Wylie's read: *What's your biggest fear about dating?*

He glanced up at his latest date—Minnie Cornwall. She wore a simple gray dress. Her thick brown hair fell in puffy curls beneath her red cowboy hat. As with many of the singles here, they'd been in high school around the same time. As far as Wylie knew, Minnie had been married three times, divorced three times, and had four kids. She was a pharmacist, so she understood science. She drove a practical minivan, went to church on Sunday, and brought her dogs in for their annual exams on time every year. She checked all his boxes, too. But…

Dang. She's just as boring as I am.

Except for the part about her marriages and her kids.

Since Minnie had four kids, she probably didn't want to have any more. And Wylie… He loved kids but having been a foster teen, he wanted to create a family that was also all his own.

"Wylie." Minnie gave him a nod. "I can't believe I'm doing this. You could probably answer this card for me. Lifelong resident. Whatever sports my kids are playing at the moment is the sport I enjoy most—currently, it's rodeo. And on Saturday night you can find me crashed on the couch surrounded by four kids, two dogs, and several bowls of popcorn." She smiled. "I imagine your Saturday nights are more exciting than mine."

"Nope." A sense of calm descended over Wylie. Minnie was his kind of boring. A friendly kind of boring. "If I'm not on a call, I'm crashed on the couch alone." No kids, popcorn, or dogs. All the things he was too busy for.

"Oh, I envy you a couch all your own." Minnie

grinned. "Just so you know, I'm not really looking for husband number four. Ronnie roped me into this when she bumped into me at the doctor's office. I figured it'd be a great excuse to get out of the house." She leaned forward conspiratorially. "My oldest insisted I shave my legs for this. I wasn't going to. That's how bad I am at dating."

Wylie chuckled. "I showered. Plus, I put in a load of laundry before I left the house."

"Laundry." Minnie rolled her eyes. "Don't get me started. I won't be able to sleep on my bed tonight if I don't put some away."

"Time!" Ronnie called.

"Good luck," Wylie said before moving to the next chair. "We old, boring people need to stick together."

Minnie gave him a speculative glance.

And the odd thing was that Wylie didn't mind.

DIDN'T IT FIGURE? Hazel's dinner bill arrived just as the speed dating event ended.

Awkward.

She didn't want to walk outside with Wylie, much less make small talk as if she hadn't witnessed his sprinting search for love. But she also didn't want to hang around the Buffalo Diner any longer. She was stuffed and ready to collapse on her bed. It had been a long day. A long few days on her drive from California.

So, Hazel followed the chatty bunch of singles

outside and navigated her way around them to the sidewalk that would lead her back to the clinic. The sun hadn't gone down yet and even though there was a light breeze, it was still hot out. The trees lining the sidewalk promised shade and she made a beeline for them.

"Hazel." Wylie hailed her. "Can I give you a ride back to the clinic?"

The group of daters turned to look at Hazel, curiosity in their eyes.

It was bad enough that she'd encountered doubt about her medical skills from patients. The last thing Hazel needed was her clientele assuming her boss was interested in finding love with her.

Hazel wielded her practiced smile and casual wave. "No, thanks, Wylie. I'll walk. Got to burn off that slice of pecan pie."

They weren't kidding when they said it was good. Made her wonder about that peach pie tartlet the speed daters had raved about before the end of their session.

Hazel slid on her sunglasses and continued down the sidewalk, sandals slapping on pavement.

"I'd like to check on that surgery patient with you." Wylie appeared at Hazel's side. He must have stretched his long legs to reach her. He brought with him the smell of an overwhelming amount of cologne.

That man is trying too hard.

It shouldn't have been endearing. But it was.

"Come on," Wylie said, taking careful hold of her arm and picking up the pace as he veered toward the parking lot. "We're going the same way."

"Why does it feel like we're running away from a garbage fire?" Hazel murmured.

The sound of dishes clattering drifted toward them from the open back door of the diner.

"It's more like fleeing a middle school dance." Wylie chuckled softly. "Everybody knows what they're supposed to do but no one wants to make more than a token move for fear of... Well, just because the opposite sex is mysterious and scary."

Hazel grinned, unable to resist. "I'm assuming that means you made your token move and you don't want to be anyone else's token move."

"Something like that." Wylie grinned right back at Hazel.

And what do you know? Her heart started pounding as if excitedly waiting for him to make a token move.

Hazel sobered.

There will be no moves. Token or otherwise.

Wylie opened his truck door for her. "I suppose seeing me speed dating was weird."

"Not for me," she sing-songed, buckling in and facing forward. From here, she could see inside the diner's kitchen. Or at least, the dishwasher's station and the billowing steam that arose from it. She imagined it was hot and muggy in there.

It's hot in here, too. Because of Wylie.

Thankfully, Wylie closed her door and came around to the driver's seat giving her space. "Did you get unpacked?" He put on his sunglasses, adjusted the tilt of his brown cowboy hat and started the truck.

"I unloaded my truck and my horse. Did I unpack? No." That would take days.

Setting the air conditioner on high, Wylie pulled out of the parking lot, turning toward the clinic. "If we're going to be working together, I think we should get to know each other better."

This was sounding an awful lot like speed dating.

"I was born in Bakersfield, California," Hazel began, falling into presentation mode. "The youngest of three. Mom's a vet. Dad's a doctor. My older sister is a plastic surgeon in New York City. Very posh practice. My older brother is—*was…would have* been—a veterinarian. Mike was in a car accident before he began his residency." Multilayered guilt rose up inside her like a rogue wave about to wash her away. Hazel rushed on. "My favorite sport is college football, which is mostly played on Saturdays. So by Saturday night, I'm ready to get away from football and chill out with a book or a movie. I don't have time for other hobbies, including dating."

That last bit might have come out like a big, bad line drawn in the sand: *Thou shalt not cross, Dr. Newland!*

"So much for you *not* offering a little sarcasm," he teased.

Something inside Hazel softened, smudging that line she'd drawn in the sand.

Dr. Wylie Newland is handsome, endearing, and *charming.*

Despite everything that had happened today and everything she didn't want to happen tomorrow, Hazel grinned. "I might not have been completely honest about *rarely* being sarcastic." Especially since losing out on Newmarket.

Wylie smiled at the road ahead. He had a nice smile. The kind of smile that reassured someone they could reach any dream they set their heart on, no matter how many obstacles appeared in their path.

They retraced the route she'd taken to the diner, passing businesses, including a fitness center, a bakery, and a bank before entering what looked like the historic district with its old homes and towering, established shade trees. At a corner house, a group of people wearing cowboy hats were hanging out on a front porch drinking what looked like lemonade while young children played in the yard. Siblings, by the look of them.

A pang of homesickness struck Hazel out of nowhere, a longing for days gone by when she couldn't imagine life without her siblings by her side. Now, her brother was dead and her sister busy with her career in faraway New York.

Wylie cleared his throat, bringing Hazel back to the present. "I've spent the last ten years running the clinic. Like you, I have no time to date."

"Hence the appeal of *speed* dating," Hazel surmised, unable to get rid of that darn grin. She hadn't expected to enjoy talking to him after the way they'd been sidestepping disagreements this afternoon at the clinic.

"Yes." He nodded. "My foster brothers and friends are all getting married and having kids."

"You have friends?" She mock-gasped.

Wylie spared her a smile. "Yes, I have friends, Miss Sarcasm."

Hazel liked their teasing banter. "I bet most of your friends are your clients. Great way to kill two birds with one stone, Dr. Newland."

"They were my friends long before they were my clients." Wylie gave her one of those inscrutable looks, a warning that she was coming to the edge of tease-territory.

"Gotcha."

Wylie pulled into the clinic's parking lot, nearer the empty warehouse building on the far side of the property than the clinic's front door. "The county fair is coming up soon. We've been getting a lot of calls from kids getting ready to show their stock and discovering something isn't right."

Hazel nodded. "I remember those days." Her hometown was located in one of California's most fertile farming valleys where ranching and agriculture were king.

"Your first call is at nine tomorrow morning," Wylie told her. "You'll take the mobile unit to a small ranch."

"Well, well, well. I earned your approval." Hazel felt a burst of pride blossom in her chest. "Where are you going to be?"

"Me?" Wylie tapped his steering wheel with one hand before admitting, "I have a coffee date."

"Ah. So you didn't give me a ride back here out of the kindness of your heart." *Or to get to know me.* That was unexpectedly disappointing. "Who did you ask out? Or did one of the ladies ask you?"

Wylie's expression closed. "That's none of your business."

"You're right. I don't need to know." Hazel opened the door and hopped out on the hot ground to the backdrop of his loud truck engine rumbling. She turned to face him. "But I can hypothesize. It's hard to step out of your comfort zone, which is why I'm guessing you didn't do the asking. Your date did." She closed the door and turned toward the clinic, laughing to herself.

Wylie's truck window rolled down. "I did the asking!"

"Sure, you did." Without turning, Hazel waved away his comment, emphasizing her disbelief.

Wylie drove off, apparently having forgotten that he'd claimed to want to check on a patient together.

Hazel visited with the cat fighters they'd kept overnight. Fiona the piglet wasn't in a kennel and must have been taken home. She made a mental note to check in on her tomorrow.

Hazel was still smiling when she got upstairs. At least, until she found Maisey snoring on the couch, a growling Fluffy in her arms.

CHAPTER FOUR

"Morning, Miss Maisey," Hazel shouted as she bolted downstairs at six the next morning.

She made sure to stomp her feet on each hollow, wooden step, retribution for the old woman's noisy nocturnal habits.

Maisey had kept the TV on until midnight with the volume loud enough to wake the neighbors down the block. Then she'd taken a bath and sang love ballads from the 1970s until 1:00 a.m. When Maisey finally retired to her bedroom, she snored with enough gusto to rattle the old windows.

No wonder Maisey was ill-tempered. The woman needed to drink less caffeine and get tested for sleep apnea.

Hazel made a mental note to shop for a pair of earplugs today.

Downstairs, Hazel checked on the two cats who'd had drainage procedures yesterday afternoon. Neither one of them looked happy to be kenneled. But at least Laramie hadn't stopped purring.

"And I won't stop smiling," she promised him, holding on to her dream of being a surgeon.

Next, Hazel went outside to feed Budge. A brief rainstorm had passed through during the night, giving the air a damp feel. The gelding nickered a soft greeting beneath his covered paddock, more than ready for his breakfast.

While Budge ate his mix of oats and healing herbs, Hazel cleaned out his paddock, grateful that it was covered since the steamy summer heat was already building. Then she put on his halter and lead rope and took him out for a walk around the neighborhood. His shod hooves may have been in bad shape but walking was good for his circulation and would help him heal.

The clinic was located four blocks south of Main Street on the other side of what looked like the historic district—blocks of Craftsman-style homes with welcoming front porches and large, established trees that cast shadows across streets in the early morning light.

"True Americana, Budge."

The gelding gummed her shoulder.

A few blocks later, they encountered an elderly woman standing on a shady corner and holding the leash of a small, white poodle. She wore eye-popping orange cowboy boots, a matching orange cowboy hat, and a blue dress with orange roses appliquéd on the skirt. "Lost your saddle, did you?"

"Something like that." Hazel stopped and explained that poor Budge's overgrown hooves weren't up to supporting a rider. She scratched his neck beneath his bright chestnut mane.

Budge stood still, as if posing for a photograph. He often did that around strangers, as if trying to be invisible, as if being seen had resulted in bad things happening to him.

"Poor boy looks like he's got a long recovery ahead of him." The elderly woman inspected Hazel next, her gaze intent but friendly. "I'm Rose. Haven't seen you around town."

"Just moved in yesterday." Hazel introduced herself and explained about working at the clinic.

"That Doc Newland is quite the catch." Rose winked as her poodle sniffed in a circle around her orange boots. "I hear he's finally ready to settle down."

"So I'm told." Hazel bit back a smile, recalling images of Wylie fidgeting in his seat while speed dating and his frown when she'd insisted that he hadn't done the asking for his coffee date.

The poodle's leash was now wrapped around Rose's legs. One wrong move and the elderly woman would topple like a struck bowling pin.

"May I?" Without dropping Budge's lead, Hazel took the handle of the dog's leash from Rose and quickly unwrapped her.

"Thank you, honey. Bruiser does that all the time. It worries my grandson, too." She chuckled. "Of course, everything I do worries my grandson.

If you aren't interested in marrying Doc Newland, are you interested in buying a partnership in his veterinary practice?"

"No, ma'am." Hazel grinned, imagining Maisey's emphatic response to that bit of speculation. "I want to go into surgery as a specialty. This is just a small stop in an otherwise long journey."

Rose nodded, taking a step off the curb, to which Budge took two steps backward, careful-like. "Well, if you change your mind and are looking to finance a partnership, head on over to the Clementine Savings & Loan. I'm the bank president emeritus, otherwise known as *retired*, but I still have an office and I can put in a good word for you with my grandson who runs the place. That's it over there." She nodded to a sturdy-looking brick building across the street.

"That's very kind." Hazel walked with the pair to the other side of the road and bid Rose farewell at the front door to the bank. She and Budge ambled on, approaching a bakery, a fitness center, and an insurance office.

"Good morning!" A brunette scurried out of Betty's Bakery with a white paper bag and a steaming cup of what smelled like coffee. "Haven't seen you before but you must be Doc Newland's new intern."

"Resident." Hazel stopped and introduced herself.

Budge stood as still as a statue once more.

"Doc Hughes. Please accept these gifts as my official welcome to town." The woman introduced herself as Katie Underwood, great-granddaughter of Betty, the bakery's founder. "We're known for my blackberry scones and strong black coffee. Compliments of the house." She handed over the bag and coffee. "Fresh-roasted joe. Fresh-baked goods every morning. I can get you creamer if you like."

"I'm good. I like my coffee plain." Budge gummed the pastry bag as Hazel adjusted the lead rope and her gifts.

Katie beamed, smoothing her apron. "We open at six, half an hour earlier than the coffee roasters around the corner."

Ah. That explains the sales pitch and free samples.

"I've got to finish stretching Budge's legs." Hazel resumed her walk. "Thanks for the goodies, Katie. I'll be by again tomorrow around the same time."

A few people in the fitness center were running on treadmills facing the road. They waved at Hazel as she passed.

"We're not in California anymore," Hazel told Budge, giving him a pat on the neck as they continued their stroll. "Californians stick mostly to themselves." Noses deep in their devices.

They walked past the Buffalo Diner, where Hazel had eaten last night. It had a good breakfast crowd. It might have been Hazel's imagination but it felt as if everyone watched her walk by. A few waved.

"You'd think they hadn't ever seen a handsome gentleman like you before," Hazel told the gelding.

They kept plodding along down Main Street. Past a brewery and the coffee roaster that was Katie's competition. Folks drove by slowly, giving them a good look-see. Hazel supposed it wasn't every day that a horse in Budge's poor shape promenaded downtown. When they reached the feed store at the end of the main drag, Hazel turned, intending to head back.

"Hey there!" A slip of a woman with white-blond hair beneath a straw cowboy hat popped out of the feed store. "Dr. Hughes, isn't it? I'm Izzy... My daughter and I brought in Laramie yesterday."

"Right. The cat fighter." Hazel came to a stop. "He's doing well this morning. Still purring. You'll probably be able to pick him up later."

"Della-Mae will be happy to hear that." Izzy pointed toward the feed store behind her. "We've got everything you need inside for your horse and to stock your closet with jeans, boots, and the like."

Hazel glanced down at her black tank top, brown breeches, and black muck boots. "Is this why I've been stared at everywhere? Because I'm not wearing jeans and cowboy boots?" She'd assumed they'd been gawking at Budge.

Izzy smiled. "Could be. Around here, you're like a parakeet in a sky full of red-tailed hawks."

"I'm not sure I like that metaphor." She'd rather be a bluebird in a sky full of parakeets.

"Apologies for that. What I meant is this is cowboy country and you're wearing English riding pants." Izzy grinned. "That's not something we see every day."

Hazel juggled her scone bag and coffee cup in order to tip her hat brim back. "My cowboy hat doesn't count?"

"Not for much." Izzy chuckled. "You should come to the Buckboard on Thursday night. Around here, Thursday is like a Friday because this is rodeo season and most rodeo cowboys and cowgirls leave for the weekend competition on Friday morning. Thursdays are our best shot to date or hang out. You can sit with me and my friends."

"Thanks. I might just do that." Hazel spotted the back of the two-story vet clinic in the distance. She said her farewells and proceeded down the street, intending to complete a loop instead of doubling back.

This side of downtown wasn't as old as the other side. Small ranch homes dotted the street, many with single-car garages, some of which had obviously been converted into living space, having windows rather than a roll-up door for cars. The trees were tall but didn't tower over everything as they did in the historic district.

Two teenagers approached on horseback at a leisurely pace. One of them was Nancy, the owner of the orange kitten that Hazel had met upon arrival yesterday. The pair of teens stopped to talk, expressing concerns over Budge's condition and asking about his recovery plan.

When their questions had been answered, Hazel asked them where they were going.

"We're headed to rodeo team practice at the high school," the boy told Hazel.

Nancy nodded. "Best part of summer besides the county fair."

Hazel bid them farewell and continued toward the vet clinic, talking to Budge about the weather and praising his progress. If she kept talking, her mind wouldn't circle images of Wylie. He was a man worth taking second and third looks at. At least, he would have been had she been in the market for romance or planning to settle in Clementine.

As Hazel and Budge passed the empty warehouse next to the clinic, Wylie pulled into the parking lot in that big, black truck of his.

He hopped out and came over to inspect Budge, tipping his brown cowboy hat back. Unlike yesterday, he wasn't wearing ratty jeans or a wrinkled T-shirt. He'd dressed to impress, in the same style he had last night—brown checked shirt instead of blue, black jeans instead of blue, a shiny rodeo belt buckle, and those black, silver-tipped boots. "Out for his morning constitutional?"

"Yes, sir." Hazel tried to look as if this was just another day at work and she hadn't ribbed her boss last night about his level of dating courage.

"How long have you had him?"

"Almost two months." Hazel stroked Budge's chest and shoulder. "He was brought into the university clinic by a rescue shelter that didn't have the resources to care for him. Dr. Reed wanted to keep him for the students to study but…"

"He's not a lab specimen," Wylie said softly.

Hazel nodded, surprised by the warmth she felt toward Wylie almost as much as by the tears gathering in her eyes. "There was just something about Budge… The way he held his head high despite being tested and prodded by everyone. I know he's old and I'll probably never be able to ride him but…" She tried to laugh, tried to smile, and finally just tried to hold herself together. A sleepless night and the stress of a job she didn't choose were catching up to her. Fast. "I want to give Budge his dignity back. Don't get me wrong. He would have been well taken care of at the university but when he goes…" She slung her arm over the gelding's withers. "When he goes, I don't want him to be dissected for science."

Budge reached around and gummed her braid, nearly bumping her cowboy hat to the ground.

"He's just a sweetheart," Hazel said gruffly.

Wylie placed what felt like a supportive hand on her shoulder.

More tears welled. Hazel struggled to blink them back.

"He's not in the best shape, obviously, but he's special. I couldn't bear to start his treatment and then leave him there." When Hazel was finally able to look at Wylie without watery eyes, he was staring at her in a way he hadn't before, a way that wasn't professional, a way that made her heart begin thudding faster in her chest.

Careful.

Hazel blew out a breath, needing to deflect that look and change the subject. "I'm sorry for teasing you last night. That was unprofessional." And she was determined that they only be professional with each other.

Wylie stared off at the horizon as if lost in thought.

"Did you know it rained last night?" Hazel tried to appear as if his intense regard wasn't unnerving. "Does it rain here often?"

"Storms blow through periodically in the summer." That faraway look pivoted to her. "Doesn't drop much water or stay too long."

Hazel held on to Budge's lead rope with both hands because Wylie made her feel unsteady. A good kind of unsteady. A tempting kind of unsteady. The kind of unsteady that knocked a woman off her career path.

Hazel couldn't let that happen. "I should put Budge up." She took a step toward the paddocks.

"Hey, after you do that..." Wylie ran a hand around the back of his neck. "I thought you should know more about your first call of the day and I didn't have time to show you where everything is in the mobile unit yesterday."

"Great." Hazel started walking away from him. "I'll put Budge back and catch up to you."

WYLIE WAS CHECKING on Laramie and Dexter when Hazel joined him in the lab.

His phone chimed with a message. He didn't check it. He'd been getting plenty of texts since they'd left the Buffalo Diner together last night. All of them asking about Hazel and romance.

She's my new employee, he'd replied to basic inquiries.

She's only here temporarily, he'd responded when it was suggested they looked like a cute couple.

She's not my type, he'd countered to those who wouldn't let it go.

Wylie stared at Hazel now, trying to see what all the matchmaking busybodies saw.

Hazel looked just as pretty as she had yesterday. Strawberry blond hair in a plait down her back. Brown riding breeches. Black tank top now covered with a pink scrub shirt. Cowboy hat. She didn't look like a Clementine resident. What made her appear to be his type to others?

How badly would they hound him if they knew

he was having a hard time looking at Hazel like a colleague? Last night on the drive back, they'd bantered like friends who could be more. And this morning when she'd talked about her bond with Budge, he'd been hard-pressed not to take her into his arms to comfort her.

He had to resist this pull of attraction. He had to remember Hazel was his resident. And a temporary resident of Clementine.

Along those lines, Wylie gestured toward the cats in the kennels. "These two should be able to go home today."

"I agree." Hazel washed her hands the appropriate amount of time and dried them with the quick efficiency of a medical professional.

There wasn't much to complain about Hazel except for her looking like an eye-catching fish out of water. And Wylie couldn't in good conscience complain about that.

Because I like the look of her.

"I like the way you've laid out your supplies in the lab, Wylie. Everything is easy to find." Hazel gave Wylie a searching look as his cell phone chimed again. "Do you need to get that?"

"No. My phone's been blowing up since last night." He hadn't meant to say that. Not that he knew what he should have said instead. "I've fielded a lot of questions about you," he admitted.

"I'd expect that, wouldn't you?" Hazel shrugged.

"Small town. People want to know about the newcomer, as well as how I fit in at your practice."

"Yep. Yes. That's it." It wasn't. Wylie didn't usually tiptoe around the truth. But he didn't want Hazel to know folks had been more curious about them romantically than Hazel as the new vet in town. "After all, there hasn't been a new vet in Clementine in over a decade."

"You were the last new vet, I'm presuming."

He nodded. "Yes. My dad died after I completed my residency and left me everything. It was…a shock."

"Him passing?" Hazel moved closer, warmth in her gaze. "Was he sick?"

"No. It was a heart attack. We hadn't been close. He had these mood swings. They got really bad after my mom left town… And I… I didn't handle that well. Consequently, I spent my high school years in foster care. And…" Wylie realized he was babbling. "That was an overshare. Sorry." He cleared his throat. "We were talking about my text messages. Out here, everyone knows everyone."

"And I'll have to prove myself," Hazel said without missing a beat. She was easy to talk to, quick on the uptake, always smoothing things over if she sensed tension. "I understand. Folks consider their animals part of the family. It makes sense that they'd be hesitant to take the recommendations of someone they'd just met. I won't let you down or hinder your search for Mrs. Dr. Newland."

Wylie laughed. And then he regarded Hazel, probably longer than was prudent, trying to analyze his reaction to her. She was sophisticated in appearance and destined for other places. Why was he wondering what it would feel like to kiss her?

"And I'll have to prove myself to you, too." Hazel nodded. A few too many times. As if she was nervous. As if *he* made her nervous. "And to Miss Maisey." She rolled her eyes.

"You bet you'll have to prove your worth." Maisey walked by, heading toward the front desk while carrying a large mug of coffee. "Thank you for the second opinion on Fiona last night, Doc."

Hazel gave Wylie a sharp look. "She called you for a second opinion on the piglet?"

"She emailed. And I messaged back that I agreed with your treatment plan. I trust you but you are my resident, not a partner." Wylie noted Hazel's small flinch but he waved the episode off. It was past time to get down to business. "Your first patient of the day is Hard Nose. He's a young bull being raised by Tad Crocket to show at the county fair. I'm told Hard Nose has a rash of some sort." He handed Hazel the file with the bull's history, which she perused briefly. "Let me show you the mobile unit."

A few minutes later, Wylie's tour of his pride and joy was over.

"This is great. You've got everything in here for emergency surgery, materials to make splints for broken limbs, and the most commonly used medications," Hazel said in a sincere tone. "I'm not surprised that this vehicle is just as well equipped as your lab. And now, it's time for me to pay Hard Nose a visit and for you to get your dating face on."

Wylie was pleased with her praise, enough so that he ignored her tease. "Call me if you have any problems."

"There won't be any problems, Dr. Newland. Enjoy your coffee date." And Hazel was off.

TWENTY MINUTES LATER, Hazel arrived at her destination—a small ranch on the outskirts of Clementine.

The two-story, white farmhouse had peeling paint and thrumming air-conditioning units in more than one window. Chickens were out and about in a coop next to a small barn. A white billy goat stood on the hood of an old red truck, watching her park.

Hazel slipped cattle treats into her scrub pockets, then got out of the air-conditioned truck and was struck by a wave of moist heat that rose up from the damp ground.

A young cowboy came out to meet her. He looked to be about fourteen. There was a sprinkling of whiskers above his lip and a blemish forming on his chin. "That's Doc Newland's rig."

"Yep." Hazel took out the truck's portable medical bag along with her backpack containing her personal medical equipment. Both contained what she'd need to perform an exam. Medications and other supplies were locked in different compartments in the truck. "I'm filling in for Dr. Newland this morning. Are you Tad, owner of the infamous Hard Nose?"

"Yep. He's gonna win a blue ribbon at the county fair." Tad frowned, tipping his straw cowboy hat back. "Or I thought he was. Now I'm not so sure. He's got—"

"Who are you?" A middle-aged woman emerged from the chicken coop with a basket full of eggs and haste to her step. She was quite tall and her straight brown hair fell simply to her shoulders beneath a wide-brimmed hat. "Where's Doc Newland?"

"He was busy this morning." Hazel gave a jaunty wave. "I'm Dr. Hughes. Are you Tad's mother?"

"Yes. I'm Janie Crocket." The woman set down her egg basket and crossed the ranch yard, her cowboy boots crunching on gravel. "You look too young to be a doctor."

"It's the curse of my mother's DNA," Hazel quipped, still smiling, although it was harder to hold on to now. "Where's my patient?"

"Hard Nose is in his paddock behind the barn." Tad led the way, hitching up his blue jeans. "Are you gonna take a picture of his rash and send it to Doc Newland?"

"Nope." Hazel pointed at herself with her thumb.

"Why would I consult with Dr. Newland when I'm *Dr.* Hughes? Also a doctor. Get it?"

Walking next to Hazel, Janie's brows were lowered. She was Team Wylie all the way.

Hazel caught up to Tad and smiled brightly. "Sorry. Not everyone likes my sense of humor."

"It's okay." Tad's face was as red as his chin blemish. "It's just that Doc Newland is the only doctor I've ever had. For livestock, I mean."

"In your lifetime, you're going to have many different veterinarians," Hazel assured him.

Tad didn't look as if he believed her.

They rounded the corner of the barn. The paddocks came into view, positioned to receive the full morning sun. Beyond them, golden wheat covered rolling fields as far as the eye could see. But it wasn't the sight of all that wheat that held Hazel's attention. There was a young bull in the nearest paddock. The only bull in any paddock. And he looked…intimidating.

Hard Nose was a good-sized young bull, black as night, with nubby horns on either side of his head. And based on the way the bull eyed Hazel— like he suspected she was about to use an electric cattle prod on him—he wasn't show-ready. Rash or no rash.

All of a sudden, the morning sun felt hotter than hot.

"I'll put his halter on him." Tad slipped through the metal fencing with all the confidence of a kid who hadn't been kicked, bit, gored, or trampled by a bull.

Hazel, who'd been on the receiving end of plenty unhappy bovine gestures in her lifetime, decided it was wiser to wait outside the paddock and try to locate the bull's rash from here. At least, for now.

"Have you treated livestock before?" Tad's mother joined her at the fence, continuing her skeptical assessment of Hazel.

"I can assure you that I have plenty of experience." Hazel tipped her cowboy hat back and looked the older woman directly in the eye. "Both in the field and in a surgery theater."

Janie grinned but it was the kind of superior expression Maisey might have wielded. They were two peas in a disapproving pod. "Just asking because you look a little swanky."

"Fashion is never a crime." Hazel tugged at a pocket of her breeches. "These pants have more give and aren't as hot as jeans. And who knows? I may start a trend here in Clementine."

"Naw. Those pants look like they'd tear when working with wire fencing and they wouldn't be much protection with stock that bites."

"Does Hard Nose bite?" Hazel studied the bull the same way Janie had been studying her. She had yet to locate that rash.

"No bites. But then again, Hard Nose earned his name for a reason." Janie was full-on trying to test Hazel's mettle now, a challenge in her tone to match the skepticism in her eyes. "You just never know what a bull is going to do. It's probably not a good thing that he's decided he only likes Tad." She leaned closer. "Don't go in. I won't be responsible for a townie getting trampled on our property."

"I'll be fine," Hazel reassured her. "You'd do better to worry about Tad showing him in the ring and damage being done to a judge or other participants at the county fair." Human and bovine. "He's got a twitchy look in his eyes."

"Point taken," Janie allowed, although she didn't warm toward Hazel. "Doc Newland is a strong, handsome fella. I hear he's looking for a wife. Is that why you're here? Are you interested in him?"

"Nope. He's my boss." And the sooner he got busy dating, the more hope Hazel had that her attraction to him would fade.

Tad secured the bull's halter and held the strap under his chin before turning toward Hazel. "His rash is under his tail."

In other words, on his behind. No wonder Hazel hadn't seen it yet.

"Great." Hazel entered the paddock, snapping on plastic gloves. "Let's have a look."

Staring at her, ears up high, Hard Nose presented Hazel with his broad side, a tactic cattle used to show they were large, capable of holding their own, and not to be messed with.

"I see how big you are, buddy." Hazel reached in her pocket for an oat and berry cube as she approached. She offered the treat to him. And when the bull took it, she ran a hand along his back toward his hip.

The bull shifted, moving his backside away from her.

"I think Hard Nose wants another treat before you do that," Tad said unhelpfully, resettling his straw cowboy hat on his head rather than correcting the bull.

"You keep a tight hold on him, Tad," Janie called from the gate. "I don't want to have to call Doc Newland to tell him his city doctor got trampled."

"Nobody's getting trampled." Hazel backed up and gave the bull another oat and berry cube. "What a good boy you are." She ran a hand along his back once more. "When did you notice his rash, Tad?"

"Two days ago when I was giving him a bath. He likes baths, don't you, boy?" By the sounds of it, Tad was enamored with the beast.

"Hard Nose doesn't like much else except Tad and the pasture," Janie quipped. "But even Tad has trouble catching him in the pasture."

"She worries he's going to hurt me," Tad explained in a quiet voice.

"All parents worry," Hazel said, thinking of her own. She eased the bull's tail up and got a peek at eighteen inches of unusual growth. She lowered his tail and rested a hand on the bull's hip just so he'd know she was still at his back end. "It's not a rash."

"Some doctor." Janie scoffed. "We described it

to Maisey on the phone yesterday and she said it was a rash."

"Those are warts." Hazel eased her way back to the bull's head, giving him another treat. "Same as any human would get." Only bigger and on a wider swath. Hazel recalled Wylie saying his ranch clients were cost conscious, so she said, "I can apply some wart remover or you can do it if you have your own."

If this visit was any indication, Janie's resting expression was a frown. "You're here, aren't you?"

"I'm here. I'll get the medication I need from the truck." Hazel walked toward the paddock gate.

The bull lunged after her, ramming Hazel's chest into the railing. The flat of his head connected with her back. His horn nubs skimmed her shoulders.

What the devil...

Air wheezed out of Hazel's lungs. There didn't seem to be any room to fill them back up.

And then, his nose sought her scrub pocket with those treats.

He's just a big baby.

Hazel might have laughed if she'd been able to breathe.

"I'm sorry, Doc." Tad tugged Hard Nose back an inch or so. "Come on, buddy. Give her some space."

"Tad, the city doctor got the wind knocked out of her," Janie said calmly. "She's blocking the gate. If one of us doesn't see to her, she'll pass out soon."

True that.

But before either of the Crockets could act on that idea, the bull tossed his head, flinging Tad to the ground. Then he shoved Hazel against the gate once more, unintentionally resetting her lungs into working order.

Hazel drew a much-needed breath of air. And despite the sun and the heat, she felt a bone-chilling, tingly cold. The kind of feeling that washed over a body before they blacked out.

"Criminy." Janie had a hand on the gate latch, ready to open it as soon as Tad had Hard Nose under control. "Thaddeus Crocket, that darn bull of yours nearly killed this sweet doctor."

"I'm fine," Hazel wheezed, managing to hand the bull another treat. She ignored the onslaught of pain in her torso and willed herself to stay conscious by taking several deep, slow breaths. "No harm done. He just wanted more food. I'll get that medicine."

Treat obtained, the bull backed off.

Janie opened the gate and Hazel stumbled through.

It hurt to breathe. It hurt to move. But no way was Hazel going to admit that. Any of that.

Not to anyone.

W‍YLIE WAITED FOR his coffee date in front of Clementine Coffee Roasters.

"Hey." Evie Grace stopped next to him on the

sidewalk. She'd abandoned cowgirl fashion for fitness instructor garb—black tank, black leggings, black sneakers. Her blond hair was in a high ponytail that on anyone else he'd call perky.

"Good morning." Wylie tipped his cowboy hat. And when Evie didn't leave, he asked, "Are you waiting for someone?"

Someone she'd met last night at speed dating, perhaps?

Wylie smiled kindly, hoping a new beau would distract her from his past oversight.

"I'm waiting for Mandy," Evie said, full of snark.

"Same." Wylie did a double take. "She made a coffee date with you, too?" Had he gotten the day and time wrong for his?

Evie laughed mirthlessly at him. "No. I'm her wingman."

"Why does she need—"

"Hi. Sorry I'm late." Mandy rushed up to them. She was dressed in a pair of green scrubs, as if she was heading into work as a dental hygienist after this. Her brown hair was in a neat ponytail at the base of her neck. "Cyrus Henry was moving his sheep from his pasture on one side of the highway to another. Who knew there'd be a traffic hazard between Friar's Creek and Clementine?" She beamed up at Wylie. "You don't mind if Evie joins us, do you?"

"No." *Yes.* "Not at all."

Evie's here as payback for me not calling her back after one bad date.

Wylie held the door open for both women wearing a smile he stole from Hazel. "This is great. Coffee's on me."

He paid for their fancy coffees and his Americana. They sat at a table near the front window, waiting for their order. Wylie took consolation that the morning wouldn't be a total loss. Hazel had taken what had to be a very challenging appointment.

Last year, Tad Crocket had raised a bull for the fair. It had been the worst-behaved bovine on the planet. Tad had named the beast Easy Money. That bull had tried to kick Wylie into the next county. Only luck and Wylie's quick reflexes had saved him. He hoped Tad's bull this year would be better behaved. The kid had to have learned something.

And yet…guilt twined with relief. Hazel could very well be in over her head. She didn't dress like any livestock vet he'd ever seen and—

Underneath the table, Evie kicked Wylie's shin. Hard. Once Evie had his attention, she jerked her head toward Mandy.

Right. I need to keep my eyes on the prize.

Wylie smiled toward his date. "Mandy, do you plan to go to the county fair this year?"

"Oh, yes." Mandy nodded. "I have to support Evie. She's entering her peach pie in the baking competition."

"It stresses me out every year." Evie nodded, sipping her coffee and smirking at Wylie. "But this year more than others. The fair's early and the peaches aren't fully ripe. I always enter a pie baked with fresh, locally grown peaches. I might have to use peaches I canned last year."

"Huh." Wylie turned his back toward Evie and her baking problems. "What about you, Mandy? Do you enter anything in the fair?"

"No. I can't bake to save my life. And crafts… Pfft." Mandy held up her hands, wiggling all ten digits. "I'm all thumbs."

And yet, you're holding up all your fingers. Not just your thumbs.

Wylie frowned. He needed to get Hazel and her brassy sarcasm out of his head. "Do you have any pets?"

"Does a bearded dragon count?" Mandy grinned. "Evie thinks he's a snake with legs but he's so much more. Smart. Loving. Curious. He sits on my shoulder while I read."

Evie rolled her eyes. "Mandy, when I offered to be your wingman and help you land a man, I told you not to mention Dragon Lord."

Scoffing, Mandy leaned forward as if sharing a secret. "Evie thinks you won't want to hear about Dragon Lord but I know she's wrong. You're a vet. You love all animals."

Nope. Nope, I do not.

Wylie drew the line at reptiles. He was willing to bet Hazel did, too.

Unaware of his opinion, Mandy beamed. "This is fun, isn't it? Getting to know each other, I mean. Speed dating is the way to go. I'm meeting Jansen for a walk around the historic district after work. And on Thursday, Zane challenged me to a game of billiards. And Lyle. He's—"

"You shouldn't talk about other men you're dating when you're on a date with someone." Evie rolled her eyes as if this was obvious.

Yes, because now I feel about as useful as a saddle made for Dragon Lord.

Mandy's slender brows lowered. She frowned at Evie. "What did you talk about when you dated Wylie?"

"We didn't *date*," Wylie hurried to say. "It was one dinner."

"And then he ghosted me." Evie drummed her peach-colored nails on the table. "Be careful that Wylie doesn't do the same to you."

"I would never do that...*intentionally*," Wylie muttered.

Thankfully, their coffees were up. He went to get them, ready to chug his down and leave.

Maybe he'd been wrong to accept this date, wrong to agree to speed dating, and wrong to think now was the time to settle down. At the very least, he'd accepted Mandy's date for all the reasons on his checklist, despite him telling Hazel he'd done the asking. And apparently, Mandy had asked half the men at speed dating last night for a follow-up. But Ronnie was right. There was no spark. Not that he could leave now. That wouldn't be polite.

After he set the drinks on the table, his cell phone rang.

Wylie excused himself and stepped outside to answer.

"Doc, this woman you sent is in a river too deep for her boots." Janie Crocket spoke in a circumspect voice, as if she didn't want to be overheard. "She didn't see that bull coming for her."

Wylie's system went on full alert. "How badly is she hurt?"

"I'm not saying she can't walk upright but…"

Wylie hung up the phone and ran toward the clinic, where he'd left his truck.

CHAPTER FIVE

"THERE'S DOC NEWLAND," Janie said, as if she'd been expecting Wylie.

Ignoring her aches and pains, Hazel glanced up from loading the treatment bag into the clinic's mobile unit to find Wylie quickly rolling up in that big, black truck of his as if he'd been called to fight a raging fire.

Dust barreled over them after he came to a stop. And then he hopped out and marched over to Hazel, looking like he had intentions.

Like sweeping me into his arms and kissing me.

Irrationally, Hazel's heart pounded.

"You need to call me when you get injured." Wylie came to a stop a few feet away from Hazel and gave her the kind of head-to-toe inspection that made a girl blush.

"Who said I was injured?" Hazel turned toward Tad and his mother with narrowed eyes.

"Your new...*person*...is just a slip of a thing." Janie spoke directly to Wylie, ignoring Hazel completely. "Thought she might have bruised a rib or two."

Hazel sucked in a breath, stifling a reaction to a stab of pain where those suspected injuries were.

"And besides, me and Ma don't think Hard Nose has warts," Tad piped up.

"And there it is." Hazel curtsied stiffly, trying to make light of the situation. "They want a second opinion, Dr. Newland." *As usual.*

Wylie took a few steps closer to Hazel, peering at her face. "Are you sure you're all right?"

"I'm great."

Far be it from me to break down and show you my soon-to-be-colorful back and rib cage.

Wylie studied Hazel's expression, then turned to the Crockets. "I have complete faith in Dr. Hughes and her diagnosis."

My hero.

And then, Wylie glanced past them toward the barn, hesitating.

The rat.

"Great," Hazel said with full-on sarcasm. "I've applied topical wart medication and given Tad instructions on how to administer it over the course of the next few days. Miss Maisey's going to *call* Janie with her bill." They didn't even have the ability to accept electronic payment while on call. So primitive. "I'm out." Hazel gave Wylie a brief salute before opening the driver's side door, pausing to say to the Crockets, "Nice meeting you. Give the clinic a call if you don't see noticeable results in three days."

She got in as Wylie turned back toward his truck.

"But Dr. Newland..." Tad took a few steps forward. "You're not going to check Hard Nose?"

"Nope." Wylie got behind the wheel and drove away in a cloud of dust.

Hazel started the mobile unit and followed him.

Her cell phone rang a few minutes later. It was the clinic's number and since Wylie was in the truck ahead of her, it couldn't be him calling. "Go ahead, Miss Maisey."

"The boss wants you to take a patient at the Done Roamin' Ranch," Maisey said in her high-and-mighty voice. "One of their bucking bulls had a run-in with another. Sounds like he'll need stitching."

"Great." Hazel contorted herself in the seat, trying to find a position that didn't jangle her hypersensitive nerve endings. "Text me the address."

"Text you..." Maisey huffed. "Everybody knows where the Done Roamin' Ranch is."

Hazel passed by a sign for that very same ranch. In fact, it was the ranch sign featured in the picture with all those cowboys that Wylie had on display in the clinic's waiting room. "You're right. Everybody knows where the Done Roamin' Ranch is." Hazel hung up, made a U-turn, then drove beneath the large ranch gates, following a gravel road that disappeared over a hill.

Her phone rang again. "Go ahead, Miss—"

"I wasn't done," Maisey said in a snit. "After that, the boss wants you to cover the office appointments. That means you have ninety minutes to get back here."

"Cover the office appointments?" Hazel drove over a rise. "Is Wylie going on another date?"

Apparently, when Wylie decided to do something, he really went for it.

"*Another* date?" Maisey gasped. "When did he have time to go on a date?"

"Last night, for one. And then this morning." Oh, it felt good to know something about Wylie that Maisey didn't.

The Done Roamin' Ranch came into view. It was a large operation with multiple houses, barns, and paddocks. There was an arena as well as one of the largest ranch yards Hazel had ever seen, complete with several stock trailers and freight-hauling trucks. A tall, lean cowboy waved at Hazel and directed her to park near a very large semitruck.

"Who did he date?" Maisey demanded. "I can't believe he didn't tell me. His last relationship was a complete bust and I thought he'd never recover."

That was more interesting to Hazel than it should have been.

"Well, recover he has," Hazel teased. "Gotta go, Miss Maisey. I'm on a tight timeline."

And if Maisey kept talking while Hazel hung up, Hazel wasn't going to admit that it gave her the best laugh of the morning.

And a much-needed laugh at that.

"How dare you?" Maisey wasn't happy when Wylie returned to the clinic. She sat behind the check-in desk, frowning.

"I know. I know. I shouldn't have done it." Wylie strode past Maisey toward the back carrying a bag of clean work clothes. He needed to change before the next patient came in.

"And without telling me." Maisey scurried along behind him, still harping. "Me, who's been here through all your heartbreak over your father and Tabitha."

Wylie pulled up short and turned. "What are you talking about?"

"Your *dates*. Plural." Maisey shook a finger at him. "You can't just go asking out any cowgirl who strikes your fancy. You're *Dr. Wylie Newland*. There are plenty of cowgirls interested in you, and you need to choose the right one. You'll need a second opinion, of course."

Wylie took a moment to let Maisey's words sink in, to consider how to head this runaway idea off at the pass. "Er... I thought you were talking about me heading over to the Crockets' place because Janie called and said their bull had rammed Hazel."

"That's terrible. Of course you should have gone

out there." Maisey drew back, a look of satisfied surprise in her eyes. "Why didn't Hazel tell me? How many bones were broken? Was there a head wound?" Maisey glanced out the windows toward the parking lot, frowning as a truck pulled in. But it wasn't the clinic's mobile unit. "Such a pity. Hazel probably won't be in any shape to work here anymore."

You wish.

This attitude of Maisey's was rapidly turning out to be more of a problem than Wylie had anticipated. And it was only the second day! "I hate to burst your bubble but Hazel said she was *great*."

I should have anticipated Hazel's response. The clinic could be on fire and she still wouldn't show her true emotions.

"That's good news, I suppose." Maisey pursed her lips, seeming to think on it before shaking herself. "Now, to get back to my earlier point." She stomped her sandaled foot. "You've been dating behind my back."

"I've been dating," Wylie allowed, although his efforts were lackluster so far. "I appreciate your interest, but that's none of your concern."

"None of my..." Maisey frowned fiercely. "I'm all you have."

That wasn't true. Wylie had his very large foster family at the Done Roamin' Ranch.

But his heart went out to the elderly woman, who was truly alone except for him.

He drew Maisey in for a hug, if only to quickly release her when she squirmed away. She wasn't one for physical displays of affection. "When I find someone I'm serious about, you'll be the first to know."

The bell clanged at the front of the clinic.

Maisey hurried toward the check-in desk. "I'll hold you to that."

Leaving Wylie to wonder if that was good or bad.

"Tornado Tom got into a little scuffle when we were loading him onto the trailer for a rodeo." Chandler, the ranch foreman, was a tall cowboy with kind brown eyes and gray at his temples. He led Hazel through a long horse barn, presumably toward the corrals where they kept their bulls.

"Is he usually a problem?" Hazel tried to focus on her patient, not the stiffness in her rib cage when she breathed or the way carrying her medical bag and backpack caused discomfort every time she took a step.

"Is Tornado Tom a problem? Not usually, although he has his own trailer, kind of like a movie star." Chandler's grin was as wry as his humor. "That's my weak attempt at a joke. But it should tell you what a diva he is. He's a hard ride for rodeo cowboys and one of our most requested bulls."

They passed a lot of empty stalls, none of which

felt as if they'd been vacant for long. The smell of hay and dung were too strong.

"Do you truck riding horses to rodeos, too?" Hazel glanced in another open stall door.

"Yes, ma'am... *Doc*." Chandler tipped his hat as if apologizing for acknowledging her gender before her profession. "We supply roughstock for rodeos—broncs, bulls, cattle, and the like—plus, stock wranglers who need a horse to ride on-site. Sometimes we work as many as three rodeos at a time."

The Done Roamin' Ranch was indeed a large operation. And perhaps, a logistical challenge.

"And you're leaving today?" Hazel recalled something Izzy had said to her this morning. "It's Tuesday. Someone mentioned rodeo folk usually leave on Fridays."

"Rodeo stock actually leaves earlier than human competitors," Chandler explained, lengthening his stride. "And we've got a rodeo starting Thursday in southeastern Oklahoma."

"Got it." Hazel pressed onward, ignoring her aches. "Tell me about Tornado Tom's accident."

"We're short-handed today and we had too many bulls headed toward the loading area at the same time." Chandler's smile fell. "I'm hoping Tornado Tom can still compete this week."

"Not if he needs stitches."

Chandler grimaced.

They exited the horse barn and entered a large

area full of paddocks, some empty, some not. Bulls and horses glanced their way.

Chandler stopped, rubbed his chin and considered Hazel. "Thanks for taking care of Laramie. Izzy is my fiancée. She hasn't had that cat long but he's a gem. So… I just wanted to thank you."

"You're welcome."

"Now…" Chandler gave a crisp nod. "If Tornado Tom gets stitches, can he compete next weekend?" He smiled at her as if they were good friends who'd just learned they'd earned free ice cream.

Hazel gaped at him. "Did you just try to butter me up with praise for my treatment of Laramie before looking to shorten that bull's recovery time?" His gaze was skyward. She shook her head. "No deal. I haven't even seen his injury."

Chandler had the grace to look remorseful. "I don't mean to sound callous, but we send bulls all over the Midwest and I need to know for scheduling purposes."

"I'll have to see Tornado Tom first." Hazel heard something behind her and turned too quickly.

Ouch. Stupid ribs.

But she covered her reaction because a bunch of cowboys stood forty feet away, watching them with grins designed to charm.

Hazel frowned. "Do they need something, Chandler?" He was the foreman, after all.

"No." Chandler made a go-away gesture with

his hand. "This delay is holding us up from getting on the road."

The cowboys didn't scatter. If anything, their smiles grew.

"Chandler? Can you ask the new vet if she's single?" asked one.

"And if she likes to dance?" asked another.

"Or if the rumor about her and Wylie being a thing is true?" asked a third.

"There's a rumor about me and Wylie?" Hazel wondered aloud, wanting to disappear. This was worse than having her knowledge challenged.

"Sorry. This is what comes of working with family," Chandler muttered. "We're all foster brothers, you see, including Wylie. Raised right here on this ranch, which is why our ranch hands don't always *mind their own business*." This last was spoken in a much louder voice.

"Yes, Hazel is single." Ronnie, the woman who'd run the speed dating event last night, came around the corner of the barn, baby bump first. "I'm sure she likes to dance. And no, the rumor about her and Wylie isn't true. Now, don't scare the poor thing away." She shooed the cowboys off before joining Hazel and Chandler. "That said, I'm still hoping you'll accept my matchmaking services, Hazel."

Shaking his head, Chandler made a beeline down the aisle between paddocks toward one with a very large bull with blood trickling down his shoulder.

"As I said last night, Ronnie." Hazel tried to be tactful as she hurried toward her patient. The clock was ticking. "I'm not staying in Clementine longer than I have to."

"So you've said." Ronnie took Hazel's refusal as graciously as she had the night before. "But if you change your mind, you can always find me here. I live in the original farmhouse at the front."

"Pay Ronnie no mind," Chandler said when Hazel caught up to him at the occupied paddock. "My sister-in-law loves to play Cupid but that doesn't mean you have to go along."

"I can handle matchmaking cowgirls," Hazel assured him. And then, she took her first good look at Tornado Tom.

The oversize, majestic bull had a long, bleeding laceration on his left shoulder and a look in his eye that said he was annoyed about it. He huffed when he spotted Hazel and turned his broad side to her, all without breaking eye contact.

Hazel swallowed a groan.

I will never complain about giving rabies shots to unruly house pets again.

Or at least, not without a reminder about what she could be doing—house calls to unruly livestock.

"I'm assuming you have a squeeze chute?" Hazel needed the bull to be cocooned in a metal cradle and immobile in order to clean and stitch the wound properly. Not to mention, safely.

"I can do you one better, Doc. We've got a *new* squeeze chute. I'll get a couple of the guys and we'll secure him in it for you." Chandler turned, only to find those same cowhands loitering near the barn door once more. "Well, you heard me. Get it done. Now."

While the cowboys scattered to do his bidding, Hazel realized Ronnie had followed them.

"You think they'd never seen a woman on the ranch before." Ronnie hooked her arm through Hazel's as if they were good friends, then led her away from the barn and Tornado Tom. "You're a novelty because you're new to town."

"That's...*great*." Hazel reached for her usual adjective. "But I should really hang around back there—"

"The guys will handle everything," Ronnie assured her. "You'll just be a distraction. Some of them can be show-offs, which is dangerous around roughstock."

"That's flattering, Ronnie, but—"

"Why are you single?" Ronnie laughed, a rich, enticing sound. "Listen to me. My husband Wade says I'm incorrigible. Always asking folks about their love life." And then she lowered her voice. "But seriously... Have you been too consumed by your job to have time for romance? Or have you just not found the right man yet? Even if I can't help you find a happily-ever-after, I'm always curious about people." Ronnie smiled. And it was such a friendly smile.

Hazel resisted its pull toward friendship and guards being let down. In fact, she tried to laugh herself. If only that didn't hurt. "You're really something, Ronnie. Does that pitch work on everyone?" Because she imagined it did and before folks knew what had happened, Ronnie would have found them a date she promised would lead to the altar.

Chuckling, Ronnie drew Hazel closer. "You're the first person to ask me that."

Hazel gave in a bit to the friendship tug, smiling more naturally. "As long as we're sharing confidences, Ronnie, when I watched you orchestrate speed dating last night, I couldn't help but think you gave yourself a goal to reach before you give birth. How many matches do you want to make before that baby pops out?"

Ronnie's mouth dropped open but only for a few seconds, barely long enough for a fly to zip in. And then, she nodded slowly. "Izzy mentioned there was something she liked about you."

"Izzy? The owner of Laramie the cat fighter and manager of the feed store? Chandler's fiancée Izzy?" Hazel asked, realizing how tight knit the community was. When Ronnie nodded, Hazel prompted, "And…"

"And yes. I set a matchmaking goal before I take maternity leave." Ronnie flashed that beguiling grin of hers. "You won't mind if I keep trying to match you, will you?"

Hazel nodded, almost looking forward to the challenge. "Not if you don't mind me continuing to refuse."

"I'm going to enjoy becoming friends." Ronnie studied Hazel closer than a textbook beneath a dim desk lamp. "So...when Wylie insisted you take the ride he offered last night—"

"Wylie didn't insist anything." Hazel tried a proverbial backpedal. "He wanted me to drive back with him so we could discuss a patient and today's work schedule. We're all business."

"I see." Ronnie nodded her head slowly once more. "So... You're not attracted to him at all? I mean, he's very handsome, isn't he?"

Hazel waited a beat too long to answer.

Smiling triumphantly, Ronnie headed off toward the barn. "That's all I wanted to know."

"But... I didn't tell you anything." And yet, Hazel was afraid her silence told the matchmaker entirely too much.

CHAPTER SIX

"You're late." Maisey frowned when Hazel returned to the clinic. "Bruiser and Gustaf are here."

Hazel hung the mobile truck keys on the hook beneath the check-in counter and her cowboy hat on a hook on the wall. She surveyed a row of containers on the counter in front of Maisey—fudge, cookies, and tiny berry tarts—berry, not peach. "Where'd all the treats come from?"

"Women who want a date with the boss keep stopping by with baked goods." Maisey scoffed, disapproving wrinkles multiplying fast on her face. She took a bite of fudge. "The nerve of these gals, thinking this will give them some sort of an advantage."

"The nerve," Hazel echoed, taking a fudge square and popping it in her mouth. It was super sweet and super creamy. "You should ask for the fudge recipe."

Maisey gave her a dirty look and a sharp dismissal. Apparently, Wylie's suitors weren't to be encouraged. "You have patients waiting in both rooms."

"I need a clean shirt first." Hazel's pink scrub had bull slobber and blood on it. She peeled it over her tank top in the hallway, groaning as her bruised ribs protested.

Darn that Hard Nose.

"Ow!" Hazel bumped into something warm and solid while her shirt was still stuck over her head and raised arms. She managed to move the scrub past her shoulders to see who—or what—she'd collided with.

And wished she'd left the scrub shirt over her face.

"We don't change clothes in the hallway in full view of the parking lot windows." Wylie blocked Hazel's way, voice deep and guarded. And the heated look in his eyes…

Dangerous.

If only because it was so tempting. *He* was so tempting.

The last thing I need is to let Wylie know I think he's adorable.

"Sorry." Backing away, Hazel freed herself from the pink scrub, ducked her head, and moved past Wylie to the lab, where she'd seen a laundry basket.

After tossing her shirt into the basket, she returned to the hallway, where Wylie waited for her. They stared at each other in silence. But his eyes… His green eyes still gave her mind unwanted images of his arms coming around her and his lips pressing onto hers.

Awkward.

Hazel reminded herself of her career goals, which didn't include Clementine. She tried to look and sound professional. "Dr. Newland, the reason I wear a tank top beneath a scrub top is so I can change anywhere. And quickly. Which is more than I can say for you." She gestured toward his unimaginative green scrub, straining her banged-up core muscles in the process. "You don't have anything on underneath yours."

His eyes flashed and that smile…

Retreat!

Hazel cleared her throat. "Dr. Newland, let me clarify. I am *not* speculating about what you do or don't wear underneath…*anything.*"

Gah! I'm just making it worse!

Wylie stared at Hazel more intensely than before.

"Not that there's anything wrong with only wearing one layer of clothing." Adrenaline numbed Hazel's aches and pains enough to allow her to bolt upstairs for a fresh scrub, this one sea foam green.

Fluffy tottered into her bedroom, pink and hairless, growling before reaching a ray of sunshine on the carpet and plopping down on it. She curled into a tight ball.

Hazel took pity on the dog and went in search of Fluffy's bed and gray blanket. She found them in

Maisey's dark bedroom at the foot of the old woman's bed—a traditional, solid oak, four-poster that must have been wrestled up those stairs by burly men egged on by a sharp-tongued Maisey.

"Here you go, Fluffy." Hazel dropped the dog bed in the widest swath of sunshine, then tented the gray blanket on top of it.

Not needing a second invitation, Fluffy grunted as she got to her feet and burrowed beneath the blanket canopy. She settled down with a sigh.

Moving stiffly, Hazel tucked the blanket snugly around the little dog, earning another growl for her efforts.

She smiled. Some dogs were just glass-half-empty.

Hazel turned and headed for the stairs, only to find Wylie in her way again. "Oh. Are you a ninja? How long have you been standing there?"

"Long enough to confirm that you're hurt and moving like a turtle." Wylie opened the coat closet outside her bedroom. "I've got something for that." He held up a hanger with what looked like a tan fishing vest. "One of my foster brothers made this for me after a mare decided cracking one of my ribs would be fun. Put this on." He handed it to Hazel, looking self-conscious. And when she took it, he walked toward the kitchen.

"This is great. Thanks." Hazel slid the large vest over her shoulders. It hung down mid-thigh. "But... Um... What's this for?"

"It's a cold pack holder to ease the ache of body blows." Wylie removed several fist-size blue ice packs from the freezer. And then he turned to look at her, frowning. "We'll need to get creative about the fit." He came over to Hazel and began fiddling with the vest—zipping the front, cinching the waist, tugging it down so hard it nearly knocked Hazel off-balance.

"Are you sure this works?" she asked, moving her feet to keep upright rather than grabbing onto Wylie's strong arms for balance.

"Yes." Wylie took a step back, inspecting the fit. Then his gaze lifted to hers. "Where does it hurt? That's where we need to put the ice packs."

Hazel pressed her lips together. No way was she going to admit she hurt everywhere. But she had to say something. "I…uh… I'm great as is."

Wylie smirked. "We haven't put any ice packs in. But your go-to response tells me all I need to know. Hard Nose squeezed you like an accordion, didn't he?" Without waiting for an answer, Wylie began dropping small blue-gel ice packs into various pockets on the vest Hazel wore.

That felt entirely too personal.

"I've got this," Hazel said, taking over the task herself, at least on the front.

"I'll get the ones in the back." Wylie went about the task methodically.

The vest was thin. The ice packs were extremely

cold. It didn't take long for Hazel to feel like a Popsicle.

A two-legged Popsicle who was melting under Wylie's persistent stare.

"Better?" he asked.

"Great. This is great." Hazel estimated she'd last about five minutes before her hands shook so hard she'd have to remove it.

The door at the bottom of the stairs opened and Maisey called, "Patients are waiting."

"That's you," Wylie said gruffly. "I've got some calls to make with the mobile unit."

And just like that, he was gone.

Hazel hesitated to follow, wanting to remove the vest. The cold was becoming unbearable. But it was a kind gesture he'd made. She'd wear it until Wylie left the clinic.

A short time later, still wearing the cold pack vest, Hazel entered the first exam room where a small white poodle and an elderly woman dressed colorfully in orange boots and hat sat talking with Maisey.

Hazel realized it was the woman she'd encountered on her morning walk with Budge. "Hi, Rose. What's going on with Bruiser?"

Maisey looked surprised that Hazel knew her patients. *Good.*

"Someone came in the bank with a Labrador puppy." Rose held the poodle in her lap. "Bruiser couldn't resist playing with him. And since then, he's been moving stiffly."

Hazel picked up Bruiser and put him on the exam table. The little poodle wouldn't lift his head. And when she tried to rotate and extend his legs, he resisted. "Rose, do you exercise? Besides walking to the bank and back, I mean."

"Forgetting who the patient is, are we?" Maisey muttered.

Hazel ignored her.

"Exercise?" Rose tittered. "Not me. It wears me out. I don't even ride anymore. Makes me sore for days."

"That's exactly how Bruiser feels after playing with a puppy. Sore." Hazel continued her exam, moving to his spine, not finding anything of concern. "You have a few options. Rest, for one. If Bruiser doesn't get better in a day or two, you can bring him back."

Rose nodded. "That's what my grandparents would choose. But even I can tell he's hurting. I feel so bad. What else can we do?"

"I can prescribe some medicine to ease his pain or…" Hazel hesitated, glancing at Maisey, whom she knew wouldn't approve of her next option. "Or I can give him an acupuncture treatment."

Maisey gasped. "Dr. Newland would never—"

"I'm licensed to perform acupuncture," Hazel went on to assure Rose as Maisey stomped out of the exam room. "Bruiser will feel better almost immediately. In either case, he needs to stay home and rest over the next few days. Ultimately, the choice of treatment is up to you."

The bell over the front door rang and Maisey called out, "Doc Newland? You're needed back inside."

Hazel grit her teeth, knowing it was too soon to have earned Maisey's trust but feeling bitter that the old woman doubted her anyway.

Meanwhile, Rose stared at Hazel blankly. "Acupuncture? I don't know anyone who's had acupuncture. Haven't heard tell of any animals receiving it either. Is that what your vest is? Are there needles in those pockets?"

Hazel explained how the vest was one big ice pack while she caught snatches of voices murmuring in the hallway.

Then the exam room door opened and Wylie leaned in. "Dr. Hughes, can I have a word?"

Tension pinched the base of Hazel's neck.

Here comes the kibosh on acupuncture.

"Excuse me, Rose." Hazel placed Bruiser in the old woman's lap. "I'll be right back."

"Hazel, your hands are freezing," Rose told her. "Are you feeling all right?"

"I'm *great*. But this vest I'm wearing is turning me into an icicle." Blowing air on her hands, Hazel left the exam room and followed Wylie and Maisey into the lab. While they turned what felt like accusing gazes her way, Hazel undid the vest's waist strap, then wrestled with the zipper. "I've reached my limit on being iced down." She was so cold, it was hard to smile. That just wouldn't do.

"Hazel, we haven't discussed offering acupuncture," Wylie said in what seemed like a reproachful tone. "I don't know if it's right for my practice and I wouldn't even know what to charge."

Naming a figure, Hazel folded the entire vest and put it in the freezer, earning a frown from both her coworkers. But with patients waiting, she didn't have time to remove the twenty or so ice packs separately.

"We aren't using our clients as pin cushions." Maisey crossed her arms over her chest. "Mumbo-jumbo. That's what it is."

Hazel ignored her, turning to Wylie to plead her case. "Acupuncture is a proven science. It relieves inflammation that causes soreness, as well as other symptoms caused by inflammation." She could use a treatment herself. "I'm licensed. I've used it on several animals, especially older ones. I don't just mention it as an option to rock the boat and upset Miss Maisey." Although she wouldn't dismiss the idea.

"Miss Maisey," the vet tech mumbled through her bulldog frown.

Brow furrowed, Wylie stared at Hazel in a detached way that told her his mind had already been made up. "I don't think our clients are the right target for acupuncture."

"They could be." Hazel drew herself up taller, realizing she wasn't as sore as she had been before donning the torturous ice vest. "Let me show you. I could give a few treatments to Fluffy and—"

"Don't you touch my Fluffy!" Maisey howled.

"I won't touch her without your permission," Hazel reassured Maisey, trying to hide her bitterness and disappointment behind a professional demeanor. "But it's what I'd recommend if she were my patient."

"It's a good thing you aren't her doctor." Maisey's frown was deep enough to become permanently etched on her face.

"All right. Message received." Hazel moved toward the door, needing to get away from all their negativity. "Now, if you'll excuse me, I have patients to attend to."

A patient that had decided against acupuncture before Hazel could tell Rose that she wasn't being allowed to offer it. Hazel prescribed a mild painkiller instead, then moved on to the next patient.

Gustaf was a chocolate Labrador with ear infections. After she'd cleaned his smelly ears and sent him home with ear wash and antibiotic, there was a string of dogs and cats in need of shots, tick removal, and severe allergy and constipation relief.

Hazel was just a vet doing ordinary vet things. Just a vet doing what she was told, no matter how many additional treatment options she could have offered. Sad to say, the stitches Hazel had given

Tornado Tom were the highlight of her day, not that she could share it with anyone who'd understand her fascination with binding living flesh to promote healing. Wylie wasn't to be found. Not that she wanted to talk to him. He was…confusing. Attractive. Attracting. But close-minded when it came to treatments outside his normal wheelhouse.

So demoralizing.

When Maisey finally closed the clinic, Hazel fed Budge, then dragged herself upstairs, removed another stained scrub shirt, and climbed slowly into bed, too tired and achy to take a shower.

"I'm not making you dinner," Maisey said, banging around the kitchen.

"I'm not making me dinner either." Hazel had lost her appetite.

Dr. Reed had been wrong. Her residency wasn't revealing a new, more appealing horizon. If anything, Clementine was blocking out the sun.

Her roommate banged around in the kitchen as if relishing making too much noise.

Argh.

And to top it all off, Hazel had forgotten to pick up earplugs today!

She punched her pillow and called out, "Miss Maisey, don't you dare snore tonight."

Maisey cackled.

Hazel shut her eyes and wrapped her pillow over her ears, thankful for one thing: *My attraction to Wylie has been seriously downgraded.*

An hour later, Hazel woke up to the smell of something burning. She hurried out to the kitchen, where she found a pot of what she assumed had been boiling pasta. But the pot had boiled over, as evidenced by the layer of water on the stovetop, and then the water had boiled completely away, as evidenced by the burned, blackened pasta on the bottom of the pan.

And Maisey?

She and Fluffy were curled up on the couch, blissfully asleep and snoring.

Hazel shut down the stove, opened a window, and cleaned up the mess, not even trying to be silent—not that Maisey woke up. And Fluffy? Well, the dog barely opened her eyes to growl at Hazel.

When Hazel finished, she changed out of her work clothes and into another sundress, her comfy sandals, and her peacock-trimmed cowboy hat. Grabbing her cell phone-wallet, she headed for the door, determined to find food and a pair of earplugs. Not necessarily in that order.

WYLIE ENTERED THE feed store after a long afternoon spent far away from his troublesome, enchanting resident. His scrub shirt was dirty, stained, and damp with sweat. He wasn't exactly fit for being seen in public when he was hoping to present himself as a catch.

But Ronnie had arranged for a mini-date with Minnie in twenty minutes at the Buffalo Diner.

Wylie had no time to go home, shower, grab a clean shirt out of the dryer and iron it. So, he'd decided to buy a new one at the feed store.

"Hey, Wyatt." Izzy called a greeting from behind the sales counter at the back of the store where she had a small line forming.

"Hey, Izzy." Wylie ducked his head, veering into the round racks of clothing, avoiding the aisles filled with various types of pet food, toiletries, seasonal items, and shoppers. "Don't mind me. I just need a shirt." Catching wind of an unpleasant aroma, he sniffed.

Ew. Maybe I should give myself a sponge bath in the diner restroom first.

He grabbed the first shirt in his size on the rack and turned, nearly bowling over Hazel. "Oops. Sorry."

Hazel righted him with a brief but firm touch, one that was retracted almost immediately. "Put that back." Rather than let him do so, Hazel took the shirt from Wylie. "It's a good thing Izzy sent me over. We assumed you needed a shirt for a last-minute date. But you'll look like a red-and-white picnic tablecloth in that." She picked through the Western shirt options while he observed the gentle swish of her teal sundress and the soft pink polish on her toes.

She was a contradiction, soft as a gentle breeze one minute, strong as a prairie gale the next—an enigma he was itching to solve. Why hadn't he put something like that on his ideal woman wish list?

"You're lucky I was in here buying a new pasta pot and earplugs." Hazel held up a hanger with a blue shirt, first in front of herself, then in front of him. She tilted her head and studied him speculatively. "What about this one?"

"It looks like every other shirt I have in my closet." The last thing he needed was another blue shirt.

"Okay." Hazel shoved the blue option back on the round rack. "Black is always good. Classy. Modern. Powerful." She held up a black shirt that had gold trim on the yoke and shiny gold buttons.

"No bling." Wylie nudged her aside and drew out a shirt that was purple. "This'll do."

"Purple?" Hazel scoffed. "That says you're settled. And the gray options...boring."

Boring? That struck a chord. Wylie hesitated.

"Wylie." A brunette joined them at the rack, a hungry look in her gaze and a seductive purr to the way she said his name. "I was just thinking about you."

Hazel slowly backed away.

Instinctively, Wylie grasped hold of Hazel's arm above her elbow, holding her in place. "Hey, Tammy. Everything okay with your animals?"

"All is well. But..." Tammy glanced at Hazel, frowning before refocusing her smile on Wylie. "I heard you're back on the dating scene. And it just so happens…" She gestured to herself with a flourish. "So am I!"

Hazel tried to free her arm but Wylie held on, going so far as to give her a look he hoped said, *"Help me with this garbage fire."*

Whatever message Hazel received, she stopped trying to free herself and tugged her cowboy hat brim low, hiding those expressive eyes from him.

Tammy grabbed hold of Wylie's free arm and gave it a shake. "You'll save me a dance at the Buckboard on Saturday?"

This was worse than the time he'd been in high school and swarmed by a group of girls who demanded he ask Tammy to prom because, *"You'd make such a cute couple."* He'd felt trapped then. He felt trapped now. Except…he hadn't had Hazel by his side back then and…

"Tammy…" Wylie heaved a sigh of relief as he realized something. "Aren't you still married to Dan?"

"Technically? Yes," Tammy admitted, almost reluctantly. "Dan asked for a divorce but we're negotiating terms and financials. Meanwhile, I have no one to dance with on Saturday nights." She batted her eyelashes. "What do you say?"

No.

But he sensed Tammy's determination wouldn't let her take a simple no as an answer. "Sorry, Tammy. I never make firm plans at night because

I'm always on call. I wouldn't want to say yes and then disappoint you."

"The way you did Evie," Tammy murmured sadly. Then her smile brightened. "I'd heard a rumor that you might be dating your intern—"

"Resident," both Hazel and Wylie corrected her softly.

"—but it seems like you just need someone with a flexible schedule." Tammy batted her eyelashes at him once more. "I'm very flexible. Text me when you get to the Buckboard next time. I'll be there in a jiffy." And with that, she flounced away.

Hazel and Wylie didn't move or speak until Tammy had left the building.

"She's on call for you." Hazel carefully extricated her arm, smiling sadly. "I'll let you pick out the shirt you want." And then she left him, too, the same way she'd left him earlier at the clinic when he shot down her acupuncture idea.

As if she was disappointed in him.

FIFTEEN MINUTES AND a quick sponge bath in the feed store bathroom later, Wylie entered the Buffalo Diner wearing the black shirt with gold bling, new blue jeans, and a cheap brand of deodorant. Trying to settle himself in the stiff clothes, he took stock of the dining room occupants.

There were couples, families, and groups of people at the diner. But no Minnie.

And surprise, surprise. There was Hazel. She sat

on a bar stool near the wall with a bowl of chili, a side of French fries, and a chocolate milkshake, a feed store bag with her purchases at her feet.

Wylie came to sit next to her. "Has anyone ever told you that you eat like a sixth grader?"

"After not eating all day, I'm not going to apologize for choosing protein and carbs," Hazel said unapologetically, giving him a quick once-over. "I see you went with my advice and chose the black shirt."

He nodded, taking note of how the late afternoon light caught the many shades of red, orange, and yellow in her hair. "You made the other options that weren't blue sound unattractive."

"About what happened at the clinic earlier..." Hazel swirled a long French fry through her bowl of chili. "I apologize for assuming I could just offer a service without discussing it with you first."

He nodded, watching her eat that chili-coated fry. His empty stomach rumbled. "Starting a new job is difficult."

"Even if you have the right staff, like you do with Maisey." Hazel's smile seemed a bit forced and her gaze guarded. "She's great. She's got everything down to a routine."

Wylie could guess where this was going. "I don't want to be the guy who says we can't do something just because I've never done it before." He'd hated hearing that when he'd been a resident.

Hazel's eyebrows rose but she said nothing.

"I realize that's what it sounded like today but you surprised me." He ran a hand around behind his neck. "We should talk about what else you'd like to do and if it's a fit with my clientele."

"We should talk," Hazel repeated slowly. "All right. In addition to acupuncture, I'd like to offer a variety of products, natural herbs, salves, and shampoos. Things that promote wellness and good health. I know it sounds heartless but you can increase your profits with an upsell."

"An upsell meaning..." He gestured toward her plate of French fries. "Would you like fries with your chili?"

"Yes." Hazel laughed a little, cutting off the sound too quickly and sobering. "You know, if you're going on a date, you should really remove the price tag." She slid her hand to the base of his neck, brushing her fingers through the fringe of his hair.

Wylie froze, tempted to...

Just a tug of Hazel's hand and his lips could cover hers.

Hazel tugged, but not in the way Wylie anticipated. She yanked the price tag backward off the neck of his shirt. "There. Now you're ready for that date."

A date he no longer wanted.

"Wylie?" Smiling, Minnie tapped Wylie on his shoulder, gaze drifting toward Hazel. Her smile

lost some of its shine. "Sorry I'm late. Are you ready?"

Wylie nodded and got to his feet, but he wasn't ready for a date with anyone but Hazel. He wanted to learn what made her tick and ask her how her ribs were doing. He wanted to admire the various colors in her hair and the diverse facets of her personality.

But he'd committed to this mini-date. So, he followed Minnie to an empty booth where they each ordered an iced tea and put soldiering smiles on their faces.

"What a day." Minnie fidgeted, looking flustered as she fiddled with the neck of her gray blouse. Her brown hair was without a cowboy hat and mussed, as if she'd run her hand through it a few too many times today. "Is it a full moon this week? Everywhere I turn I encounter drama."

To be agreeable, Wylie nodded, gaze drifting toward Hazel. She had her head propped on her hand and was leaning over that bowl of chili as if she didn't want to be disturbed.

Except…to him, she looked lonely.

"First thing this morning, my ex-husband Kirby came into the pharmacy demanding I sell him prescription flu medication because he's certain that he has the flu." Minnie huffed, staring at her clasped hands on the table. "Can you imagine? He was married to me. He knows I'm not a doctor and can't dispense prescription medication without a physician's approval."

Wylie nodded.

Their iced teas arrived.

Minnie apparently needed to vent because she ignored her iced tea and continued, "At lunchtime, my ex-husband Mario came in asking if I knew where his birth certificate was. He accused me of having it. Can you imagine? We haven't been married for nearly a decade. Why would I still have anything of his?"

Wylie shook his head and murmured, "The nerve."

"And then, right before we closed for the day, my ex-husband Jay *just dropped by*—" she made air quotes with her fingers "—and remembered that I owed him one hundred dollars. Although he couldn't remember when or why I might have borrowed that amount. And he wouldn't leave when I told him no." Minnie's gaze swerved toward the parking spaces outside the window where they sat. She gasped. "Tell me that isn't Jay out there now. *Argh.* No need to say anything, Wylie. It's him. He must be desperate for money. Again."

And before Wylie could say a word, Minnie slung a gigantic black leather purse to her shoulder and scooted out of the booth spouting all kinds of apologies before she trotted out the door.

Wylie sighed, watching Minnie until he could be certain she wasn't going to accost Jay with that big purse of hers. But she simply shouted at Jay and then got in her minivan and drove away.

Date over.

Wylie's gaze caught on Hazel's.

She sighed just as heavily as he had earlier and waved him over, an invitation he couldn't refuse because...

He didn't want to think about why.

Instead, he brought his iced tea over, sat down on the stool next to Hazel and swiped a French fry. "I think that date was faster than my speed date with Minnie the other night."

"Do I want to know what happened?" Hazel stirred her bowl of chili with her spoon.

Wylie shook his head. "She had a bad day. Enough said. Except..." He sighed. "This dating thing..."

Hazel lifted her gaze to his, lifted her lips in a smile. "I guess you didn't need to buy a new shirt and blue jeans, after all." All spoken with that sneaky bit of sarcasm.

He was growing fond of that tone. "I can always use a non-blue shirt." Wylie reached for another fry.

But so did Hazel. Their fingers touched and sparks flew in his head, launching themselves like fireworks above them and announcing love was in the air.

They both sat back. They both said nothing.

At least, not with their lips.

But their eyes... Their eyes had a different story to tell.

They said: *Those sparks could mean something.*

They said: *This feeling is new and exciting.*

They said: *There's something here that could be important.*

That is, if they both planned to stay in Clementine.

WYLIE'S GOING TO kiss me.

And Hazel wasn't going to stop him, even if some tiny part of her brain was telling her this was foolishness. He was her boss and she didn't plan to make Clementine home.

But she was lost in his green gaze and leaning in closer, encouraging him to make his move.

And then...

Something brushed lightly over Hazel's toe, a whisper of a touch.

She assumed it was Wylie getting playful with his feet. But...

Hazel stilled. Wylie had been wearing boots. And cowboy boot footsie wasn't light. It would have felt more like a bump on her bare toe.

Hazel glanced toward the floor and shrieked, *"SNAKE!"* Then she leaped off the bar stool and onto Wylie's back.

Wylie must have caught sight of the snake, too. He leaned away from her former bar stool, lost his balance, and they both went tumbling to the floor.

Almost immediately, they scrambled to their feet and retreated to the diner's door.

"What happened?" A thin, elderly woman darted out of the kitchen. She'd been Hazel's waitress the night before.

"Snake," Hazel said again, pointing toward the corner where the counter met the wall.

A relatively small black snake extended its head upward, tongue darting out toward the counter and her dinner.

"A snake?" The elderly woman grabbed a kitchen rag and headed their way. "Are you sure?"

"Kevin!" A cowboy of about ten clomped over to their former seats before the cook could. "See, Mom. I told you he wasn't lost." The kid picked up the fifteen-inch snake and coiled it around his wrist. "Hey, Doc Newland. Meet Kevin." He thrust his snake-covered wrist toward them.

Hazel ducked behind Wylie, waiting a second or two before peeking around his shoulder. "Is that your emotional support animal, kid?"

"We don't allow those," the elderly cook grumbled, coming to a halt a safe distance away. "Or snakes of any kind."

"But Coronet, this is Kevin." The pint-sized cowboy tenderly stroked his snake. "I found him in our pasture. We came into town to get him a cage at the feed store but they don't have any. I'm gonna keep him in a shoebox tonight. Mom says we'll try Friar's Creek tomorrow."

"He should have been in a shoebox that you left in your vehicle, Cassidy." Coronet inched past the boy, bent in the corner, and wiped her rag on the floor beneath the bar stools.

That won't wipe away my memory of Kevin.

Wylie scuffed a boot on the floor, glancing toward the door.

"It's too hot to leave animals in the truck," Cassidy told anyone who'd make eye contact. "Especially in a shoebox. That wouldn't be right."

"After roaming around your pasture, Kevin's not going to be happy in a little shoebox," Hazel told him, glancing up at Wylie, whose face was as white as an empty sheet of paper.

"That's what I told him, too." A cowgirl of about Wylie's age joined them near the door. She laid her hands on the little cowboy's shoulders. "Sorry for the scare, everybody. I don't suppose you have a spare terrarium at the vet's office?"

"Nope," Hazel answered, having nosed around the place.

"If you don't have a proper home for Kevin, that's all the more reason to put him back in the pasture," Wylie said gruffly.

"But Doc… He loves me." Cassidy held up his snake-wrapped wrist once more. "See?"

Wylie leaned back into Hazel and said weakly, "Check, please."

Hazel chuckled. "Mine, too." She hadn't finished

her meal but she wasn't comfortable sitting in the same café as a boy and his snake.

A few minutes later, she and Wylie were outside the diner. She stared at him. He stared at her.

And then, they both started laughing.

Hazel didn't know for sure why Wylie was laughing. But she found it hilarious that they'd almost kissed in front of everybody in the Buffalo Diner, and had been interrupted by a runaway snake.

By what seemed like mutual consent, Hazel and Wylie went their separate ways, Hazel toward the clinic with the bag with the pan and earplugs she'd purchased at the feed store. Wylie toward the parking lot and heaven only knew where.

Hazel's sandals slapped the hot pavement. She was very much aware that she'd dodged a bullet with Wylie. A kiss... Heck, a *relationship* with him would only complicate her stay in Clementine. Maisey would be hopeless to work with, more so than she was now, if that was possible. And Wylie...

Those kisses might be worth the trouble.

Hazel scoffed.

Keep things professional, Dr. Hughes.

That was Dr. Reed's voice in her head.

A familiar black truck pulled up next to her, engine rumbling. The driver rolled down the window.

"Get in," Wylie said in a no-nonsense tone. "I'm hungry and we need to talk."

And despite her better judgment, Hazel did just that.

CHAPTER SEVEN

"So, this is the local honky-tonk." Sitting in a booth across from Wylie, Hazel glanced around the Buckboard.

Because looking at the bar was preferable to looking at her very handsome, very smart, very tempting boss.

A man who shares my fear of reptiles.

Shared fears was just one more in a growing list of similarities between them. They were both smart doctors who cared about animals and enjoyed the challenge of surgery. A match made in...

Pfft. That could describe me and Dr. Reed.

She'd never felt attracted to her mentor professor. Not in the slightest.

Hazel took stock of the Buckboard. The bar nearly ran the length of the place, from the front door to the dance floor and stage in the back, which she faced. Booths lined one wall. Wooden tables and chairs filled the middle. The decor was rustic barnwood and antlers with a come-as-you-are atmosphere. Country music played at a level where you could hear each other talk but could also sing along, if you were so inclined. Hazel was more the head-bobbing type.

Izzy had invited Hazel to join her and her friends here on Thursday. And now that she'd seen the place, Hazel was inclined to accept. After all, she needed somewhere besides the Buffalo Diner to eat. The Buckboard wasn't filled with single cowboys the way Maisey had made it out to be. And the other patrons had plates of food in front of them—steak, pot roast, burgers.

Hazel's stomach grumbled. She hadn't eaten enough at the Buffalo Diner before a snake stole her appetite. It was coming back full-force now.

"We need to talk about what happened at the diner." Wylie's deep voice brought Hazel's attention back around to him. He'd tipped his brown cowboy hat brim upward, revealing sharp, commanding features. And he was looking at her like her employer, not the man who'd almost kissed her.

That's a shame.

Hazel felt like rolling her eyes. She didn't, choosing instead to soldier a smile. "You want to discuss our mutual fear of Kevin?" The small snake that had brushed her bare foot. She shivered.

"Nope." Wylie didn't so much as blink those sharp green eyes. "You know what needs to be said."

Still smiling, Hazel clasped her hands and rested them on the edge of the table. "Okay. We're not going to admit a snake phobia. But you know that by morning Maisey will have heard about it." Hazel may have only been in Clementine a few days but she knew how small towns worked. "She'll have a field day over our reaction." How Hazel had leaped onto Wylie and how they'd both fallen to the floor, only to scramble to their feet and scoot as far away from Kevin as possible, while a kid came to their rescue.

"Maisey is the least of our worries." Wylie leaned forward. "I'm more concerned with how we…" His voice faltered and he turned his head toward the bar, a crease between those black brows, as if he didn't want to complete that sentence.

Yes, let's not speak the K-word out loud, please.

"Oh, that." Hazel tsked and waved his concerns aside, attempting to sweep their attraction out the door and to a curb neither one of them frequented. "Nothing happened at the diner." Even if they'd been a tick of the clock away from kisses happening.

Wylie's gaze caught on something behind her. His frown deepened.

Let him look as unhappy as he wants to, as long as he doesn't dissect that almost-kiss.

It was Hazel's turn to frown. It wasn't like her to be anything but decisive, especially where her career was concerned. But since she'd met Wylie in person, she'd been waffling between wanting and *not* wanting to lock lips with him.

Wylie got out of the booth, stared down at Hazel as if he was considering hightailing it out of there, and then came to sit beside her. "Shove over."

"Shove over?" Hazel didn't move. Not until his hip touched hers. And then she practically leaped to scrunch herself next to the wall. "This isn't a good idea."

Ronnie appeared at their table, hands cradling her baby bump. A sturdy cowboy stood behind her. "I spotted you two when we came in. Hazel, this is my husband, Wade. Wade... Hazel. She's the new vet in town. May we join you?" And without further ado, Ronnie eased her pregnant girth into their booth and removed her cowboy hat.

"Wade is my foster brother," Wylie said to Hazel. *And the reason I'm sitting beside you,* Wylie's expression silently communicated.

Hazel shouldn't have felt disappointed that he'd sat next to her just to make room for another couple. But she did. Although she tried to hide it behind a smile she turned toward Ronnie's husband. "Are you another brother from the Done Roamin' Ranch? How many kids did your parents foster?"

Wade grinned. "Mom says a passel. No matter the number, we're a family who support each other and share interests. We all ride. We all learned to rodeo. And most of us stayed local," Wylie's foster brother said with a smile, curling his arm around Ronnie's shoulders and bringing her closer to him. "Just FYI. We came into town for dinner and to discuss business with you, Wylie. Although not the matchmaking kind."

Ronnie smirked. "At least, not at first. I am always working for my clients." She gave Hazel a knowing glance.

Like she knew we almost kissed?

Hazel tensed.

"Hmm," Wylie said, looking toward the bar.

A server came over and took their orders—cheeseburgers all around. Ronnie ordered extra pickles, a side of chicken fingers, and a cup of country gravy.

"So much for me being the only one you know who eats like she's twelve," Hazel quipped to Wylie at a volume only he could hear.

"Try getting pregnant and see how much your good food habits regress." Ronnie grinned at Hazel, smoothing her long, dark hair over one shoulder. "Don't look so surprised that I caught your comment, Hazel. I read lips. It's a very helpful tool when you work at an elementary school. And I will admit to this baby's stomach-rejecting aversion to broccoli and other vegetables. I used to love to eat them raw. Now it's all carbs, carbs, carbs."

"Ain't that the truth." Wade stared at his wife with an endearing look in his eyes. "Every word she said. The other night, Ronnie asked me for pepperoni pizza and ice cream."

"I put a spoonful of vanilla ice cream on top of

each pepperoni." Ronnie touched her fingers to her lips and blew a kiss. "Five stars."

"Pass," Wylie said.

Hazel agreed. "I'm hungry and even I don't find that appealing."

Somehow, Wylie's hand found Hazel's beneath the table. His fingers twined with hers, an oddly easy-connection considering the pitfalls of their doing so. "What's the business you have with me, Wade?"

"Someone sent word to the county fair committee that the Done Roamin' Ranch cowboys should step down from judging. *Permanently.*" Wade frowned his disapproval. "You were set to judge large livestock—"

"As usual," Wylie said succinctly, his grip on Hazel's hand suddenly as tense as his expression.

"—and I was going to judge bull and bronc riding," Wade continued, discontent in every syllable. "But someone complained that there are too many young cowpokes entering events with ties to the Done Roamin' Ranch. Whoever this was, they challenged our impartiality if it's our niece or nephew out there competing."

"That's like questioning my honor," Wylie said sharply, falling back in the booth but not letting go of Hazel's hand. "As well as your honor, Wade. Why would this come up when there are less than ten days before the fair begins?"

"It's the worst timing." His foster brother nodded. "I talked to Dad about it today. He doesn't want us to roll over and quit. Said it was like letting a disagreement fester between family."

"His idea of family stretches wider than mine most days, all the way to the county line, apparently." As Wylie spoke, his thumb stroked a path over the back of Hazel's hand. And as he did so, she felt his grip loosen until it became more tender and—

What are we doing?

Hazel tried to be the smart one here, tried to ease her hand free. At least, she tried until she noticed Ronnie's curious glance and Wylie's frank look that said, *Relax. Don't attract any more of Ronnie's attention.*

Hazel stilled. What happened—or didn't happen—between herself and Wylie was their business, not the local matchmaker's.

And it's not like we're making out. He's just holding my hand through a difficult time.

"In a small town, everybody knows everybody." Wylie rubbed his forehead with his free hand. "If the fair committee applies this rule to everyone, they won't have any judges left."

"What about Hazel?" Wade nodded her way. "She's new to town. Can she judge the large livestock in your place?"

"I have no experience," Hazel blurted. She never took on any task she wasn't qualified for.

"You're a veterinarian," Ronnie said simply.

"I'm sure you know how to judge an animal's confirmation and behavior."

Behavior? Hazel was reminded of Hard Nose's misbehavior. She hadn't been aware of more than a dull ache around her chest from her bruising but now the sharp reminder of pain came back as if the bull had just rammed her. "I'll pass," she said.

"Who questioned our integrity?" Wylie demanded, resting their joined hands on his thigh. "I look forward to supporting the fair every year."

"Why?" Hazel asked. If Wylie was going to hold her hand, she felt entitled to some answers.

The fire in Wylie's eyes dimmed and he began speaking slowly, softly. To Hazel. "When my mom left and my dad became…*inconsistent*…I was grateful for my found family at the Done Roamin' Ranch. Like Wade said, there are a lot of us. And Clementine…" His voice deepened…roughened. "They supported me and my dad. There could have been talk about me being a problem at home. And that would have been true." He hung his head. "And there could have been talk about my dad being a problem. That would have been true, too. But at the fair… I was just another local kid. Welcomed. Encouraged. Cheered."

"At the fair you felt like your whole life was ahead of you, full of untainted possibilities." Hazel moved her other hand to cover their joined ones, imagining she felt Wylie's strength, his compassion, his honor—all through that touch. "And you want to give back, perhaps be the light some kid needs even if they don't realize they need it."

Wylie nodded, glancing down at their hands and then at his foster brother. "Who raised this issue? Who wants us out as judges?"

Wade shrugged, and then seemed to realize that Ronnie had fallen asleep on his shoulder. He lowered his voice. "If you want answers, we'll need to attend the fair committee meeting next Tuesday."

"I prefer answers over the unknown." Wylie's gaze found Hazel's. "In all things."

Including me?

Hazel gulped.

"I HAVE PLANS for you," Ronnie told Wylie as Wade helped her out of the booth after dinner. "All these mini-dates are getting us closer to something truly meaningful."

Since Wylie had once more claimed Hazel's hand under the table, he merely nodded before bidding the couple good-night.

And then—*finally*—he and Hazel were alone once more.

It was late, close to nine. There was hardly anyone left in the Buckboard at this hour midweek. Just Chet the bartender and a couple he didn't recognize at the far end of the bar.

"We should get going, too. Long day tomorrow," Hazel said, although she didn't try to tug her hand free or push him out of the booth. "Thank you. This has been…great."

"Great." Wylie shook his head, turning slightly to look directly at Hazel. At her long, strawberry blond hair and her winter-gray eyes. At that unshakable smile she used like a shield. "There's just one problem with leaving now. We haven't talked about that feeling between us. The one I imagine neither one of us wants but neither one of us can ignore." That sense of attraction and rightness.

"A feeling…" Hazel seemed to gather herself, to put emotional distance between them, although she kept her seat and her hand in his. "But we can ignore it, Wylie. We can shift things into the work-friend zone. We can—"

Wylie kissed her. He kissed her uncaring of the gossip chain. He kissed her uncaring—*mostly*—that she didn't want to call Clementine home. He kissed her uncaring of her logic and offer of a work-friend zone.

Wylie kissed Hazel because he had to. He had to know if the attraction between them could be something more…something that would make him revise his ideal image of a soul mate…something that might make falling in love a whole lot riskier.

And when the kiss was over, he had his answer.

And it wasn't good.

"Oh, my," Hazel murmured, eyes still closed. "That is bad news."

"The worst," Wylie agreed, taking her delicate

chin in his hand and tenderly tilting her pretty face up toward his.

He wanted to imprint her features in his memory.

Because he was one hundred percent certain that if he wasn't careful, Dr. Hazel Hughes was going to leave and take his broken heart with her.

KISSES LIKE WYLIE'S didn't come along every day.

But Hazel didn't want to dwell on her boss's kiss.

So, when Wylie started to scoot off the bench and out of the booth at the Buckboard, she grabbed hold of his arm.

Wylie stared at her hand on his sleeve and then into her eyes, green eyes wary. "This isn't a good idea."

"Agreed." Hazel released his arm. "I want you to understand something… No. I *need* you to understand something—*why I can't stay here in Clementine.*"

Wylie shifted to face her, tilting his cowboy hat back in that way of his that put every inch of his gorgeous face within her purview. "Go on."

"It's about my brother." Hazel squared her shoulders, not even trying to smile because there was too much at stake here. "As kids—Nina, Mike, and me—we were each a year apart in age, thick as thieves, if nerds could be thieves." A bit of her humor tried to slip in. "But it was Mike I was closest to. While Nina went off to human med school,

Mike and I focused on veterinary med school." Her shoulders felt stiff, perhaps because the last time she'd tried to explain this to someone, it had been her mother and it hadn't gone over well. "Since we grew up around the family veterinary practice, Mike and I were naturally a bit ahead of other vet students and fascinated by things Mom didn't offer at her small-town practice." Here, she floundered.

"Like experimental surgery practices," Wylie guessed, taking her hand once more.

"And alternative medical practices." Hazel nodded, wondering why her hand in his always felt so right.

"You have a curious mind." Trust Wylie to understand.

"We both did." Hazel nodded again, faster this time. "My brother was accepted for a residency at what I consider the best veterinary hospital on the planet." Newmarket, England. "But he died before he ever got there."

"You said Mike was in a car accident." Wylie cradled her hand in both of his, the way she'd done with his earlier. And that strength...

That strength she'd imagined earlier returned to her.

"Yes. I was two years into vet school when he passed away. I came home to be with Mom." To see to the funeral and grieve. "It was tough on everyone in the family, especially on my mother. So I stayed and helped her through her grief, working with her at her small-town practice. I applied for a gap year in school but was turned down." That had been a bitter blow. "But during that time in Taft, I realized I wanted to carry on with my studies...with the studies Mike and I had talked about."

"New, exciting procedures. You want to honor him by continuing the journey you planned together." Wylie's gaze never left Hazel's face. "You had expectations about small-town practices because you'd grown up in one. You didn't want to come here."

"True," she admitted thickly. "On all counts."

"And you don't want to stay here," Wylie said quietly. "You'll continue to look for a more cutting-edge residency."

"Also true." Hazel met his gaze evenly, although she didn't want to. But she couldn't stop there. Wylie had to know. He had to know everything. "I have dreams I need to fulfill. For Mike."

"And for yourself. Which is why you don't want to kiss me again." Trust Wylie to cut right to the point. "You don't want to let anything stand in your way of leaving."

"Exactly." Hazel shouldn't feel guilty over admitting as much. "My mother doesn't understand. She wants me to return to Taft and take over her practice, even if I manage to get into a surgery center or premier veterinary hospital for my residency."

"She asked you to settle. And you think I'll ask

you to settle, too." Wylie's hands slipped away from hers. "We've only just kissed."

"We've only just *met*. But yes." Hazel felt cold. Somehow, she found her smile, stinging as it was to hold on to. "I just want to be clear, Wylie. Whatever that kiss hinted at… I can't spend time discovering what it leads to."

"I had dreams like yours once," Wylie admitted, staring at his hands. "For different reasons perhaps and I still…" He ran a hand around the back of his neck. "This is my life now and… It's enough."

Hazel didn't believe that.

And when Wylie finally looked at her, his expression was clear. He didn't believe it either.

CHAPTER EIGHT

THE WEATHER SATURDAY morning fit Wylie's mood.

A thunderstorm was traveling across the plains. Lightning. Thunder. Slivers of light through an occasional break in the clouds. The air was charged, as if Mother Nature couldn't decide what to do.

Wylie could relate. He couldn't decide what to do about Hazel and the unwelcome, but increasing, feeling that she could be what he hadn't known he was looking for.

He pulled into the ranch yard at the Done Roamin' Ranch and hurried into the horse barn, intent upon walking out the back to check on Tornado Tom and the stitches Hazel had given the bull earlier in the week.

"Didn't expect to see you here." Frank Harrison, Wylie's foster father, came out of a horse stall, pushing a full wheelbarrow. "Thought you had office hours on Saturdays."

"My new resident is handling appointments this morning." Because Wylie had several mini-dates today, dates he wasn't looking forward to. His lips seemed to want only Hazel's. "I thought I'd stop by and check on Tornado Tom."

Wylie took over wheelbarrow duties from Dad, moving out to the compost pile.

"I hear we're going to the county fair board meeting this Tuesday." Dad had followed Wylie outside where the wind was whipping every which way. "To defend the ranch's honor and your own."

"Yes, sir." Wylie set the wheelbarrow aside and walked over to the corral where Tornado Tom stood.

Stitches ran a good six inches down the bull's shoulder, so neat they could have been made by his foster mother when she quilted.

Hazel has skill, same as Tabitha.

His heart panged a little. That didn't bode well.

"Something's bothering you," Dad said, coming to stand beside Wylie. "Something besides a complaint about you being able to be a fair judge or Ronnie trying to find you a wife."

Wylie shrugged, returning to the wheelbarrow. His foster father had a way of seeing what wasn't always said. "How many more stalls need to be cleaned?"

"None by you." Dad gestured to Wylie's black going-out boots. "You're dressed to impress, not muck stalls. It's about to dump buckets again though. Let's get a seat inside and you can tell me what's on your mind before you conquer the dating world."

Wylie stared at his boots, and then at the sky. And then he took a good, long look at his foster father. Frank Harrison never seemed as old or as weary as he did today. Izzy had mentioned his foster parents were slowing down, but Wylie hadn't really believed her. He was seeing it now. "We can talk while I muck stalls."

"Now, see..." Dad removed his wide-brimmed, white cowboy hat and scratched what little white hair he had left on his head before setting the hat back in place. "You're stepping on the edge of my pride, making like I can't clean a stall on my own ranch anymore. That's nearly as bad as someone saying one of my boys won't judge a county fair event impartially."

Big drops began to fall, quickening and thickening until the rain sounded like applause for Dad's arguments.

"Let's talk about this inside." Dad led the way into the barn and toward the tack room on the far end where there were metal folding chairs. He took a seat and tossed his white cowboy hat over the horn of a nearby saddle. "Something's bothering you."

Wylie found himself telling Dad about his unexpected and unwanted attraction to Hazel. About her desire to be a veterinary surgeon of the highest caliber. About her need to explore the newest procedures and treatments for animals, for both herself and her dead brother.

And when Wylie finished, Dad sat back and considered him in a silence that stretched uncomfortably. Finally, Dad said, "You know, this reminds me of one of the reasons you came to live here in the first place. Your biological dad had very specific plans for you."

"Yeah." Wylie removed his hat and slowly turned it around in his hands, thinking about the past and the baggage it held, luggage he hadn't delved into for years. "He wanted me to be just like him."

"Unresolved parental emotions don't work so well with the pendulum swing in a fella's teenage years," Dad said quietly. "You coming here gave your father some grace to recover from your mom's leaving."

Wylie nodded. Outside of the classroom, he'd been a wild teen, needing an outlet for the emotional roller coaster his mother's leaving had put himself and his father on. Some locals had labeled him *a caution*. And his father... Well, he'd been somewhat steady when on duty at the clinic. But afterward, he was as agitated and volatile as a herd of wild horses surprised by a lone wolf.

"Now, when you talk about your Hazel—"

"She's not *mine*," Wylie blurted dejectedly.

"—I get the impression that you're a bit envious that she's determined to pursue her dream of being a surgeon. More from knowing you than listening to what you had to say today."

Am I that transparent about my unfulfilled dreams?

If his father saw it, Hazel must have as well.

Wylie studied his hands, then the silver tips of his boots, then the smudge of dirt on the barn floor. "I gave up that dream of being a veterinary surgeon in exchange for having my family around." His found family. There were no other Newlands that he knew of. Wylie lifted his gaze and his chin. "It was the right choice."

"Perhaps," Dad allowed. "At the very least, it probably eased some of that remorse you carry about not mending that fence with Paul before he died."

"I don't carry regrets about that," Wylie said in a tone that didn't even convince himself.

Dad heaved a head-shaking sigh. "We both know that's not accurate."

Wylie set his jaw, reminded about how he'd told Hazel the room upstairs was his father's. Reminded about the day Tabitha left, driving away alone to chase their dreams while he stood at the clinic window reliving every argument he'd ever had with his biological father. Reminded about the last time he spoke to his dad—on the phone inviting him to attend his veterinary school graduation. His father had abruptly cut him off, refusing, citing a busy schedule at the practice. That had stung and Wylie had hung up without saying goodbye.

Or I love you.

"Now, I don't want to get in trouble with Ronnie." Dad chuckled a little. "But I don't think you should be looking forward, toward finding a real partner and having a family, until you look back and make peace with any troubling feelings you have about the past."

Wylie nodded, putting his cowboy hat back on. "That's good advice."

Solid advice.

But he wasn't in a position to take it.

HAZEL TOOK BUDGE out for a walk after her first cup of coffee on Saturday morning. The clouds and rain had rolled past, giving way to bright sunshine.

Given how restless Maisey had been every night since Hazel had arrived and the ineffectiveness of the earplugs Hazel had purchased at the feed store, Hazel wasn't feeling her best. She was going to need multiple cups of coffee to get through the day. Again.

Over-caffeination is par for the course in Clementine.

She'd like to blame her perpetual exhaustion on Maisey. That was better than blaming her sleeplessness on that stellar kiss from Wylie four days past. She'd been avoiding him ever since, easy enough since Wylie seemed to prefer making ranch calls while Hazel settled into the ho-hum routine of healing house pets, neutering young animals, and continuing Budge's recovery regime of walking and acupuncture.

As far as Wylie's client base was concerned, Hazel was still an oddity and an outsider. Folks took note of her breeches with a disparaging expression. Her diagnoses were still questioned and Wylie's opinion sought, even by Maisey. Especially by Maisey.

Annoying, that bit.

Hazel had taken to cooking her meals in the upstairs apartment instead of out and about town where she might run into Wylie and his dates, an opportunity Maisey had pounced upon. The vet tech had mooched a little something from every meal Hazel prepared. In fact, last night, Hazel had cooked enough for both of them, telling herself it was preferable to having Maisey fill the apartment with smoke since she seemed to burn everything she tried to make other than frozen microwavable meals.

On the street, Wylie drove past, headed toward the clinic.

Hazel raised a hand in acknowledgment, trying not to allow the memory of his kiss to resurface.

It did anyway in what felt like a slow-motion replay. The surprise of his lips on hers. The spark ignited by his touch. The way she melted when he was near.

One kiss doesn't feel like enough.

But if his kisses became addictive, like her relationship with chocolate, everything would be complicated. She couldn't believe that the leisurely stroke of his thumb over the back of her hand meant they had all the time in the world. She knew they didn't. They had a year, at most. Less if an opening appeared at a surgery center. But kisses like Wylie's…

Well, kisses like Wylie's made Hazel want to toss her career goals aside in favor of a chance at love. But deep down, Hazel knew she couldn't settle for less.

Budge nudged Hazel's shoulder, as if he didn't like to walk in silence. His white whiskers tickled her bare shoulder.

"You're lucky I've had a few days to heal from being pancaked by a bull." She'd worn the dreaded ice vest several times a day since Wylie had given it to her. And she'd blown off Izzy's invitation to line dancing on Thursday at the Buckboard. She hadn't been up to dancing. But now, Hazel was finally feeling less creaky and more like herself.

And Budge…

The blacksmith had carefully trimmed the front of his hooves yesterday and given him a new pair of shoes. The chestnut gelding was still walking on his heels but less so. Today, he had a spring to his step, as if just half an inch of hoof removed up front had given him hope for what lay ahead—a potential short gallop in a long pasture.

"You've got to have dreams, Budge. And you've got to work toward them." No matter the obstacles.

A dog barked somewhere down a side street.

Budge's ears swiveled like a satellite dish, trying to pick up a signal, but the dog went silent.

Their path took them out from beneath a shady patch of road into the sunshine.

"It's going to be another sunny, hot day, Budge," Hazel predicted with good cheer, vowing that it wouldn't be hot between her and Wylie ever again. "A good day to be in the work-friend zone."

The No-Kissing Zone.

Budge nibbled on the brim of Hazel's straw cowboy hat, as if he disagreed.

"You know I'm right." Hazel gently pushed his head away.

"He's filling out nicely," a familiar, deep voice said. Wylie came up from behind them, having followed them from the clinic. He was wearing his dating clothes again—black boots, crisp blue checked shirt, new blue jeans. He turned his attention to Hazel with that all-encompassing green gaze that sent her pulse and her mind racing.

I do. I don't. I will. I won't.

He cluttered her head. Hazel set off walking at a good clip.

With Wylie right beside her, bookending her between him and Budge. "I imagine this is how city couples walk their dog. I should have brought a cup of coffee along."

"I'm getting mine from Katie at Betty's Bakery." Hazel spoke begrudgingly until she looked over into Wylie's troublesome green eyes and felt the seeds of attraction she'd been dodging, scattering in every nook and cranny of her core.

How thrillingly annoying.

Hazel blew out a frustrated breath. "Aren't we supposed to be avoiding each other except at the clinic?"

Wylie smirked. "I don't recall having a discussion about avoiding you."

"We didn't need to say it outright. There was..." She lowered her voice to a whisper, not that anyone was near. "...the agreement to be in the work-friend zone." Because despite this marvelous and unfortunate attraction, Wylie was a skilled vet and could probably teach her a thing or two.

Budge crowded Hazel toward Wylie and the curb, having spotted a truck coming their way.

Wylie cleared his throat. "Actually, I've been giving you space while taking some myself to consider things. Because our kiss required a lot of consideration."

"No, it didn't." Hazel wasn't certain where Wylie was going with this. But she was determined, if at all possible, not to ride along. "I know you can diagnose our predicament and come to the same treatment plan I did. You're very good at diagnosing patients and prescribing the proper course of action, in this case, each to our own neck of the woods."

"Thank you," Wylie said, instead of acknowledging her implied boundaries. "I think you're good at your job, too. I swung by the Done Roamin' Ranch this morning on my way into town and checked on Tornado Tom."

"You checked on my work?" The daily tension caused by mistrust of her abilities jolted through her, manifesting itself in a small, brittle smile. "Again?"

"I *admired* your work," Wylie corrected, studying Hazel with a crease between his black brows. "This is a residency, after all."

"I'm used to more autonomy," Hazel mumbled.

"I probably understand that more than most," Wylie allowed. "Tornado Tom needs a few more days until the stitches can be removed. But you… You could have been a plastic surgeon. Where did you learn to stitch like that?"

"My grandmother taught me how to embroider." Tension diffused, Hazel smiled at the fond memory. "I could make you a sign to go in the lobby. How about a sampler that says *Happiness is being a veterinarian*?"

"There's that cheery sarcasm I've been without all week." Wylie grinned.

It was the good smile. The one that struck Hazel from head to toe as remarkable, like a bite of chocolate truffle. So good, it had to be savored.

"I'm not going to kiss you again," Hazel blurted, although a part of her mourned. Wylie was a fabulous kisser.

"Fair enough." Wylie huffed, similar to the way Budge huffed when she was too slow retrieving a treat from her pocket, like he was impatient and pleased at the same time. "Fair enough. That's what my dad used to say when I'd tell him I was never going to help him again at the clinic after a cat scratched me or a dog's cyst burst and covered me in…" He chuckled, earning an ear swivel from Budge. "Well, you get the idea. I was a teenage boy with an abundance of pride."

It was Hazel's turn to huff. "You're trying to be charming and distract me."

Wylie claimed her free hand, fitting their palms together too easily. "Is it working?"

Hazel wanted to say no. But Wylie had indeed enchanted her.

Could kisses be far behind?

Hazel gave herself a mental shake. "There will be no more kisses."

Wylie laughed, removing his brown cowboy hat and fanning himself as if this conversation made him hot. His hair stood up in at least three places.

Hazel bit back a laugh, along with the desire to smooth those locks back into some semblance of order.

"Good morning," Rose called from the corner ahead. Today, the elderly woman wore a pair of purple velvet slacks, a flowery blouse in an iris print, purple cowboy boots, and a matching cowboy hat. And instead of having Bruiser on a leash this morning, the little white poodle sat in a small doll stroller, bright blue bows attached to the hair on his ears. "Look, Bruiser. Your doctors are here."

Hazel greeted Rose and brought Budge to a halt a few feet away. The gelding stood as if he was in the show ring. Very still. Very proud. Hazel stroked his coppery neck.

"Good morning, Rose." Wylie put his hat back on, then released Hazel's hand to lean over and scratch the poodle behind his ears. "How is Bruiser today? Still walking stiffly?"

Rose nodded. "He's as rusty as my husband's ancient Cadillac door hinges. But we're not the shut-in kind." She gestured toward the retreating clouds. "We both needed some blue sky after that storm. Quite a bunch of boomers."

Wylie agreed, sending Hazel an inscrutable look.

"Now, if Bruiser's no better by Monday," Rose continued, "I might give that acupuncture thing a try."

Wylie seemed to stiffen.

"I'm always open to a discussion about patient needs." Hazel gave Budge a fond pat on the shoulder when she wanted to give Wylie a nudge on the shoulder and point out how opinions of his clientele could change, if given time. And perhaps, his opinions should shift along with them. "Are you taking Bruiser for a walk toward Main Street, Rose? If so, we can join you crossing the street."

"We're counting on it." Rose eased the dog stroller over the curb. "Best to cross in packs. You never know what kind of yahoo will go speeding through town."

"I haven't seen any yahoos yet." Still, Hazel looked both ways before cuing Budge into a walk.

Wylie walked at her side but he felt different… Distant. Because Rose had mentioned acupuncture?

"Rose, are you still on the fair committee board?" Wylie asked, baldly changing the subject and reminding Hazel about the brouhaha surrounding his fair judging role.

"Yes, I'm still on the board." The elderly woman gave Wylie a speculative look. "I suppose you want to talk about the letter we received regarding you as a judge."

Wylie nodded briskly. "I do."

"You're in luck," Rose said, chuckling. "I have the entire morning free. Take a stroll with me."

"Okay, but…" Wylie gave Hazel an apologetic look. "I'm sorry, Hazel. I meant to walk with you."

"Oh, no. Don't worry about me," Hazel told him quickly, simultaneously relieved and disappointed that he was leaving her. "I have Budge to keep me company. You go straighten this thing out." And more importantly, go on those dates Ronnie had no doubt made for him today.

Wylie nodded. "Thanks. I... We'll talk more later."

Hazel thought it best not to promise they would. Wylie might be getting swept up in his feelings with her now, but Hazel wanted to keep her eyes on her future.

She and Budge continued on their way to Betty's Bakery, where Hazel took money out of her pocket and waved at the window until she caught Katie's eye.

The baker hurried outside with her regular order. "Black coffee and a blackberry scone. Are you open to trying something new?"

"Your scones are great," Hazel told her effusively. "But... You can surprise me with something new anytime."

"I'm testing out a new cannoli recipe. The dough isn't cooperating." Katie gave Budge a pat. "He looks happier today. And so do you." She darted back inside before Hazel could ask what made her look happier.

I'm not happier. I'm grumpier.

She was sleep deprived and at risk of falling in love with the right guy at the wrong time.

Hazel's cell phone rang. She had to put her coffee cup on the ground and the scone bag on top of it in order to answer.

"Dr. Hughes." Dr. Reed's somber voice reached her. "How are you getting along in Oklahoma?"

"I'm great," Hazel said with false cheer. "And Budge seems to like it. Don't you, boy?"

Budge stretched his nose toward her scone before she eased his head away from her breakfast.

"How are you doing, Dr. Reed?" She hadn't heard from him since she'd left California close to two weeks ago.

"I'm busy getting ready for the summer term and screening a few interesting cases." There was something comforting about his steady voice and the familiar, predictable schedule of the university. "But I called you with some news that might be upsetting."

"Nothing you say could upset me, Dr. Reed. Remember that you're the peas to my carrots. We work well together."

He was silent for a moment while Hazel imagined him counting to ten and adjusting the set of his black glasses on his nose. He'd never truly appreciated her humor or terms of endearment. "Dr. Hughes, there's been an accident at the surgery center in Newmarket. One of their residents was kicked during a procedure with a racing stallion. They tell me the wounds are very serious."

"Oh, that's horrible. I hope they recover soon." Hazel was sincere in her sentiment. "Thanks for letting me know."

"Well…" Dr. Reed hesitated. He wasn't one for

hesitating, which made the pause all the more curious. And then words seemed to tumble out of him. "The truth of the matter is that they don't think this resident will return and they inquired about you."

"Me?" Hazel squeaked, so high-pitched that Budge turned his head to stare at her. She, in turn, glanced over her shoulder toward Wylie and Rose.

Not that her favorite professor was finished talking. "But I know that Dr. Newland was in great need of a resident and I don't want to undercut him." Dr. Reed went silent once more. Waiting, perhaps, for Hazel's reaction.

Hazel didn't know what to say. She faced forward once more, unwittingly staring at the horizon, where dark clouds were disappearing.

"It's a quandary," Dr. Reed admitted when she didn't say more. "I know you had your heart set on Newmarket. And I know that Dr. Newland is at the breaking point handling his workload alone. I care about you both. I suppose I could propose Dr. Newland taking on a new resident. Perhaps there's someone else who would like a change from their placement and is looking for a lower-risk environment."

An image of Hard Nose's nubs framing her shoulders came to mind, not low risk by any means.

"I don't know what to say," Hazel murmured. But she knew what to think: *If Wylie gets a new resident, I can move on without feeling like I left him in a lurch.*

But her heart... Her heart wanted to weigh in with feelings. Feelings about Wylie that she didn't want to acknowledge because they'd struck too hard, too soon.

"Maybe saying nothing is for the best at this point," Dr. Reed said, unwittingly providing Hazel with good advice. "Newmarket wants to give their resident a chance to heal and think about things. There may be a spot opening and there may not be."

"I see." And Hazel did see. She recognized this push-me-pull-you, will-she-won't-she cycle too well. It was the same roundabout she'd been circling with Wylie. Nothing was certain. Every off-ramp had both positives and negatives. "I know it might not be professional in terms of my current placement, but I'd like to keep the door open at Newmarket, if I can. The horizon here is...*isn't* for me."

CHAPTER NINE

"Rose, you're saying someone lodged an anonymous complaint about me as a judge at the fair?" Wylie couldn't believe it. "Just me? Not Wade?"

"Just you. For nepotism." Rose bobbed her purple cowboy hat-topped head. She pushed her dog stroller slowly along the sidewalk with the white poodle a well-behaved passenger.

Hazel and Budge disappeared around the corner by the Buffalo Diner and with them a nebulous feeling of belonging. Which was ridiculous on some level. But true on others. And that feeling was clouding his interest in finding more appropriate marital candidates.

Even Ronnie had noticed. Just yesterday, she'd told him she would continue to limit him to mini-dates until further notice. Not that he was disappointed. Shorter meet-ups meant he could politely move on if there was no spark.

There won't be any sparks if it's not Hazel.

Unaware of his thoughts, Rose continued to talk

about the fair judging issue. "Although the complaint wasn't specific—"

"And was anonymous." That seemed important. It had been made by a coward.

"—the committee's knee-jerk reaction was to clear the decks, so to speak."

"Which is why you considered removing all judges connected to the Done Roamin' Ranch," Wylie said flatly. "Wade was guilty by association."

"Yes. I know this comes as a blow but nothing has been decided." Rose slowed, staring up at Wylie with faded blue eyes. "You've been a good judge, not to mention you've refused any compensation for your work. We truly appreciate you."

"And you'll still want me to health check animals upon arrival next week," Wylie surmised wryly. "Even if I'm not judging."

"If you're still willing," Rose said graciously, dipping her head.

Wylie dutifully mumbled something about it being the right thing to do. And then he sighed. "I just... I can't think of anything I've done that hasn't been aboveboard in terms of judging. Frankly, there haven't been many kids showing animals that can claim a connection to the Done Roamin' Ranch. My foster nieces and nephews are more likely to compete in the junior rodeo competition." Which was where Wade was a judge.

Rose nodded. "We know. It's why we tabled the

issue. Can you come to the meeting Tuesday night at the fairgrounds?"

Wylie nodded. "Wade and I already planned to."

"You're a good man, Dr. Newland." Rose patted his cheek. "Your father would be proud."

"My...biological father?" Wylie made a weak gesture back toward the clinic.

"Both your dads. Back in the day, I helped Paul obtain the financing to open his clinic and Frank money to expand the Done Roamin' Ranch." Rose wheeled her dog stroller in a circle, heading back the way she'd come.

Wylie was drawn back around with the elderly woman, curious about his biological father because folks rarely talked about him. To Wylie, anyway.

"Paul and I were friends," Rose continued. "He was so proud of you wanting to open a surgery center after you graduated. He talked about you all the time. Bursting with pride, he was."

"He never told me..." Wylie swallowed his surprise. "I thought he wanted me here. I thought he resented my leaving." His house. This town.

"No." Rose scoffed, stopping in front of the bakery, and leaning over to fuss with one of Bruiser's twisted blue hair bows. "Paul mentioned more than a few times that he was exploring how to sell the practice when he was ready to retire."

"Really?" Wylie scratched the back of his neck. "He never said any of that to me."

"Frankly..." Rose stared up at Wylie, a compassionate expression on her petite features. "I think he talked himself out of having a relationship with you. You know how he could be after your mother left. Second-guessing every decision until he was tied up in knots. He wanted you to live your own life."

And I chose to live it here.

"Now, you might be wondering why I haven't told you that before," Rose said in a businesslike tone of voice. "You're always in such a rush. At the fair. At your clinic. And I don't see you at other places." She gave him a somber look. "Might want to think about that now that you're casting about for someone to spend the rest of your life with. Relationships take time."

Wylie's jaw dropped open. He *was* busy. He knew that. And even with Hazel at the practice, he still worked long days. He didn't hang out with his foster family unless it was a holiday.

Wylie thanked Rose for her insight and headed back toward the clinic, walking slowly. His first date of the day wasn't for another hour and he needed time to process what Rose had told him.

He knew his father had struggled with communicating his feelings sometimes. But why hadn't he told Wylie he was proud of him? Why hadn't he given Wylie his blessing to forge his own path elsewhere?

A weak breeze ruffled leaves overhead. Wylie lifted his gaze from the sidewalk beneath his feet and was struck by a thought: *This is home.* Clementine and his father had shaped him into the man he was today. Ronnie was right. Wylie wasn't a big talker. He was stuck in his ways and on the boring side. But family and community were important to him.

This is where I'm meant to be.

The choice he'd made—to stay in Clementine and take over his father's practice—was right for him. If only he could show Hazel that she could live a professionally fulfilling life here, too.

A squirrel scolded him before racing up a tree.

"Yeah, I get it." He didn't have a prayer. Or the right to ask.

Maisey was at the front desk when he returned to the clinic. She took him in from top to bottom. "You look like someone clipped your wings."

Wylie briefly explained about someone wanting him removed as a fair judge.

His vet tech showed very little sympathy for him. "You should be grateful. If you don't judge, you'll have a lot more free time. With a little rest, you might be better able to spot the right tree in the forest that has become Clementine women showing an interest in you." Maisey gestured toward the canisters of goodies on the counter. They'd multiplied since Wylie had been here last. "Someone tried to drop off a plate of cookies before you came in."

"Tried to?" Wylie frowned.

"The minx claimed her oatmeal raisin recipe included an herb often used as an aphrodisiac." Maisey harrumphed. "Reminded me of Hazel's new treatment nonsense." Maisey uncovered a plate of chocolate chip cookies and offered him one. "Don't worry. I sent her on her way. All I need is for you to eat a cookie and then go all googly-eyed for the next woman who walks before you."

He bit into the sweet treat. "I suppose I'm lucky to have you filtering my prospects." And even if his heart wasn't into pursuing anyone other than Hazel, he'd made a commitment to meet women today. He'd go through with those mini-dates but he likely wouldn't end up encouraging anyone.

A sound outside had Wylie moving toward the windows. Hazel was returning from her morning walk with Budge, coming around the empty warehouse.

Wylie couldn't explain this attraction. He only knew that deep down, a vital part of him believed that she was the one.

Maisey joined him, holding a very large mug of steaming coffee. "I never thought I'd say this but I'm getting used to the sight of them."

Me, too.

"I slip Budge oat cubes when she's busy with patients," Maisey admitted in a low voice. "He was someone's heart horse, I bet." Meaning a human had once loved him to the moon and back, more as a loved one than a working animal. "Those connections don't come around often."

"Not for animals or humans," Wylie mused, feeling sentimental. He draped his arm over Maisey's shoulders. "What was it like working for my father?"

"Why are you asking me that?" Maisey compacted herself and drew away, even with his arm around her. "If you really wanted to know, you would have said something years ago."

"Maybe I wasn't ready before," Wylie said in a quiet voice, a contained voice. Maisey wasn't the only one to get tense at the mention of his father.

"You won't find me saying anything bad about Paul," Maisey groused. "He was a fair boss, a good vet, and a good father, not that he'd toot his own horn. That wasn't like him."

"No. It wasn't." And for once, Wylie didn't feel all tangled up inside when speaking about him. Impulsively, he dropped a kiss on top of Maisey's white head. "Thanks for sharing."

His vet tech skittered away, cheeks red. "My goodness. You'll be having me bake for you next."

A car pulled into the lot. A German shepherd's head poked out the window.

"That's Victor." Maisey shuffled files on her desk. "I'll get him checked in and ready for our intern."

"Resident," Wylie said softly as he headed to-

ward the back of the clinic, Hazel, not Victor, on his mind.

"Good heavens," Maisey snapped. "Look at that. Donna didn't just bring Victor. She brought a basket of tomatoes. I forgot she dumped that no-good husband of hers last winter. A few more thoughtful love-gifts for you and we'll have enough for a feast. Although… I wouldn't complain if someone dropped off a side of beef next."

"I would." He was uncomfortable with all this attention. Wylie ducked into the lab and headed straight out the back door to the paddocks, where Hazel was giving Budge a good brushing, her back to Wylie. "Can I ask you a question?"

"Depends on the question, I suppose." Hazel didn't turn around. She wore black breeches today and an orange tank top. Her strawberry blond hair was in a loose bun at her neck beneath that worn straw cowboy hat that she wore when working. Contradicting that relaxed bun, her shoulders seemed tense and her brushstrokes brisk.

She was in no mood for questions.

Wylie switched tactics from getting to know Hazel better to telling her more about him. "I'm a workaholic."

Hazel glanced at him over her shoulder, purplish-gray eyes alight with humor. "That's a question?"

The gelding swung his head around to stare at Wylie, as curious about Wylie as his owner.

"I used to have a life outside of the clinic," Wylie continued, encouraged by Hazel's humor. "I competed in rodeo, although I wasn't good enough to win more than an occasional, small purse. But I enjoyed being around my foster family and doing something just for the fun of it."

Hazel moved to the other side of Budge, where she resumed brushing him with her head down, expression hidden by her curled cowboy hat brim. "Your family? The ones who competed or the ones who supplied roughstock for the rodeo?"

"Both." Wylie was heartened by her interest. "My pace isn't healthy. Nothing to balance my hours at the clinic. My dad... He had a heart attack here." Upstairs in his office. "He was a workaholic, too."

"Hazard of the business," Hazel said frankly. "My parents are the same way. Always on call. Never a vacation. And when disaster strikes..."

She didn't finish that thought but Wylie recalled something she'd told him at the Buckboard. "They couldn't take time to grieve after your brother died."

Hazel lifted her head, revealing tears glistening in her pretty eyes. "My mother... She had the hardest time processing what had happened. I stayed a week, then a month. And suddenly, I was taking a gap year, which as you know, is highly frowned upon. But that's when I decided to study acupuncture." Hazel's chin came up, almost as if she was daring Wylie to pick apart her decision or, more likely, her field of study. "And that was one of the reasons Dr. Reed accepted me as a third-year student at a different university."

He wanted to talk more about alternative medicine and her experience getting into a different vet school. But there wasn't much time to get into anything. He had a mini-date in thirty minutes.

And at any moment, Maisey was going to burst through the door and demand one of them come treat their next patient.

Forcing himself to take it slow, despite the ticking clock, Wylie moved closer to the paddock, leaning his arms over the rail. "When I was in veterinary school, acupuncture wasn't something we acknowledged as a legitimate area of study. I've read more about it since." Although he was still uncertain of its effectiveness. "I'd like to see its results."

Hazel chewed on the inside of her cheek. "You're asking me to prove it to you rather than taking me at my word."

Too late, Wylie realized his mistake. He'd been trying to establish trust between them and gone about it all wrong.

The door to the clinic was flung open.

"Is no one showing up for work today?" Maisey demanded.

"I'll be right there, Miss Maisey," Hazel said with her usual smiling demeanor.

"Victor is waiting," Maisey snapped. "He chased a rabbit into a blackberry bramble and punctured the pad on his hind foot. We can't stop the bleeding."

"I'll be right there," Hazel repeated, exiting the paddock and walking past Wylie.

He thought Hazel would head inside without another word but she stopped with her hand on the door handle. "Good luck with your dates today. You deserve to find the right woman." Hazel turned her head, although not far enough to face him directly. "You deserve someone who loves Clementine and this clinic as much as you do, because they're both special. Just like you." And then she disappeared inside.

Special like me?

How could she say something like that and run away, leaving Wylie more regretful than ever that he'd agreed to see any woman other than Hazel.

HAZEL WAS CONVINCED it wouldn't take long to stabilize Victor, even if he was an ornery patient. That is, if she could get Maisey to cooperate with her method of treatment.

Two ornery beings in an exam room was one too many.

Hazel missed being top dog. Or at least, one of the top dogs at university.

After Hazel conducted a brief exam, she excused herself and went into the lab.

Maisey followed Hazel and began her critique, dropping her clipboard to the counter with a clatter. "Your patient is bleeding. I put gauze and bandages in the exam room. You should be wrapping Victor's paw. If Dr. Newland hadn't already left, I'd get him in there ASAP and then *you* could help hold Victor down while he does the work."

Hazel opened a cupboard where she'd stored some of her healing herbs on a high shelf. "I'm preparing something to calm Victor down so we can stop the bleeding." Because the German shepherd wasn't allowing Hazel or Maisey to touch him for more than a few seconds.

"All our tranquilizers are in the locked cupboard." Maisey stomped over to the glass case and spread her arms from top to bottom. "I don't know what you're looking for over there."

"I'm not subduing an eighty-five-pound dog with a heavy dose of meds. We'll never get Victor back in Donna's vehicle safely." Much less guarantee the dog's safety when she got him home.

Hazel's cell phone rang, the distinctive clang of a video call. The only person who ever contacted her on video chat was her mother when she was feeling blue.

Hazel answered, propping her phone up against a glass jar of dog treats. "Mom, I'm with a patient. Can I call you back?"

"Must you?" Mom said mournfully. She was sitting in her office at the clinic. The large picture of Mike they'd displayed at his funeral sat on the credenza behind her. "Gosh, you look really good. Are you happy?"

"Yes, Mom." It was Hazel's standard answer and her standard smile. "I'm great." Hazel sprinkled bits of chamomile on a bone-shaped lick mat.

"What a shame," Mom murmured.

"Happy? Dr. Hughes?" Maisey came up behind Hazel until she was in the video frame, frowning her disagreement. "As if."

"Oh, you aren't happy?" Mom brightened. "Is that your vet tech? Daisey or Lacey or something? Hello. Vet techs always know the truth, don't they?"

"It's *Miss Maisey*." Hazel spread a thin layer of creamy peanut butter over the lick mat, disguising the herb's presence so that Victor wouldn't notice. "Miss Maisey is like a storm cloud to my burst of sunshine. Pay no attention to her."

Maisey scoffed, facial features setting in her usual, disapproving bulldog folds.

"Will you look at that. This is fascinating." Mom leaned forward, displaying uncharacteristic interest, until only her face was visible on the screen. "You haven't won Miss Maisey over, Hazel. How can that be?"

"She's a hard case, Mom." Hazel closed the chamomile and peanut butter containers, returning them to the cupboard. "She tricked me into cooking for her and she still doesn't like me."

"Chicken casserole, grilled cheese, and quesadillas do not a friendship potion make." Maisey had her nose in the air, fully prepared to try and put Hazel in her place.

"Miss Maisey's like a cactus, isn't she?" Mom grinned. "All prickly on the outside with the good stuff hidden deep inside."

Maisey huffed.

Hazel wasn't convinced Maisey had good stuff inside. "I've got a patient bleeding in an exam room, Mom." She lifted the lick mat, tilting it for her mother to see. "Gotta go. Love you."

"Love you more. Call me later." Mom rested her chin on both fists. "And bring the storm cloud."

"Will do." Hazel disconnected, leaving her phone on the counter and returning to the exam room.

"She's just like you," Maisey said, dogging her heels.

"I suppose." Hazel entered the exam room and laid the peanut-butter-coated lick mat on the floor near the spot where Victor lay.

The dog was being comforted by his teary, stressed-out owner, Donna, who held a bloody rag to his rear paw.

Hazel bent down to Donna's level. "While Victor enjoys a snack, I'm going to put some glue over that puncture wound and then give it a pressure wrap."

Maisey made herself helpful for the first time

ever, and handed Hazel the glue and an antiseptic pad, then moved into place at the dog's hips when he stood to lick the mat.

By the time Victor licked the mat clean, Hazel had the wound cleaned, glued closed, and athletic tape wrapped twice around his paw.

"What a good boy." Hazel praised the dog but her smile was for Victor's owner. "We're going to leave you alone for a few minutes to decompress." She shooed Maisey toward the door.

Perhaps sensing the worst of his day was over, Victor plopped down in front of Donna, who hugged him and started to cry openly.

Hazel shut the door behind them and breathed a sigh of relief. And then she shook her finger at Maisey. "Now you've done it."

"Done what?" Maisey honestly looked flummoxed.

"Isn't it obvious?" Hazel led her back to the lab. "You've become my mother's new favorite obsession." She held the door open for Maisey. "Let's call her back."

Mom answered the video call right away. "Nice work," she said when Hazel briefly recapped their patient's situation and treatment. "Make sure you both eat and hydrate."

"I'm getting water for us both now," Maisey said, filling two glasses she took from a cupboard.

"How sleep deprived are you, Miss Maisey?"

Hazel stared deeply into the older woman's eyes. "What brought on the nicey-nice?"

Scoffing, Maisey handed Hazel her a glass. "I've got beef sticks in the fridge. They're packed with protein."

"And sodium." Hazel propped her phone on the treat jar once more.

"You'll sweat it out," Maisey insisted. Tossing Hazel a beef stick.

"You've both got valid points," Mom said, ever the peacemaker. "Are you always at each other like this?"

"Not at all," Maisey said before Hazel could answer differently. "We're establishing a pecking order, is all, just like horses in a herd."

"Do tell." Hazel bent at the waist, propped her elbows on the counter, and her chin in her hands.

Mom laughed.

Maisey edged close to Hazel so that her face was in the video frame. "I've never done a screen chat before."

"Welcome to the new millennium," Hazel quipped. "Mom, why did you want Miss Maisey on this call?"

"I wanted to see for myself how a top notch vet tech and a top notch resident work together." Mom beamed at Maisey.

Maisey beamed at Mom. Then she nudged Hazel. "Unlike you, she knows how to spot talent."

"I know how to spot talent," Hazel grumbled.

"I told myself on the day we first met that you ran this place."

Maisey's eyebrows rose. "Really?"

"I trained her well, Miss Maisey." Mom fiddled with her phone. "Well, Dr. Reed and I trained her well. He was her mentor professor last year. He's smart and very kind."

"She means handsome," Maisey whispered.

Hazel cut Maisey with a sharp look. And then she shifted her attention to her mother's image on the screen. "When did you form such a stellar opinion of Dr. Reed? You met him once."

Mom tsked. "Honey, we've talked on the phone many times."

"About me?" Hazel was horrified.

"No. She's dating him," Maisey whispered.

"My mother isn't dating Dr. Reed." Hazel peered at her mother's smiling face, unable to tell anything.

"She smiles just the way you do," Maisey continued, still in hushed tones. "Not giving anything away."

She's right.

Hazel peered at her phone screen and her mother's angelic expression.

No way. My mother might be dating Dr. Reed!

Mom leaned closer to the phone. "I'm not dating Dr. Reed. We're colleagues, just like Miss Maisey and I are colleagues. You need a network of peers,

Hazel. People you can talk to. People who understand what you're going through."

"I have that," Hazel assured her.

Maisey harumphed.

The landline rang at the front desk.

"You can get that," Maisey told Hazel, flexing her office authority. "Your mother and I need to talk."

Hazel's jaw might have dropped. What was happening here? It was *her* mother. *Her* phone.

But in the end, Hazel did as she was told and went to the front desk to answer the call.

After all, Hazel's time here was temporary. Maisey was the boss and always would be.

CHAPTER TEN

WYLIE PARKED IN front of the renovated farmhouse at the Glover-Malone Ranch.

Bess Glover was engaged to Wylie's foster brother Griff Malone. The couple coached the high school rodeo team together and had—for reasons Wylie had never probed for—decided to coach younger kids to participate in the goat obstacle course. He'd been told they'd constructed a course in the ranch's arena, and had enthusiastic sign-ups practicing nonstop for the relatively new event at the county fair next weekend.

At Ronnie's request, Wylie was meeting Doreen Bader here. Her daughter owned a goat and was part of what looked like the twenty or so kids on the practice squad.

Doreen waved from a spot near the arena gate. She was the town's recently-hired librarian, blonde, sporty, and loyal in appearance. She wore a Clementine High School baseball cap, sneakers, jeans, and a T-shirt that proclaimed her *The World's Best*

Mom. Unlike Hazel, everything about Doreen said she was here to stay.

Wylie waved back and walked up the incline to the arena, determined to make a friend if not identify a future soul mate. "Good morning, Doreen."

"Good morning, Wylie," a middle-aged woman behind Doreen said cheerfully. She wore a denim sundress and a calculated smile. "We're so happy to see you."

"We?" Wylie had a bad feeling about this minidate. A very bad feeling. He took a step backward and tugged his cowboy hat brim lower.

"Mom." Doreen turned on Lilac Stoddard, owner of a pair of Siamese cats and a client of Wylie's. "I told you to wait for me over at the bleachers."

The Glover-Malone Ranch had covered bleachers, which provided participants, parents, and siblings with much-needed shade in the summer. The sun's rays had already dried up the soil from this morning's rain shower. Shade was needed today.

"Doreen, your daughter wants a sibling and you've always said you'd like a large family." Doreen's mother came forward and hugged Wylie, going so far as to whisper in his ear, "Doreen's a gem but if I let her, she'd spend her entire life in the library with her nose in a book. You have shoulders that seem strong enough to attract her attention."

If Wylie had learned anything in nearly a week of dating, it was that women came with a posse—

friends, relatives, and exes. But this... This was over the line.

"Mother." Doreen pointed stiffly at the small rows of bleachers on the far side of the arena. "Go back to your seat. Now."

Wylie had to untangle Lilac's arms from around his shoulders because she just kept holding on. "Nice to see you again, ma'am." What were her cats' names? He couldn't remember.

"Such good manners." Doreen's mother squeezed Wylie's biceps before he could leap out of manhandling distance. Lilac's dark brown hair was pulled back into a severe ponytail and her inspection of Wylie felt like he'd been placed in a police lineup.

"Mom, you make me want to quit this matchmaking thing altogether." Doreen grabbed onto Wylie's wrist and towed him away from danger toward a row of trees at the rear of the arena. "Sorry about that. My mother's intentions are good, but her tactics are over the top." She released Wylie, released a breath, and bestowed him with a smile that looked forced. "Mom contacted Ronnie, who ambushed me when I opened the library the other morning. Not that I don't want to date. Or date *you*," Doreen rushed to say, her cheeks turning as red as a ripe apple. "But my life is content and my mother otherwise manageable when I don't date."

Doreen seemed about as enthralled by the idea of dating Wylie as he was about dating her.

Good.

But that didn't mean he could just head for the hills. That wouldn't be polite.

Wylie gestured toward the arena. "Which competitor is yours?"

"Sabrina." Doreen spun around and pointed. "She's wearing the pink checked shirt and competing with Oregon, the big white goat."

Sabrina was a sprig of a girl with straight brown hair that barely brushed her shoulders. Her straw cowboy hat had a red band and looked like she had a year or two to grow into it. Despite her size, she had a good grip on her goat's lead rope and enough friendship bracelets on her wrist to imply she was popular with her peers.

Nice, like her mother.

"They both look like goers," Wylie said because he had no idea what a goat obstacle course was or what made a good competitor in the event.

He took inventory of the items in the arena. A four-by-four beam spanning at least twelve feet sat atop two concrete bricks, creating a bridge barely a foot in the air. Poles had been planted in the dirt a few feet beyond the bridge. Six poles, each spaced about three feet apart. Beyond the poles, large plastic hoops were suspended by wooden frames, dangling several inches off the ground. There was a seesaw without handles and a plastic tube, large enough for a goat to run through, that snaked across ten feet or so. The obstacles were spread far enough apart that the competitors broke into a run in between each one.

"You know nothing about this event, do you?" Doreen laughed, making Wylie feel less like he was an avocado in a bin her mother had been picking through and more like a living, breathing person deserving of a little respect.

"I know nothing about this event," Wylie confirmed, smiling at Doreen. "What are the rules?"

"I've been told our format is different than in other counties because someone put Griff in charge of making the rules." Doreen looked more comfortable now. Her entire being looked relaxed. "It's not about obedience as much as time, which makes it fun."

Having grown up around Griff, Wylie knew firsthand that anything his foster brother touched turned into something high energy and amusing. "Fun? That explains why Griff volunteered to coach."

"Essentially, it's dog agility with goats." Doreen hung her arms over the top arena rail as if she'd grown up on a ranch instead of in town. "Go get 'em, Sabrina!"

Her little girl waved back.

Bang! Something solid and heavy clattered onto the metal bleachers. And then another *bang!*

Wylie caught sight of a small cowboy jumping on the bleachers, despite several adults telling him not to.

Bang! Bang!

A small brown goat on the far side of the arena fell over sideways.

A little girl nearby screamed, "She's dead!"

Several members of the audience on the bleachers got to their feet, jockeying for a better view. Ronnie was among them.

Just when Wylie was about to hop the fence and come to the collapsed goat's rescue, an unexpected touch to his shoulder had him flinching back.

"I'm guessing you're a forty long in jacket size." Doreen's mother had a cloth measuring tape in her hands. She'd been taking the length of his arm. "What do you think of powder blue as a tuxedo color for the wedding?"

"Mother." Doreen snatched the measuring tape from Lilac's hands and stuffed it into her jeans pocket. "No one gets married in powder blue tuxedos anymore. And instead of helping me make a connection with Wylie, because of you, he probably doesn't see me as marital material."

Both women turned their gazes upon Wylie, awaiting his pronouncement.

"I…uh…" Wylie cleared his throat. "I think it's early days yet, don't you, Doreen?"

I should just come clean and admit my heart is engaged elsewhere.

"Ruined your chances?" Lilac elbowed her daughter, cackling gleefully. "I've increased them. Wyatt likes me. You have nothing to worry about,

Doreen. Between me and Ronnie, you'll be hitched by the new year."

Yikes.

Wylie eased out of Lilac's reach, fearful of another lasting hug.

"Mother." Doreen rolled her eyes, not even blushing, which said a lot about her mother's behavior today and every day: *This is par for the course.*

"Now, Wylie…" Lilac leaped forward, linking her arm with his before leading him away from the arena. "As you can imagine, Doreen, Sabrina, and I are a package deal. Doreen is a good cook. Sabrina's a bucket of sunshine. And me?" She chuckled again. "I'm the wild card that keeps things lively."

"I bet." At which point, Wylie realized that Doreen hadn't followed them.

I'm alone!

And Doreen didn't seem intent upon rescuing him. Nor did Ronnie seem to be running to his aid.

I'll remember that if Ronnie ever asks me to babysit.

Lilac had her arm hooked through his good and tight. "I'm the best of babysitters. A live-in nanny, only asking room and board in return." Lilac stopped and gestured toward Bess and Griff's farmhouse with its fresh coat of white paint. "We'd like to live on a ranch of our own. I know you've taken on the old Jardspur place but I hear that's more a hobby ranch than a legitimate venture. I've had my sights on something bigger, grander. All for my daughter's and granddaughter's sake, of course."

"Of course." Wylie tried to dig in his heels but Lilac just kept on dragging him farther and farther away from his date and deeper and deeper into her happily-ever-after fantasy. He needed an escape. Pronto.

As soon as Hazel pulled the mobile clinic into the ranch yard and saw Wylie's big, black truck, she had a bad feeling about this emergency "house call." Experience had told her that if Wylie was around, folks didn't need her.

Hazel got out of the truck anyway, slinging her backpack and the clinic's equipment bag to her shoulders.

Ronnie waved Hazel over, looking more pregnant than ever, but adorable in a red maternity sundress and red cowboy hat. "One of the competitors wants you to check out their goat." Ronnie led the way toward the arena.

"A goat competitor? Is someone roping goats?" Hazel could see several goats in the arena but they were all on lead ropes and there were no horses in sight.

Ronnie explained about the timed goat obstacle course as they walked the rise to the arena.

"Is a goat in distress?" It didn't feel like it. No

one was frantically waving Hazel over. "Is Wylie around?"

"Oh, Wylie's here somewhere," Ronnie said in that vague, cheerful, don't-ask-me-too-many-questions way of hers.

A woman in a baseball cap smirked at Ronnie as she approached.

A dissatisfied customer? That seemed unlikely given Ronnie's optimistic demeanor.

The woman rested her hands on the shoulders of a little girl with a significant amount of friendship bracelets on her wrist and a too-large-for-her-head cowboy hat on her wispy brown hair.

"Have you seen Wylie, Doreen?" Ronnie asked as she and Hazel passed the pair.

"Not since my mom got a hold of him." Doreen's smirk morphed into a grin.

Odd, that. But Hazel had no time to ponder the woman's comment. Ronnie was leading her through the boisterous crowd who all seemed to have goats. There was activity in the arena—a young cowboy ran next to a brown-and-white goat past a set of poles. The goat bounded in and out of the poles, earning cheers from the crowd sitting three rows deep on the covered, metal bleachers.

At the far end of the audience, a little girl with tear-stained cheeks sat cross-legged on the ground with a small brown goat in her lap.

"This is Aliyah," Ronnie said when she reached the girl, leaning over to pat the little cowgirl on the head, and then do the same to the small goat. "And this is Jo-Jo."

"Jo-Jo fell over in the arena before I had a turn." Aliyah scrunched her face as if she was about to cry again. "And *Tommy-Know-It-All* said she's a fairy goat and can't compete."

A fairy goat?

Hazel had never heard of such a thing. Regardless, the baby goat looked healthy.

"Don't call your brother names, Aliyah," a woman gently scolded from a seat in the bleachers a few rows above Aliyah. She held a small, sleeping baby in her arms and rocked from side to side, ignoring Aliyah's additional complaints about Tommy to greet Hazel. "Thanks for coming, Doc. Ronnie told us it was Wylie's day off, so we weren't to bother him. Seems like the whole town is talking this week about him looking to settle down."

"Which is why I called you," Ronnie said, giving Hazel a too-satisfied smile before moving a few feet away to watch the happenings in the arena.

Ronnie's up to something.

"Jo-Jo is sick," Aliyah interrupted Hazel's thoughts. She cradled her goat as if it was a beloved rag doll. Not that Jo-Jo seemed to mind.

Hazel set her backpack and equipment bag on the gravel, then sat on the metal bleacher next to her patient, gently discouraging a white goat from having a taste of her backpack straps. She'd start with collecting some background on her patient. "How old is Jo-Jo, Aliyah?"

"I dunno. My daddy fixed someone's engine and Jo-Jo was how he got paid." Aliyah gave the brown goat a tender squeeze. "I love her."

Jo-Jo blinked calmly at Hazel. She looked to be several months old. She was either feverish or had fallen in love with her human.

Hazel stroked the goat's head. Jo-Jo's fur felt soft and healthy, not oily. The goat's head wasn't hot.

Jo-Jo's clear brown eyes opened wider and she extended her muzzle toward Hazel's straw cowboy hat, as if prepared to take a bite.

"Many a beast has tried to snack on my hat, Jo-Jo." Hazel tipped her cowboy hat back and out of reach. "How long have you had Jo-Jo, honey?" She eased the little girl's arms out of the way so she could conduct a more complete inspection of her patient, searching for abrasions or swelling on the goat's torso.

"She's been with me a week and I wanna do the course with her because my stupid brother Tommy has his own goat and he does everything." Aliyah pouted.

"That's not true, Aliyah," her mother said from her seat above them. "Tommy doesn't do everything."

"Seems like it anyway." Aliyah wasn't giving ground. Her lower lip was still thrust out.

Hazel smiled at the little girl, liking her spunk.

A theory about Jo-Jo began forming in her head. "Was there a loud noise before Jo-Jo fell?"

Aliyah nodded, a big, grand gesture for a pint-sized thing. "My brother was jumping on the bleachers."

"And did Jo-Jo get right back up once you gave her some lovin'?" Hazel asked, fingers moving to explore Jo-Jo's legs.

"She got up slow, like my grandma when she wakes up from her nap." Aliyah's eyes welled with unshed tears. "Is Jo-Jo gonna die?"

"No, honey." Hazel drew the small goat to her feet, staring into the kid's steady brown eyes. "I think you have a very rare goat here. I think Jo-Jo is a—"

"Tennessee fainting goat," a familiar, masculine voice interrupted Hazel.

She glanced up to see a pair of warm, green eyes and a gentle smile. "Dr. Newland. You are one hundred percent correct." Hazel wasn't annoyed that he'd interrupted her diagnosis because just his presence made everything around her brighter… lighter. Plus, he was being surrounded by nosy goats on slack lead ropes, as if they knew Wylie was goat-friendly.

But she could think about his appeal to herself and animals later. Right now, Hazel had to finish her appointment. She turned back to Aliyah. "Jo-Jo isn't a *fairy* goat. She's a *fainting* goat. And she's going to be around a long time if you take good care of her."

Aliyah's mouth dropped open. "Really?"

"Truly." Hazel adjusted Aliyah's cowboy hat to a jauntier angle. "I hope that makes you feel better."

Aliyah gave another one of her big, expressive nods. This time with a toothy grin. "Did you hear that, Mama? Tommy is wrong."

Her mother paused her chastisement of Tommy long enough to nod.

"I'm sorry you came all this way," Wylie said to Hazel, gently easing goats away from his legs. "I could have saved you a trip." He gave Ronnie a reproachful stare.

"You were busy." Ronnie cradled her baby bump and looked smug. "I called the clinic and Hazel came right over."

"Ronnie insisted on calling," Aliyah's mother added, adjusting the baby in her arms. *"And then she told me she'd foot the bill."*

"How considerate of you," Wylie deadpanned.

Hazel didn't know whether to laugh or gnash her teeth because Ronnie had indeed been up to something—no good! She'd gotten Hazel out here on false pretenses. Hazel made a mental note to tell Ronnie more emphatically that she wasn't looking to be matched with anyone, including Wylie.

But one fact remained. "There's no need for a bill when I didn't do anything." Hazel turned to Wylie for confirmation.

He nodded, then moved to stand next to Ronnie, speaking in a voice too low for Hazel to hear.

Hazel returned her attention to her young client. "I think Jo-Jo is ready to take on that obstacle course. But you need to know, Aliyah, that when Jo-Jo gets scared, she falls down and plays dead. That's what a fainting goat does. Now, unless she's bleeding when she gets up or walks stiffly for a long time afterward, you just need to give her some reassurance that she's safe and continue the course."

"You mean we can compete?" Aliyah got to her feet and did a little shimmy.

"That's exactly what I mean." Hazel reached into her scrub pocket and gave Jo-Jo a small oat cube.

Almost immediately, Hazel was surrounded by other goats, large and small, pressing their noses on Hazel as they searched for her cache of treats.

A large hand took hold of Hazel's arm and plucked Hazel to her feet. "You nearly started a goat stampede with those treats of yours." Wylie drew her against him. "Kids, control your goats."

A smattering of small cowboys and cowgirls reeled in lead ropes.

"Hey." Hazel felt the need to defend her use of treats. "Doling out goodies moves you up in the animal pecking order and makes them more likely to obey."

Wylie rolled his eyes.

"Doctor! Doctor!" Aliyah waved at Hazel from over by the arena gate. "Come watch me."

"Yes, stay," Wylie said in a low voice meant only for Hazel. "It'll give you a good laugh. Heaven knows I need one after the morning I've had."

Hazel wasn't feeling jovial. Not with Wylie's chest at her shoulder and his hand still on her arm. She was feeling like she should turn around, lift her head, stare into his green eyes, and wait for his kiss.

That was a scary thought.

Maybe I should take a page from Jo-Jo's book and faint.

But Hazel had no time to regroup because Wylie was guiding her to the arena rail while Aliyah entered the ring with her dear Jo-Jo.

"I need to leave after this, Wylie. Maisey has me on a tight schedule." That said, Hazel stood close enough to feel the warmth of Wylie, a welcome feeling even if it was growing hot enough to fry an egg ringside.

"You have time for a little girl," Wylie said gruffly. He caught the attention of a scruffy cowboy running things in the arena. "Hey, Griff. Aliyah's ready to give the course a go."

With a nod, Griff took charge of Aliyah and Jo-Jo, walking them through the obstacle course.

"When you were a kid, did you compete in rodeo or gymkhanas?" Wylie had placed both forearms on the top rail and rested his chin on one wrist, angling his head to look at Hazel.

"I did." Hazel nodded, wondering why she didn't feel self-conscious when Wylie gave her his complete attention.

Because we have good kissing history.

"I only competed in pole bending though." Which she'd given up on in middle school, spending time at her family's practice with her siblings instead. "You?"

"I didn't rope seriously until I went into foster care." Wylie's smile seemed to say he saw every asset and flaw in Hazel and could love them all equally.

"It's hot out here, isn't it?" Hazel tried to back away from Wylie because clearly the heat was getting to her if she was reading love in every glance Wylie cast her way.

He placed a hand in the middle of her back and drew her forward. "And, yet you seem like you want to stay."

Oh, how wrong he is.

And yet… Hazel didn't retreat.

Aliyah and Jo-Jo took their places at a rope laid across the ground, as if this was the starting line. When Griff shouted, *"Go!"* Aliyah trotted over to a raised wooden rail and encouraged Jo-Jo to hop up on it, which the little thing did, happily bouncing across.

"Did your parents come watch you compete?"

Wylie asked, low voice easing into Hazel's consciousness like a soft caress.

"No." The answer popped out of Hazel's mouth before she could think about it. How sad that made her childhood sound. "I always loaded up my horse in a friend's trailer. Her mom drove us. I guess that's because the competitions were on Saturdays and my parents always worked on weekends." And it felt as if her siblings had never watched her either.

Jo-Jo leaped down on the other end of the bridge, much to Aliyah's delight.

"My dad never came to watch me compete in anything, either." Wylie's words oozed a melancholy that drew Hazel's gaze. Hurt shadowed his eyes. "But I remember my dad asking me about my competitions. And I have this impression that he regretted not being there."

Aliyah led Jo-Jo through the poles. Literally. The little girl wove her way in-and-out of the course with Jo-Jo trailing behind her. The parents and other children who watched laughed in amusement.

"Good job, Aliyah and Jo-Jo," Hazel called out, sensing they needed encouragement.

The competitors moved to the plastic hoops. Griff helped Aliyah cue Jo-Jo through them.

"I've been thinking a lot lately about my dad," Wylie said, still in that low voice meant only for Hazel.

She liked when he talked to her like that, as if it

was just the two of them. "Is that because you're ready to settle down?"

Wylie nodded.

It was approaching noon and he had the beginnings of a five-o'clock shadow forming on his face. Hazel's hand itched to feel his whiskers. She wouldn't mind him brushing them over the sensitive part of her neck beneath her ear.

She gave a wistful sigh.

Gaze on her face, Wylie continued, "I think it was hard for my dad to carry the burden of being solely responsible for the family, running the vet practice, and being a good husband and father. I think he gave up on fatherhood when I ran away on my fifteenth birthday." His gaze shifted toward the arena, where Aliyah and Jo-Jo were moving toward a seesaw. "Like he just accepted the fact that I'd be better off if he was in the background or out of the picture. I should have made more of an effort to keep our relationship alive."

"You were a kid." Fifteen was young. He'd have been testing the boundaries of independence.

"Just because I was young and didn't know any better doesn't mean I don't have regrets." Those telling green eyes came back around to Hazel, seeking something.

Of what, she wasn't certain.

Hazel turned her attention to the young competitors about to enter the snaking plastic tunnel.

"I don't think you can go through life without regrets of some kind. Don't be so hard on yourself."

Wylie touched her shoulder lightly. "Will you do the same?"

"What?" Hazel spared him a quick glance. "Not have regrets concerning my past? That's impossible."

A boy with Aliyah's dark hair gave a shout of laughter. "Look at my sister go!" He banged a stick on the arena rail—*bang-bang-bang!*

Jo-Jo keeled over.

The audience began to chuckle, then laugh.

Instead of tending to her little charge, Aliyah stood rigidly, hands fisted at her sides as she yelled, *"Tommy! You did that on purpose!"*

Amid the increasing laughter, Hazel hurried into the arena and to Jo-Jo's side. "Aliyah. Jo-Jo needs you to comfort her. Like this, see?" Hazel stroked the goat's head and neck, speaking softly. "Come on, Jo-Jo. If you get back up, I'll give you a treat, baby girl."

Jo-Jo rolled upright, eyes wide and blinking at Hazel and earning another small oat treat.

"Jo-Jo!" Aliyah bent to hug her goat. "You didn't die."

The crowd gave a collective, *"Aw."*

"Thanks for the save," Griff told Hazel before patting Aliyah's hat. "Let's finish the course, cowgirl."

Meanwhile, other goats began to skirt between

the rails, straining against lead ropes and breaking free as they tried to get to Hazel and her supply of goodies.

"No-no-no. Make all the goats go away," Aliyah cried. And then, the tears began to flow. *"It's my turn!"*

Hazel managed to get to her feet before she was overwhelmed by goats.

"Kids! Control your...*kids*!" Griff laughed as he struggled to grab lead ropes.

Aliyah's mother entered the arena, cradling her baby in one arm and letting in a herd of goats dragging little kids behind them. "Tommy, don't ever do that again. Aliyah, you're a rock star. All you need to do is finish the tunnel, baby. And then we can go get an ice cream."

"What a great plan." Hazel gave the harried mom a thumbs-up, as Wylie reached her side, capturing more than his share of lead ropes.

"I might not be the best mom on the planet," Aliyah's mother confided in Hazel. "But I'm trying to be prepared for every contingency and be everywhere all at once for my little love bugs."

Hazel didn't think that was possible. But if she could be by Wylie's side and also work at a leading-edge surgery center, it would be worth it.

"You don't need to escort me to the mobile unit." Hazel was trying to walk faster than Wylie. "Enjoy your time off."

Wylie stretched his legs to keep up with Hazel because he'd been enjoying their time together and wasn't ready for it to end, unlike his time with Lilac that was supposed to have been with Doreen.

Wylie reached the mobile unit first and opened the door for Hazel. "Did Maisey take any more appointments for today?"

"You know she did." Hazel eased into the opening without touching him and slung her bags onto the driver's seat. "But don't you worry. Go on and give all those single ladies a good shot at you."

"You're talking about me as if it's open season on Dr. Wylie Newland." Wylie moved closer to Hazel. "And yet, you don't have me in your sights." He tucked a stray lock of Hazel's strawberry blond hair around her ear beneath her cowboy hat, then cupped her cheek. "I find that to be a crying shame."

Hazel leaned into his touch. For all her talk, she was as helpless to resist their attraction as he was.

"You know why I can't date you." Hazel stared deeply, longingly into his eyes before sighing and saying, "I'll see you later if you come by the clinic. Monday, then, if you don't."

But his cheeky cherry tart didn't move. Not an inch.

Then Wylie did what he'd been wanting to do since he'd seen Hazel walking Budge this morning. He closed the distance between them and kissed her tenderly.

Hazel sighed and leaned into Wylie, head tilting back so far her cowboy hat tumbled to the dirt.

And yet, neither one of them eased apart to pick it up.

Because we could kiss forever.

Footsteps sounded on the gravel, coming closer. Only then did hey end the kiss.

Hazel stared up at Wylie as if she was entertaining thoughts of forever kisses and happily-ever-afters, the same as he was.

If only the timing was better.

"There you are." Ronnie came up to them, face red and not from embarrassment. She was panting. "Wylie, can you give me a ride home? I'm feeling a bit out of sorts and I don't think I should drive myself back to the ranch, Wade being out of town at a rodeo and all."

"Of course." Wylie bent to retrieve Hazel's hat, hitting it against his thigh to get the dirt off before setting it back on her pretty head.

"I'll just wait over by your truck." For whatever reason, Ronnie gave Wylie and Hazel a sliver more of alone time.

"We shouldn't be doing that again," Hazel said, predictably, although without the trademark smile she'd shown up to town with.

"And yet, we might do that again." Wylie backed away, grinning. All-in-all, it had been a good morning, nightmarish mini-date aside.

"No. Don't say that." Hazel caught his hand.

"There's… There's a chance I might be leaving soon."

Leaving soon? Reflexively, Wylie's fingers curled tighter around hers.

Hazel explained how there'd been an accident at the surgery center she'd had her heart set on working for in *England*. "There might be a position open."

In England?

He'd just assumed she'd been talking about a premier veterinary hospital in the States.

"You'd leave so soon?" Everything inside Wylie was as tight and tense as his grip on her hand. "Now?" After she'd kissed him like that?

Hazel brushed her free hand over their entwined fingers, not that it soothed him in any way. "Presumably, there'd be a switch. So… Someone else would come to work for you."

"But that someone wouldn't be…" *You.* He checked the ground to see if he was experiencing an earthquake but it was just his knees going weak. "Will you…" His gaze found Hazel's. "Will you come back here afterward?" *To me.*

"If I return to a small-town clinic…" Hazel's brow clouded. "I'd have to return to my mother's. She's all alone and—"

"Wylie?" Ronnie called. "I feel a little like Jo-Jo."

About to faint, he thought she meant.

Wylie reluctantly released Hazel. "We'll talk about this later."

And then he hurried over to his truck, where Ronnie was waiting because that's what he did when he was uncertain in a situation. He went or stayed where he was needed.

And Hazel didn't need him.

"You're late." Maisey was sitting behind the counter at the clinic when Hazel returned.

Or rather, she was located behind a counter filled with what was beginning to look like a holiday party buffet. At least three dishes had been added since Hazel left for the goat emergency.

And had been kissed senseless by a handsome vet.

"AJ is waiting in exam room two." And despite the elderly vet tech's disdainful tone, she held out a Rice Krispies Treat to Hazel. "You look like you have low blood sugar. I talked to your mother on our main line after you left. Deborah said you never eat until the end of the day. That's not good for you."

"Coffee is a fifth food group." Hazel bit into the marshmallow square. Normally, sugar was among one of her favorite comfort foods. And after her post-kiss conversation with Wylie, she was in need of a little comfort. She moved to the nearly-empty plate of fudge, needing a stronger dose of sugar.

"Why are you talking to my mother without me, Miss Maisey?" She bit into the fudge.

"Because you weren't available, obviously." Maisey sniffed. "She's lonely and grieving."

"I know." The fudge wasn't going to soothe the pain in Hazel's heart that kissing Wylie had caused.

"Deborah told me about your brother and—"

"I'm sorry, Miss Maisey, but I've got a patient waiting." Hazel had no time to dissect her mother's grief when she had to keep a tight handle on her own, which now included grief over a love that would never be.

With Wylie.

CHAPTER ELEVEN

"You, Dr. Wylie Newland, are my biggest matchmaking challenge ever." Ronnie sat next to Wylie on a bar stool in the Buckboard before six that evening. "I thought something might click with Hazel but even you admit she's not going to stay. This requires more mini-dates."

She'd claimed to have had a nap and hydrated. At least, she looked refreshed. Wylie had gone on two other mini-dates over in Friar's Creek, both duds. Not that he'd given them much effort.

And now, when they should be debriefing and he should be telling Ronnie he was really only interested in one woman who wasn't interested in staying in town, Ronnie wanted him to date some more?

Wylie frowned.

Ronnie frowned back at him, fidgeting in her seat as if that baby she was carrying was making her uncomfortable. "I'm starting to believe you aren't serious about finding someone special."

"You know that's not true," Wylie reassured her

but he didn't look at Ronnie when he said it. "I don't want to be in a rocking chair when my kids have grandkids. I need to get a family started or the rest of the Done Roamin' Ranch cowboys will leave me behind." And he wanted to get that family started. Now. With Hazel.

"Starting a family isn't a competition," Ronnie said crisply, resting a supportive hand on his shoulder. "If now isn't the right time, there are still plenty of single cowboys with roots at the Done Roamin' Ranch you can compete with in the baby-making department next year or the year after."

"It's not a competition." Wylie scoffed, feeling out of sorts. "I want my kids to grow up with your kids."

Ronnie looked like she might cry.

Didn't make Wylie feel any less off-kilter.

He'd felt that way since Hazel had told him she might be leaving. And not just because she might be leaving but because she might go to a prestigious surgery center. That hub in Newmarket was a hub for experimental procedures for most of the world. It made Wylie a bit envious, just as his foster father had said.

And that envy...

How could Wylie want Hazel to stay when this was an opportunity of a lifetime? One he'd gladly pursue himself?

Because I'm falling in love with her.

And that acknowledgment was where Wylie hit a brick wall, uncertain how to proceed.

"I don't know Claire all that well," Ronnie was saying, sipping a ginger ale. "And she lives on the far side of Friar's Creek, so she's a bit out of your immediate sphere, which means she has her own circle of friends. But maybe that's all right."

"I wish you'd stop making me dates," Wylie muttered. "You can cancel that date with Claire, whenever it is."

"Are you feverish?" Ronnie laid a palm on his forehead beneath his hat brim.

Wylie swatted it away. "I'm fine."

It was Ronnie's turn to scoff. "And yet, you haven't heard a word I've said. She's about to walk in the door."

Wylie shook his head, wondering how he could have fallen in love with a stranger and disrupted all his best-laid plans in a handful of days.

Hazel isn't a stranger. I know her. I know her well.

He knew how hard she'd worked to get this far in her career, because he'd traveled that road. He knew about her guilt over leaving her mother to pursue a dream, because he'd traveled that road, too. And he knew what it was like to be forced to choose between a relationship and a career. And yet, he wanted Hazel to make a different choice than he had, take a different fork in the road.

I want her to choose love.

"And here she is." Ronnie slid off the bar stool and might have stumbled if Wylie hadn't caught her arm. "Claire, this is Wylie. Ten minutes together is all I ask. I'll be over there with my friends if you need me." Ronnie made her way over to a booth next to the dance floor where Izzy, Allison, and Hazel sat together.

Wylie had been so lost in thought that he hadn't seen Hazel come in.

"Hey, you seem like your head's in the clouds." Claire took Ronnie's seat and ordered a beer from the bartender. She wore a fancy black dress, short, black cowboy boots, and a black cowboy hat. Her hair was dirty blond and her eyes a knowing brown. "Maybe we should do this another time," Claire offered, not that she moved to leave.

"No. I promised Ronnie ten minutes." Wylie tried smiling politely but it felt more like a grimace. "And I seem to recall you came a long way."

Claire nodded, crossing her legs and swinging her foot as if nervous. "I don't do blind dates. Like...*ever*. But I ran into Ronnie at an antique store in Friar's Creek a few days ago and the next thing I knew, I was agreeing to meet you."

Wylie nodded. "Tell me about yourself." Because in the mood he was in, he didn't think he could muster a lot of chatty conversation.

Claire started talking.

Wylie didn't hear a word. And it wasn't because someone had started playing music for the line dancing hour. And it wasn't because Hazel, Ronnie, Izzy, and Allison had moved to the dance floor. It was because his brain was jammed with thoughts and feelings and ideas all targeted toward convincing Hazel to set aside a professional opportunity of a lifetime. If only she'd said she'd consider returning here after her residency was completed.

"And I was wondering how to decide if I was in love with him or not," Claire was saying, drawing Wylie's attention back to her. "Which is why I came to meet you. To see if there was a spark."

Wylie's jaw fell open. He'd missed the thread of the conversation. But what he'd missed… He had no idea.

A shadow at his shoulder indicated they were no longer alone.

"Really, Claire? You went on a date so you could decide if you were in love with me or not?" The tall cowboy standing at their backs was young, red-faced, and angry, if that scowl was any indication. "We've been together six years, Claire. You should know if you love me after six years. I expected you to say yes to my marriage proposal last weekend. Not *I don't know*."

Uh-oh.

Wylie eased back on his bar stool, preparing to see where this went. Hopefully, there'd be a happily-ever-after here for Claire.

Or not.

Claire's face had drained of color. She stared at her boyfriend, her mouth forming a little O.

"I love you, Claire," the cowboy choked out.

"Um…" Perhaps Claire didn't love the man back. She turned her blank stare on Wylie.

Who suddenly felt as if he needed to defend his date.

"Why don't you head on home?" Wylie said slowly, turning on the bar stool to face Claire's admirer. "Call Claire tomorrow so you can talk about it rationally."

"Love isn't rational." The cowboy pushed Wylie's shoulder in the universal preamble to a fight. "Stay out of this, you home-wrecker. I love Claire and she needs proof of that love. So… Let's go." He held up his fists and stood like an experienced boxer.

"None of that now." Chet, the gray-haired, handlebar-mustached bartender, hurried toward them.

Conversation in the bustling honky-tonk went bust. People gawked and jostled one another for a front row view of whatever was about to happen.

Wylie held up a hand toward Chet, getting to his feet. He'd gotten into his share of scrapes. He could handle himself. But violence was never the answer. He'd learned that the hard way. "Listen, friend. You've proved to Claire that you love her just by showing up and telling her again. There's no need to exchange blows with me."

The cowboy took a swing at him anyway.

Wylie ducked and stepped back. But his path wasn't clear. He tumbled into someone. On top of someone. And fell to the floor.

The crowd went wild.

HAZEL GRUNTED, ELBOWS AND tailbone stinging from falling on the hard floor. She pushed on Wylie's shoulders until he rolled off her. "There's not too much difference between being rammed by Hard Nose and being a crash pad for Dr. Wylie Newland."

"Hazel?" Wylie scrambled to his knees while several cowboys held on to the man who'd taken a swing at him.

They dragged the young cowboy toward the door while Wylie's date followed, sobbing.

"Hazel?" Wylie repeated.

"That's me." She extended her arms and legs, making a human X and trying to decide if she'd taken more damage than a few bruises to her elbows and tailbone. She'd worn her favorite yellow sundress tonight. Thankfully, she wasn't flashing anybody. And her cell phone-wallet was still in her dress pocket. "You're a lucky man, Wylie."

"How so?" Wylie retrieved his cowboy hat. And hers. His black hair was in a rumpled tangle, as usual.

"Growing up around a rural veterinary practice, I'm something of an experienced crash dummy."

Meaning Hazel knew better than to put her hands out when she fell. "Usually, I drop and roll out of harm's way." She hadn't counted on Wylie's legs getting tangled with hers and them toppling like movie stunt doubles.

"I'm sorry. I didn't see you come up behind me." Wylie set his cowboy hat atop his head and hers on one of his knees. "I thought you were on the dance floor."

"I thought I was coming to your rescue." Hazel rested a hand on his other knee and mustered a smile. Aches and pains aside, she'd live, she decided. "I'm very good at diluting tension with humor and a pleasant expression."

"I've noticed." Wylie grinned down at her. "Do you need help getting up?"

"Wouldn't mind it." She placed her hand in his, belatedly noting that the women she'd been line dancing with were clustered on the dance floor far enough away that they didn't intrude and near enough that they could hear since the music had stopped playing.

Wylie got to his feet, easily bringing her to hers.

"Oh...head rush." Hazel closed her eyes, resting her forehead against his chest and that blue checked shirt of his. "Why did that guy want to deck you?"

"Apparently, Ronnie set me up on a date with his almost-fiancée." There was a smile in Wylie's voice that she didn't need to open her eyes to see was also on his face.

The world continued to spin. Or perhaps being in his arms again had her head spinning. She wanted to stay there forever.

"Almost-fiancée?" Hazel sighed. "Everybody raves about Ronnie's matchmaking savvy. Do you think all the emotions and hormones raging while being pregnant has Ronnie off her game?"

"I heard that," Ronnie said, but she laughed after she said it.

Hazel opened her eyes to find Wylie's arm around her and her palm resting over his heart. "Your heartbeat is slower than mine." Which was still pounding excitedly. "Doesn't it bother you that we were almost in a fistfight?"

"We?" His dark eyebrows shot up, along with his smile.

Hazel had the strongest urge to remove that brown cowboy hat of his and run her hand through his unruly black hair. She smiled at him instead. "It's good to see you unscathed."

"Right back at you, sweet thing."

Sweet thing?

Be still, my heart.

The music started again.

Behind her on the dance floor, feminine voices and laughter became less distinct.

"Do you want to dance?" she asked Wylie.

"Nope." And without another word, he plopped

her cowboy hat on her head and hustled her out of the Buckboard into the heat and the soft evening light of summer.

Once they were outside, Wylie took Hazel's hand and headed for the sidewalk.

"Isn't that your truck over there?" Hazel asked, pointing behind them.

"Yep." He kept walking away from it.

"Do you have some destination in mind?" Something romantic and secluded. Something cool because the day's heat clung to the air. Somewhere that Hazel could forget a part of her wanted to be across the ocean, thousands of miles away, fulfilling her and her brother Mike's dreams.

"Nope." Wylie kept walking, boots striking the pavement with purpose, despite his answer.

They strolled a few blocks, entering the historic district with its charming little Craftsman-style homes and tall, spreading trees with shade to spare. The sidewalk felt several degrees cooler in this neck of the woods.

"Where are we going?" Hazel asked when she couldn't remain silent any longer.

"I'm walking you home." Except Wylie stopped at the steps of a quaint little church and glanced up at the closed double doors. He veered away from the sidewalk and went to take a seat on the top step, patting a spot next to him. "We have a problem."

Oh, don't I know it.

But they'd tried talking things through. She

couldn't say any more plainly that she was leaving—if not sooner, then later. And yet...

"Chemistry keeps pulling us together," she said softly, sitting next to him and smoothing her yellow sundress skirt over her knees. "And as doctors, we know how powerful chemical reactions can be."

"Chemistry," Wylie grumbled, leaning back to stare at her. "It's the greatest of ironies that I have the worst luck when it comes to choosing women to fall in love with."

Air burst out of Hazel's lungs in a rush, seemingly disinclined to return.

"Love?" she wheezed, simultaneously pleased and concerned.

"Don't argue." Wylie grumbled. "You can't kiss me like that and not—"

"You hired Ronnie to find you a suitable wife," Hazel pointed out, finding air and her voice. "Emphasis on *suitable*."

"You suit me." Wylie stared at the canopy of leaves above them.

Oh, how much she wanted to echo his sentiment. But there was Mike's memory, hovering like a reminder at the back of her mind, and the work at Wylie's clinic, so lacking in any real challenge.

"When I was a kid," Wylie said in a muted voice, still staring up into the trees, "I used to think that everything would be so simple when I was an adult. And the reality..."

"Has been quite the opposite." Hazel nodded.

Despite her better judgment, her hand found Wylie's. She examined the scars on his fingers, faded now but indicating he'd weathered more than one scared, hurt patient in his lifetime. "Every choice comes at a price."

How well she knew that. She'd introduced Maisey to her mother and they'd become fast phone and video-chat buddies today. Maisey had been trying to mother Hazel all afternoon. She'd much prefer their sparring.

Wylie shook his head. "And the price of every choice involves giving up something else you want." He sighed, his heavy green gaze finding hers. "I chose to stay in foster care when I could have returned to my father without acknowledging that hint of regret inside me. Or knowing that regret would blossom into something complicated I'd have to carry with me later."

"I chose to return to veterinary school knowing I wasn't going back to my mother's practice. Ever." Hazel couldn't stare into those eyes of his. It was too hard.

Coward.

She noted a small bird in the branches above them, flitting about as if it couldn't decide upon a direction.

How much she had in common with a little bird.

"I chose to stay here with my found family in my hometown instead of leaving with Tabitha." Wylie's words had a solemn quality, like a confession of a long-held secret. He eased his arm around Hazel's shoulders and drew her closer. "I don't know if I'd make the same choice twice. This time... I'm going to follow my heart."

Hazel stiffened. "You can't mean that." That he'd follow her to Newmarket. "We've hardly known each other for five days and—"

"Yet we know deep down that this is something important." He didn't look at Hazel as he spoke.

"Something that could be important," Hazel repeated, half under her breath. Adding in a louder voice, "Or it could be our biggest regret." Bigger than the guilt she carried for disappointing her mother. Or he his father.

"I have an idea." Wylie stood and drew her to her feet. "Why don't we let chemistry do its thing? You might not get an invitation to go overseas. We could just be our own science experiment. Here. In Clementine."

Hazel opened her mouth.

She opened her mouth intending to say: *Yes!*

But something stopped her. Not one thing, but many—all involving dreams. Hers, Mike's, Wylie's, even Mom's. And none of them meshed. None of them fit like a set of puzzle pieces.

And so, she said, "That won't work."

And walked the rest of the way home. Alone.

CHAPTER TWELVE

WYLIE WASN'T ONE to ignore a hunch, whether it involved a patient diagnosis or his personal life. He was convinced that Hazel was the one for him.

And therefore, he stopped accepting dates Ronnie made and began driving into town early and taking a morning walk with Hazel and Budge.

Oh, Hazel heaved a few heavy sighs at first. But after the first two days, she no longer gave Wylie the silent treatment. And other than holding her hand, he didn't press her for any more kisses. He was out to prove what was between them was real.

"Pretty soon, Budge is going to need a pasture," Wylie said on Tuesday morning.

Hazel nodded. She walked between Wylie and Budge, one hand on the chestnut gelding's lead rope and one hand nestled in Wylie's.

"I have a nice pasture at my place," Wylie continued in what he hoped was a nonthreatening tone. "And I don't snore." He knew Maisey sawed logs like a power tool. When he'd first returned to Clementine, he'd stayed in the room Hazel was sleeping in.

"I ordered sleep earmuffs," Hazel said levelly. "And Budge still has a few more weeks before he'll be up to open spaces and moving at a faster clip than a walk without risking joint injury."

They rounded the corner and approached Betty's Bakery. The sun was still low in the sky but the day promised another scorcher.

Katie stepped outside of the bakery with two coffees and one bakery bag. "Good morning, my regulars."

And as had become habit, Wylie handed her a bill and told her to keep the change.

Further down the street, Wylie and Hazel stopped at a sidewalk bench, sat down, drank their coffee, and ate Katie's latest attempt to make cannoli.

"Her filling is spot-on delicious, as usual," Wylie said. Couldn't go wrong with peanut putter as far as he was concerned.

"The pastry is still a bit gummy," Hazel admitted.

Budge stood tall and proud, waiting patiently for them to finish, as if he'd never been neglected and had spent his life among them.

Hazel could do important things in her life.

Develop a new surgery technique or a breakthrough treatment for some disease.

If she goes.

Wylie wasn't at a point yet to watch her do so. He was still learning about Hazel, discovering facets of her character on their morning walks before Maisey and work put distance between them.

"I used to eat peanut butter and cornflake sandwiches for breakfast," Wylie confessed. He held up the last bite of his cannoli. "The texture of this brought back fond memories." The gumminess. The way the food stuck in his teeth.

"Your mom didn't cook you breakfast?" Hazel was intent upon eating more filling than pastry. A bit of ricotta cheese filling plopped at her feet. "Oops." She swiped it up with a napkin and tossed it into a nearby trash can. "My mom was big on breakfast. It used to make me sleepy in school. It's probably why I barely eat in the morning."

"My mother..." Wylie hadn't talked about her much. "She didn't like things messy. And cooking anything created a mess. Breakfast was anything quick I could make when she was around. I couldn't leave for school until I'd put my dirty dishes in the dishwasher, wiped down the kitchen and bathroom, and made sure every hair on my head was in place."

Hazel lifted his cowboy hat before setting it back on his head, smiling as if she knew a secret.

"Yes, I have more than one cowlick on my head." But back then, Wylie wasn't allowed to wear a hat to school. "When she left... Things were a bit less spick-and-span. And Dad took me on more calls to ranches, which was the best. I used to think he was a miracle worker. He hardly ever lost a patient."

"I remember those days." Hazel gazed up at the sky. "Since my dad was a human doctor, I couldn't watch him work. But my mom… I thought she had superhero skills when it came to saving animals."

Wylie nodded. "For decades, I locked the good memories of my father away. But now… Now, I think about them more often. We had some good talks and good laughs." More than in later years.

"I get that." Hazel's smile misted. "My siblings and I would scramble to help Mom, which often led to teasing and laughter. My brother had a little spot on his head where no hair grew." Hazel pushed her finger beneath her straw cowboy hat brim as if locating her brother's bald spot. "It was no larger than a pencil eraser but it was still fair game in the teasing wars."

Wylie enjoyed listening to her stories and liked to imagine she enjoyed listening to his. "As an only child, I wasn't an active participant in the teasing wars." That was something Wylie had learned about at the Done Roamin' Ranch. "Were you a math and science nerd? Or did you find a love for it when you were in high school?"

"With two older, nerdy siblings, what do you think?" Hazel drained her coffee and stood, tossing her empty cup into that nearby trash can. "In our house, academics were more important than arts and crafts. Although I remember finger painting a picture of the ocean." A small smile worked its way onto her face. "Gosh, I couldn't have been more than six. I was so proud of that painting. I came home and removed my math worksheet with the gold star on it from the fridge. And then I put my finger painting up there only to have my siblings make fun of it."

That was deserving of a hug.

He stood to give her one.

And while Wylie held on to her, he whispered, "I guess you won't be one of those helicopter parents who hovers over their kids to make sure they excel." And because he couldn't trust himself to ease out of that hug without bussing those tempting lips of hers, he hung on, much the way Lilac had to him at the goat obstacle course a few days prior.

"Kids is a concept that seems very far away at the moment," Hazel whispered, a note of remorse in her voice. "If ever."

If ever?

Wylie backed away, all thoughts of kissing dissipated.

Hazel isn't sure she wants kids?

Wylie was gobsmacked. "Come on, Budge." He took the lead rope from Hazel, heading off without looking back. Because looking at Hazel always gave him hope. He could find it in the purplish-gray of her eyes or nestled in a new shade of orange he discovered in her hair. But this…

I want kids.

Every conversation about their pasts seemed to reveal another obstacle to their future together.

Hazel caught up to him, saying nothing. Explaining nothing.

Wylie turned to business. "We'll need to get to the fairgrounds early on Thursday to perform health checks on all the animals."

"Will I have time to walk Budge first?" She took tentative hold of Wylie's hand.

Wylie glanced at their joined hands and then into Hazel's purplish-gray eyes. "I hope so."

Because he couldn't imagine a day started without their time alone together. Even if—increasingly—it felt like it had an end date.

"W<small>E HAVE AN</small> emergency coming in," Maisey announced midmorning, yelling upstairs where Hazel was refilling a coffee mug. "Car accident. It's Biff."

"Who's Biff?" Hazel asked, running down the stairs and spilling coffee on the front of her yellow scrub shirt.

"Labradoodle. A year old as I recall. Sounds like a broken leg." Maisey hurried back to the front of the clinic. "I'm sorry, Deuce, but we're going to need to reschedule that annual exam. Emergency coming in."

The woman who'd brought in the terrier Deuce for an annual exam scurried out the door. "Prepare for the worst." Wylie propped open the lab door. He'd been restocking the medical kit for the mobile unit, getting ready to spend the rest of the day out and about. "Car accidents are never pretty."

Hazel knew that. What she didn't know was... "Who does Biff belong to?"

"Izzy and Della-Mae." Wylie looked grim and went to the front door, as if waiting to retrieve the injured animal himself. "First Laramie and now this."

A few minutes later, a truck pulled into the lot with a squeal of tires.

Wylie rushed out of the clinic, Hazel right behind him. He flung open the passenger-side door.

Della-Mae was sobbing, her white-blond hair as limp as the gangly, black Labradoodle in her lap. He was wrapped in a red blanket. "It was an accident. I shoulda had him on his leash."

"Don't worry. I've got him." Wylie scooped the dog from the little girl's arms, blanket and all.

He and Hazel ran with Biff back to the clinic and into the surgery room, laying the dog gently on the operating table and removing the blanket.

Biff whined but accepted their help without complaint.

Wylie took the lead, calling out commands that Maisey and Hazel rushed to follow.

Maisey started an IV. Hazel gathered tools for surgery. Everything happened so fast.

But it was a good speed. A lifesaving speed.

And despite Hazel being the new member of the team, the three of them worked well together.

"Biff is doing great," Hazel told Izzy and her daughter, Della-Mae, nearly two hours later.

The pair was huddled in the waiting room, joined by a tall cowboy that Hazel struggled to place a name to and a small boy about Della-Mae's age.

"Chandler," Hazel said when the Done Roamin' Ranch foreman met her inquisitive gaze. He sat beneath the picture of the foster cowboys. "Izzy's fiancé."

"Yes." Izzy kissed the back of his hand. The hand that held hers so tenderly. "Sam is his son."

"We're the same age," Della-Mae whispered. Her cheeks were tear-stained. "He's raising Rusty, Biff's brother."

"Oh." Hazel approached the foursome, lowering herself to her knees in front of them. "Biff has internal bleeding. We've taken care of that." Mostly. "And Dr. Newland is setting his leg right now." His rear leg had snapped cleanly, thank heavens. "We're going to keep him here for observation. Maisey will come and get you when he's ready for visitors. Do you have any questions?"

Della-Mae wiped away her tears. "Is he going to be able to run again?"

"He is," Hazel assured her. "But he might need that kennel you've got Laramie in when he comes home. He can't run for a long time. We put what's called a Schroeder-Thomas splint on his leg. It's made of metal and customized just for him."

"Cool," little Sam said.

Hazel grinned at him. "It *is* cool."

"Laramie's due for his recheck tomorrow." Izzy gave her daughter a warm hug. "How long will Biff be here?"

"I want to consult with Dr. Newland but I'm thinking two nights just to make sure he's stable." Hazel gave them all reassuring smiles. "Maisey and I live upstairs so someone will be here round the clock."

A sound in the hallway had Hazel turning.

Maisey and Wylie stood in the hallway. Wylie's green scrub shirt had a sickening amount of blood on it. Unlike Hazel, he hadn't changed scrub shirts before coming out.

"I'll take you back to see him now," Maisey said, gesturing toward the lab and the kennels within.

Hazel hurried to Wylie's side, turning him around and easing him toward the apartment stairs. "Come on. You need a fresh shirt."

He didn't argue.

"You have a good bedside manner," Wylie said, easing the stained scrub over his tense shoulders in front of the apartment's coat closet.

"Thank you." Hazel dug in the coat closet for one of his clean shirts, handing him one from the bottom of the pile. A blue shirt that had been his father's. She shook it out and handed it to him.

Wylie hesitated before taking it.

From her bedroom, Fluffy gave a barely audible growl.

"Something wrong?" Hazel was trying not to look at his bare chest.

Wylie fought the urge to smile and put his father's scrub shirt on. It felt well-worn and comfortable. Unexpectedly so.

"One thing I enjoy about a small practice is the personal relationships with pet owners," Hazel admitted, bundling up his stained shirt. "You really only see an animal and their owners a few times at a surgery center before they're out of your lives forever."

"I like that, too." Wylie gently caught her chin with one hand, forcing her to look at him. "What's wrong? Things went well in there."

Hazel nodded, expression somber. "*We* worked well in there."

"And that's a bad thing?" Wylie ran a hand through his hair. "I asked you if you wanted to stitch him up inside and out because your stitchwork is better than mine."

"I didn't expect to be such a big part of the process, I guess." Hazel looked at a loss.

"Did I do something wrong?" Wylie probed again because this wasn't the Hazel he knew. She was somber and quiet.

"We were good together," she said again, only this time her distinctly gray eyes glistened with tears. "Like a team who'd worked side by side for years, not days. And it felt right." She backed away from him. "It felt right." And then she disappeared downstairs.

Because working together made her want to stay?

Wylie wished he wasn't tied down here, by family and community obligation. He gripped the hem of his scrub shirt, fighting an urge to take it off. To shed his Clementine legacy and search for his own. In Newmarket, if he had to.

Voices from below drifted to him. The high-pitched, loving sound of a family grateful to have their fur baby alive and on the mend.

We did that.

Other cases crossed his mind. Ones where he'd done surgery just with Maisey. Ones where he'd assisted his father as a kid.

Confront the past before you face the future.

That was the gist of what his foster father had told him.

Wylie stared across the apartment at the office where his father died. His chest felt heavy. His feet didn't move.

Whatever awaited him inside, he'd allowed it to fester for nearly two decades.

Hazel didn't let anything fester. She charged ahead, telling the world—and him—what she wanted and where she wanted to be.

But performing surgery with me rocked that belief.

Determined to confront the past, Wylie crossed the apartment. Opened the office door.

The room had a dusty, disused feel to it. One wall was lined floor-to-ceiling with dark wood bookcases that were packed with books—paperback thrillers his father had loved, medical books and journals. The spines were cracked and worn, as if each volume had been read more than once. The surface of the large, dark walnut desk was empty except for a brown coffee mug Wylie had made for him in eighth grade. Dad's cowboy hat hung from a coat tree in the corner. Dad's diplomas hung on the wall, along with a picture of him and Mom on their wedding day, and Wylie on his high school graduation.

There was a framed certificate propped against the wall behind the door—acknowledgment of Dad as a fair judge. Wylie had forgotten his father used to judge livestock at the fair. And hanging above it was a smaller certificate. An award given by the university where Dad had earned his veterinary degree. An award for surgical recognition.

If Wylie had known of his father's skill in surgery, he'd forgotten it long ago.

A small growl behind him let Wylie know Fluffy was curious about the room as well.

He scooped up the little dog, earning a bit of grousing. "There's nothing here to see, Fluffy." He closed the door. "A man's legacy can only be seen in his children." In the choices they made and the memories they kept.

"I WANT THE lady doctor."

Hazel was coming out of the lab later that afternoon when she heard the small voice from the lobby. She hesitated.

"The only doctor Breezy has ever seen is Dr. Newland," Maisey said in a voice less tetchy than usual. "Have a cookie. Dr. Newland will be right with you. Look. He just pulled up outside in the big, fancy truck."

Hazel glanced out the window, barely registering the meek mew of a feline in distress.

Wylie got out of the clinic's mobile unit. He was covered in dust, head to toe, and his green scrub shirt looked like a large animal had used it as a sweat rag. He removed a baseball cap and swiped a hand through his sweat-damped hair. For once, none of his dark locks were out of place. He crossed the parking lot slowly, as if he was spent. He'd had to put someone's horse down.

Hazel's heart went out to him. She knew she'd driven a wedge between them this morning when they'd talked about having kids. But their relationship was like a roller coaster. They'd done that emergency surgery, working together so well… It had made her reconsider leaving for England, made her wonder what Mike would have thought if she decided to stay in Clementine.

He'd tell me not to stay.

Wylie's shoulders seemed to fall even more.

Mike would tell me to keep my distance emotionally, to keep my eyes on our dreams.

She stared at Wylie instead. For years, he'd run his practice alone. Lived alone. Perhaps given up on dreams.

"I recommend the sugar cookies with sprinkles," Maisey said to whoever was in the lobby.

For at least a decade, Wylie had run the clinic without another doctor to tag team with when he needed a break. Maybe he didn't have the energy to dream because he was always on the run, booked solid. He looked like he needed time to reset. How often had he pushed himself to a physical and emotional limit? She didn't know.

Hazel strode toward the lobby before she realized what she'd decided to do. She came to stand beside the vet tech's chair. "Hey, Miss Maisey. I'm taking Dr. Newland's appointments for the next hour."

"Is that so?" Maisey's frown didn't achieve its usual deeply wrinkled, bulldog status.

"Yes, ma'am. He needs a coffee break." Or a power nap. Hazel snuck a glance at the approaching Wylie before turning toward the little girl in the lobby, the one who sat next to a gangly teenage boy in sports shorts and a wrinkled green T-shirt.

A portable cat carrier sat at their feet. A small

gray face retreated from the bars, releasing that heartbreaking mew.

The little girl gave Hazel a shy wave. The teenage boy ignored her.

Hazel winked at the girl. "Who's next, Miss Maisey?"

"Breezy." Maisey handed Hazel a folder without complaint, possibly also having caught sight of Wylie's defeated silhouette. "Sounds like Breezy ate something that disagreed with her—a bug or a mouse or something. Got an upset tummy or some such."

"Let's go, Breezy." Hazel led the way to an empty exam room, assuming the kids would follow her.

They did, filing in quietly while Hazel studied Maisey's loopy, handwritten file notes. Breezy was a six-month-old female and up-to-date on her shots. The teenage boy placed the cat carrier on the exam table, then went to sit in the visitor's chair, a sulky expression on his face.

"I hoped we'd get to see you." The little girl came to stand in front of Hazel, beaming up at her. Her blond hair fell in cheerful ringlets around her face. "I'm Olive. My friend Aliyah said you saved her goat. That's how I know you'll help Breezy."

The teenage boy sighed, slouched, and tugged his cell phone out of his pocket, intent upon starring in the uncaring older brother act.

Something Wylie had mentioned to Hazel about the importance of being a good role model and inspiring young kids came back to her. Hazel felt compelled to try and do the same.

"Nice to meet you, Olive." Hazel shook the girl's hand. Then she extended her hand to the teenager. "I'm Dr. Hughes."

"Russ." The boy gave her a handshake as short as his name.

Breezy mewed pitifully.

"Have you ever conducted a pet exam?" Hazel still faced Russ. "I only ask because you seem to care about Breezy and we might be looking to hire a part-time vet trainee."

Russ straightened in his seat, interest flashing across his face. "What kind of experience do you need to have for a job like that?"

"No experience." Hazel opened the cat carrier door, peeking in at a panting gray cat. "You just have to be willing to learn and want a paycheck, of course."

Russ got to his feet. "Let me get Breezy out for you. She can be stubborn sometimes."

"Sure." Hazel stepped back and winked at Olive.

"See, Russ," Olive said with a little sister's pride. "I told you she was great."

TUESDAY NIGHT, WYLIE ENTERED Exhibit Hall A at the county fairgrounds ahead of Wade and his foster father, Frank Harrison.

Metal folding chairs had been placed in neat rows in front of a long table where the county fair board was holding a public meeting. There were only about twenty people in attendance, which meant their late entrance didn't go unnoticed. Whatever the board had been discussing before their appearance, they'd stopped talking when the cowboys filed in.

Wylie went to sit front and center.

"Really?" Wade whispered as he sat next to him. "The front row?"

"How do you think I got good grades in school?" He'd always sat up close, even when he'd been staying out late with so-called friends and making mischief in town. A part of him had always known his circumstances could change with an education.

Dad claimed the chair on the other side of Wylie, removing his wide-brimmed, white cowboy hat and setting it on his knee. "No sense beating around the bush." He raised a hand, although the board was already staring at them. "Sorry we're late. We're here about the judging. Not sure if you've talked about it yet."

"We haven't." Rose sat to one end of the table, the doll stroller with Bruiser behind her. "But I move we table the discussion about heating repair to fair buildings until we've obtained three cost estimates."

"Second," someone sitting at the table said.

"All in favor…" Sheriff Underwood glanced up and down the table, presumably counting raised hands and assent. After years of being a baking judge, the sheriff had taken on the role of head of the board at the end of last year's fair. "Motion passed. Next order of business..." He consulted a sheet of paper, then raised his gaze to Wylie and his crew. "Livestock and rodeo judging." He turned toward Rose. "This is your bailiwick."

"We had a complaint about nepotism." She held up a sheet of paper with large, loopy scrawl. "Unsigned. But claiming that cowboys who were fostered, work, or have worked for the Done Roamin' Ranch shouldn't be allowed to judge anything given their children are now competing in livestock and rodeo events."

"Sounds right to me." That came from a woman behind Wylie.

When he turned around, he found Evie smirking at him.

"Quiet in the gallery." Sheriff Underwood turned his intent gaze upon Dad. "Frank, how many employees have you had over the years?"

"Gosh." Dad ran a hand over the sparse white hair on his head. "Over forty years in business... Must be close to two hundred cowboys and a mess of cowgirls. That's not counting all the suppliers and their employees we've done business with."

The sheriff jotted something on a notepad. "And how many fosters do you reckon you've had?"

"Well...some longer than others but somewhere over fifty." Dad spoke those words with pride.

Wylie hadn't spent the majority of his childhood

at the Done Roamin' Ranch as a foster. But those few years that he had when he was a teen were some of his fondest. He'd become a man there. A good man. He'd found family there. In Frank and Mary Harrison. In the guys he'd shared rooms with, rode horses with, even been thrown in the dirt trying to ride bucking broncs and bulls with. Without them, he'd have no family. And for that, he was eternally grateful.

In the audience, metal chairs squeaked and voices whispered. No doubt, they were realizing what Wylie already knew: It was a powerful legacy Frank and Mary Harrison would someday leave behind. A notion which only brought more weight to Wylie's shoulders. He carried his biological father's legacy, as well.

"I've been saying this for years now," Evie piped up. "We should hire judges across all fair categories. Judges should be impartial, not local."

Wylie turned to face his peach-pie-making dating nemesis. "Did you write that letter?"

"Quiet in the gallery!" Sheriff Underwood demanded in a booming voice that echoed through the room. And then he leaned forward. "Evie Grace, did you write that letter?"

"No." She tossed her long blond hair over her shoulder. "It looks like doctor scribbles to me."

"But that letter has a valid point," Mandy piped up from her spot next to Evie. She wore green scrubs and an abashed expression, shrinking back when everyone looked at her, even from Wylie, who'd left their mini-date to rush to Hazel's rescue from Hard Nose without apology. "Doesn't it?" Mandy asked in a subdued voice.

"No." Rose lifted a stiff-legged Bruiser from his stroller and placed the cute fella in her lap. "We're a tiny county, so small that we can't afford to operate the fair with paid judges. Unless we drastically increase our entry fees, including for baking entries." The elderly woman fixed Evie with an uncompromising stare. "And before you give us another impassioned speech about impartiality, Miss Evie Grace, I'd like to remind you that you won the baking competition several years in a row under the existing judging system. You only started complaining when you fell into a losing streak."

The room went quiet. Wylie bit back a smile.

"Jeremy..." The sheriff turned his attention to an older cowboy at the opposite end of the board's table. "What's the county population?"

"Last count was less than twenty thousand," Jeremy said. "Spread over three small communities."

"Huh." The sheriff stared at the sheet of paper in front of him. "Now, I'm no accountant but it seems like the amount of folks directly related to the Done Roamin' Ranch is two or three percent of the county population. Does anyone know what percentage of our livestock and rodeo entrants are related to the Done Roamin' Ranch?"

The board and the audience were silent.

"Must be inconsequential, then. I'd say this question is without merit." The sheriff glanced down the table toward Rose.

Who seemed to take direction well. "I move to dismiss the unmerited concerns regarding our choice of livestock and rodeo judges."

"Seconded," somebody said.

"All in favor..." The sheriff glanced up and down the table. Nodded, then smiled at Wylie and crew. "Motion passed."

Wylie sat back with relief. If only all his problems could be resolved as easily.

CHAPTER THIRTEEN

"FLUFFY!" MAISEY'S MOURNFUL cry filled the apartment above the clinic Wednesday evening.

Hazel bolted upright in bed, roused from her after-work power nap. "What happened? What's wrong?" She swung her legs over the edge of the mattress, trying to orient herself to the place—Clementine—and the day-part—early evening. There was no acrid smell of food burning. That was a good sign.

"She's frozen," Maisey called.

Things were beginning to come together. "Fluffy's frozen? Did you put the ice pack vest on her?" Hazel got to her feet and hurried out to the living area. "That's a bold move."

Maisey was in the kitchen, Fluffy standing at her feet. The dog's back was arched upward. She faced the sink. And only her eyes moved when her attention shifted from her owner to Hazel.

She's in pain.

And Maisey... Maisey was nearly as immobile as her dog.

She's afraid.

Hazel eased closer, giving the elderly woman a reassuring smile and searching for something to diffuse the tension. "Miss Maisey, did you teach Fluffy to pose like a black cat on Halloween?"

"Don't try to out-snark me," Maisey cried, tears in her eyes. "Humor isn't welcome during a time of crisis."

"Duly noted." Hazel knelt down in front of the tiny, pink hairless dog. "Symptoms?"

"She won't move." Maisey clung to the counter, knuckles white, as if she'd fall if she let go. "I need you to prescribe some medicine. Pain relief. Maybe that new arthritis medication."

"It hasn't come in yet." Hazel ran her hands over Fluffy. "Give me a moment to make a diagnosis."

Maisey sob-hiccupped. "She's in pain. I just know it."

"Prescribing pain relief meds before we know what's wrong with her would be bad doctoring," Hazel said in a gentle voice. She tried to ease Fluffy into a more comfortable position, but the dog wouldn't move a muscle. She probed Fluffy's abdomen with her fingers next, but everything inside felt normal. She checked the dog's pulse—slightly elevated—and gently plucked a bit of skin—not dehydrated. "I suspect severe arthritis or sciatica."

"I thought as much." Maisey sniffed. "Pain meds, it is."

And, although it felt like Maisey considered this a dire medical situation, Hazel noticed that Maisey hadn't called Wylie.

Hazel got to her feet, considering what to say next. But knowing she had to offer the one thing Maisey openly rejected. "What if we try acupuncture?"

"No!" Maisey's eyes widened and her wrinkly facial folds...

They didn't crease more than her usual resting expression.

Hazel took that to mean the old woman was considering it. "Acupuncture works faster than most of the pain meds we have without making animals loopy."

"No." Less effusive this time.

Hazel wondered if she was risking an injury by placing her arm around Maisey's waist. They'd been on better terms since the office manager had bonded with Hazel's mother. But still... "Look at Fluffy. She's suffering. We'll know in twenty minutes if it helps or not, maybe sooner."

"I..." Maisey's lower lip trembled. "What if it makes things worse?"

"It won't. I promise. You've seen how well Budge takes it." Hazel released Maisey and headed toward her bedroom. "I have my kit in here." Hazel opened her closet and dug into a suitcase.

Maisey shuffled along after her, sitting on the

bed and holding a still-arching Fluffy in her lap. "Don't you dare tell me to put her down."

"The bed is fine."

"The bed..." Maisey puffed out air like a steam engine coming to a full stop. "I meant, we're not putting Fluffy to rest permanently."

"Oh." Kit in hand, Hazel turned to face Maisey, whose expression was tense. "I hadn't even considered that."

"Okay." Maisey drew a shuddering breath. "Okay. But if she's in any pain—"

"I'll stop immediately," Hazel agreed. She removed a small pack of disposable needles from her kit and opened them up. "But let it be noted that Fluffy hasn't growled at me once. That should be a benchmark of our success or failure."

"Okay. That's *our* treatment goal," Maisey whispered, staring at the ceiling as if she couldn't bear to watch Hazel work. "This dog doesn't put up with any guff. I want her to growl at you again."

"I can take growling." Hazel stroked Fluffy's hairless skin, occasionally pausing to insert the tip of a very fine needle into the dog at various energy points. "I can even take the occasional bite or cat scratch. But I want you to promise me, Miss Maisey, that if a little boy named Cassidy calls in asking us to examine his pet snake Kevin, that you'll tell him to go elsewhere. I draw the line at reptiles."

"Deal." Maisey sniffed juicily, still staring at the

ceiling. "Tell me when you start. I want to make sure Fluffy doesn't move. You'd probably poke her and cause her to be paralyzed."

"I'm done." Hazel stepped back. She'd inserted a dozen needles. Their little orange grips stuck out of Fluffy at all angles from her neck to her haunches.

"Done?" Maisey stared down at Fluffy.

Her dog drew a deep breath and arched a smidgeon less than before.

That a girl.

"I thought she'd flinch," Maisey said slowly. Thickly. "Oh... I feel faint."

Without warning, Maisey slumped backward on the bed, hands falling to her sides.

Hazel checked her pulse.

Satisfied Maisey wasn't dead or dying, Hazel sat down, carefully lifted Fluffy from Maisey's lap, and settled her into her own, and then she gently rubbed the little dog's ears. "Fluffy, your mama is the first client to pass out on me. I don't think I'll let her forget it."

Fluffy turned her head to look at Hazel and growled.

"AND THEN FLUFFY pranced right out of Hazel's bedroom," Maisey said to Wylie early Thursday morning as they walked toward the stock entrance at the fair. "And Fluffy was moving like she was two years younger this morning when I took her out."

Wylie made the appropriate, supportive noises,

curious about the science behind acupuncture the way an engineer was curious about the science behind an electric car engine.

"There's that proof you were looking for, Dr. Newland," Hazel said from behind Wylie, not without a bit of false modesty. She wheeled a portable plastic box filled with the clinic's medical records for those animals they'd been told would be at the fair—from rabbits to heifers. "Two cases, if you count Budge." Who was also receiving acupuncture treatments.

Wylie grunted, feeling over-ruled.

"I'm going to call Rose this morning," Maisey continued as if oblivious to the tension between Wylie and Hazel. "And put Bruiser on the schedule this afternoon. He needs this fabulous new treatment, too."

"Last I heard, this was still my clinic," Wylie said, half under his breath. "And the one in charge of who works here."

Hazel and Maisey had told him they were hiring Russ Winston, a local teenager, as their tech trainee.

"That's odd." Hazel chuckled. "I knew from the moment Miss Maisey greeted me that she was the one in charge."

"Darn straight," Maisey said, uncharacteristically full of good humor and smiles. "Now, Hazel and I will take the livestock. We'll send you over to the small animal barn."

"With the rabbits, guinea pigs, and the like?" Wylie scoffed, stretching his legs so he was in front of his vet tech as they passed through the fair gates.

"It's for your own good," Maisey tsked when he tried to argue. "Hear me out. A review of our records indicates the parents of the small animal exhibitors are mostly married, while the livestock crowd is populated by single parents."

Wylie had to admire that logic. Despite having pressed Pause on Ronnie's matchmaking efforts, single women were still dropping off gifts at the clinic. Just yesterday, he'd received a pair of knit socks and a finely beaded hatband, both of which he planned to return as soon as he had a spare moment.

They parted ways—Wylie headed toward an exhibit hall while the ladies veered toward the covered holding pens.

But Wylie couldn't help but feel that he was the odd man out in their little unit. And he didn't like it.

MAISEY FOUND A chair at the table where young exhibitors checked in their livestock and were assigned paddocks in one of the covered, open-air pavilions. They had to show proof of inoculation to be allowed in.

Meanwhile, Hazel was tasked with doing a visual inspection of every animal just to make sure they didn't look sick.

It was chaos.

The livestock pavilions were buzzing with activity. Kids and their animals were being checked in faster than Hazel could keep track. Sheep, pigs, goats, dairy cows, and young bulls. All were being brought in. The three pavilions were organized from the largest animals in the farthest corner to the smallest closer to the entrance. The horses were being held in portable corrals in a field across the road. Hazel planned to do those inspections later in the morning.

"There's a familiar face." Hazel approached a teenage boy walking a large, black bull.

"Hey, Doc Hughes." Tad tipped his straw cowboy hat.

"Hard Nose is looking good." Hazel took note of the young bull's clear eyes, healthy nose, and well-behaved swagger. "You've been working with him on a lead?"

"Yes, ma'am." Tad slung his arm over his bull's neck. "Hours and hours until Mom was convinced he'd be well-behaved at the fair."

"It shows." Hazel took an oat cube out of her scrub pocket and offered it to the bull, who snorted, then scooped it from the flat of her hand. She walked around to his rear end and took a peek. "And better back here." Although not completely cleared up.

"I know what you're thinking, Doc." Tad gave Hard Nose an affectionate pat. "Even if his warts aren't all gone, my coach said I can talk about taking care of his condition during the interview portion of showing."

"I'm sure you'll do fine." Hazel marked Hard Nose as clearing the visual inspection. She moved on.

Several minutes later, Hazel walked in between two pavilions.

"Yippee! It's my doctor!" Aliyah ran toward Hazel, leading Jo-Jo behind her. And she didn't stop running until she collided with Hazel's legs, wrapping her little arms around them. "We're at the fair."

"I see that." Hazel accepted the girl's hug, then dug in her pocket for a small treat for her little brown goat.

There was a loud *BANG*, like a big animal slamming against a railing.

Jo-Jo fell over, legs sticking stiffly in the air.

"Hey!" someone shouted.

Hooves pounded. Voices cried over each other.

Hazel was busy reassuring Aliyah and Jo-Jo when the sound of racing hooves approaching had her turning...

In time to see Hard Nose bearing down on them.

"Look out!" Wylie had been coming to check on Hazel and Maisey when he saw disaster about to strike.

A big, black bull charged at Hazel, who knelt

next to Aliyah and her fainting goat. She'd only just looked over her shoulder to spot the danger.

I can't get there in time.

Wylie sprinted toward them anyway.

The bull snorted, kicking up his heels in his charge.

Hazel leaped to her feet, tossed her clipboard toward the bull, held up her arms, and cried, "No, Hard Nose. No!"

The bull skidded to a stop, lead rope dangling at his front legs. He snorted once more and stomped his front feet but otherwise didn't trample Hazel, Aliyah or her small goat.

"What a good boy," Hazel said in a calm voice, smiling that professional smile of hers. She handed the bull an oat treat, then took hold of his lead rope. She spared Wylie a glance before reassuring those closing in on her that, "We're fine. Hard Nose just got jealous because he saw me offer Jo-Jo a treat."

Jo-Jo continued to play dead. Aliyah stood behind Hazel, peeking around her leg at the bull.

Wylie slowed down. But he didn't change his destination or his intention. He needed to hold Hazel in his arms to make sure she was okay.

She handed Tad the lead rope a second before Wylie embraced her, uncaring of who saw him do so.

"I'm great," Hazel spoke into his chest.

I'm great?

Wylie held her at arm's length, this wonderful,

brave woman. And he refused to filter his next words. "Hazel, be honest with me, love. I know when you say *great* you really mean you're grinning and bearing it."

Hazel unleashed a more natural smile. A smile just for him. "Dr. Newland, how are things over at the small creature barn?"

"Boring."

"I could use a little boring. How about we switch?" And without waiting for him to answer, Hazel returned her attention to Aliyah and her fainting goat.

"WYLIE." RONNIE FOUND him inspecting sheep in one of the fair's pavilions. She wore a floppy hat and frilly blue sundress, but for once she didn't wear fancy footwear. Her feet were in white sneakers. Her ankles looked swollen. "I know you wanted a break from dating but there's a wonderful, professional woman I want you to meet. I left her over at the coffee kiosk."

"Ronnie." Wylie escorted her to a shadier section of the pens. "I'm working right now. I smell like…animals. And I… I don't want to date anyone…" But Hazel.

"Humor me. I'm getting a good handle on the kind of woman you like." Ronnie wiped a hand over her sweaty brow. She looked overheated.

"Does Wade know you're out and about in this heat?" Wylie fanned her with his clipboard.

"No. Wade left for a rodeo this morning." Ronnie flapped her ruffled dress skirt. "Doc Nabidian assured me this baby wasn't making an appearance for another week. And you know Wade. Always eager to rack up the points on the bucking bronc circuit."

"Points?" Wylie muttered. "You need to go home and put your feet up. Right now." He'd call his foster parents, if need be, to keep an eye on her.

Ronnie clutched his arm. "Only if you go meet Caitlyn for coffee."

"How can you ask that when you know I'm not serious about dating anyone but…" Huffing, Wylie glanced up, looking for another single cowboy to send in his place. "I'll stay until you can find someone else."

MAISEY INVITED HAZEL to take a coffee break midmorning.

To say that was unusual…

Hazel didn't want to tease Maisey about it and ruin their apparent truce.

"The fair always has the best coffee cart." Maisey led the way through the maze of fairground paths crowded with workers and exhibitors, all seemingly in a hurry. "Strong coffee. Not burnt like some of those big-city chains. And they use fresh cream in their lattes."

"I didn't realize you were such a big specialty

coffee lover." Hazel slowed to watch a man testing a bungee cord contraption.

He strapped himself into a harness and leaped off a platform, fell in the bungee toward the ground, only to shoot back upward a few seconds later.

"I suppose you fancy being flung around on an oversize rubber band." There was the Maisey that Hazel was used to. Snarky and disparaging. "Have a death wish, do you?"

Hazel scoffed. "I was thinking about volunteering you to test it out for the man."

They chuckled as they continued on their way toward the coffee cart.

"Whoa." Maisey grasped Hazel's arm, bringing her to an abrupt stop. "Who's that?"

Hazel followed the direction of Maisey's gaze to find Wylie sitting at a table with a woman. They were both drinking coffee.

Hazel was struck with a bolt of jealousy.

WYLIE WAS BORED. He sipped his coffee, nodding his head, waiting for Fletcher to finish unloading rodeo stock on the other side of the fairgrounds and take on this date Ronnie had been intent upon arranging.

"And then, I told my boss that he was mansplaining. You know what mansplaining is, right?" Caitlyn didn't wait for Wylie to answer. She drew a quick breath before barreling on. "Mansplaining is when a man explains something to a woman that a woman knows by virtue of being a woman. And that reminds me of the time…"

Wylie's mind wandered to how confidently Hazel had stood up to a charging bull and how his heart had practically dropped beneath his muck boots.

"…I don't care if you are a judge." Caitlyn laughed.

There was nothing wrong with her laugh, if you appreciated controlled humor. It just wasn't full-throated and joyous, like Hazel's. On paper, he supposed Caitlyn looked good. Mid-thirties, short, dark brown hair, and intelligent eyes. Full figured and fashionable. Caitlyn was a lawyer and seemed extremely intelligent.

But she's not Hazel.

A flash of strawberry blond hair caught Wylie's eye. Hazel and Maisey sat at another table, casting sidelong glances his way.

Ronnie appeared next to Wylie holding a large plastic glass of what looked like ice water, half-consumed. "I hope you two enjoyed meeting each other. I promised Caitlyn I'd come get her after twenty minutes."

Has it been twenty minutes?

Wylie's mind must have wandered for at least fifteen of those minutes. He couldn't remember much about Caitlyn. But… "What happened to Fletcher?"

Ronnie shrugged, not apologetic in the slightest. The mom-to-be probably hadn't called him over.

He frowned at her, silently making note of words he'd have with his matchmaker later.

Caitlyn's phone chimed with an alarm. "Right on time, as usual, Ronnie."

As usual? Was Caitlyn a regular client of Ronnie's?

Caitlyn gathered her large, black leather purse. "The time has sped by, hasn't it, Wylie? You're quite the talker."

The smile Wylie gave the woman held no warmth. He hadn't said anything after introducing himself and he certainly didn't want to misstep and encourage her.

Ronnie and Caitlyn walked away, arm in arm. Ronnie's head was tilted toward the lawyer as if she was telling her something secret.

She better not be telling her I looked smitten.

Wylie moved over to sit next to Hazel.

She leaned sideways, giving him a long, unhurried inspection. "I thought you weren't taking any more dates from Ronnie."

Perhaps something good had come of sitting with Caitlyn after all—Hazel was jealous.

"She trapped me." Wylie tried to take Hazel's hand but she was having none of it, emitting proper jealous vibes. He took some satisfaction in that since it meant her feelings were more than casual.

"The boss doesn't look like he's been lovestruck," Maisey said slowly. She angled her head toward Hazel, not Wylie, as if he wasn't here and couldn't hear them. "He's always been a man of few words but it didn't look as if he could get a word in edgewise with that woman. Can you imagine her accompanying him in the middle of the night when a pregnant mare's in distress?"

"Not in those heels." Hazel sipped her coffee.

"She was wearing heels? I didn't notice." Wylie rested his forearms on the wooden table.

"He'll be having us believe he didn't notice her fancy skirt either," Maisey quipped. "Poor man is so overworked that he can't see an attractive woman when she's sitting right across from him."

"Oh, I disagree with that statement." Wylie caught Hazel's eye. "Because I can see an attractive woman right now, sitting next to me."

Hazel's cheeks turned an attractive shade of pink.

Maisey was waving to Rose and didn't seem to notice.

ON SATURDAY MORNING, Maisey and Hazel stood flanking exam room one, ears practically pressed to the closed door, listening to their new protégé.

Wylie was off judging livestock at the fair.

Russ was inside the exam room with a patient. His first solo check-in. He'd already taken the cat's weight and temperature.

"And what are we seeing PJ for today?" Russ asked.

"He sounds so professional," Hazel murmured.

"I taught him that," Maisey murmured back.

"How long has PJ been limping?" Russ asked.

"Great job," Hazel whispered.

"I taught him that," Maisey whispered again.

Hazel rolled her eyes.

"I did," Maisey insisted in a louder voice.

"You *and* my mother." Hazel gave Maisey a sly smile. "Don't forget you used my phone for that video chat you organized for Russ with Mom."

"She did great role playing as the client." Maisey crossed her arms over her chest.

Russ came out of the room and shut the door behind him. "PJ is ready for you, Doc." He handed Hazel the cat's chart before walking toward the front of the clinic.

Maisey scurried behind him. "Do you have any questions?"

"Nope. I'm good, Miss Maisey," Russ cheerfully replied.

"I know I taught him that," Hazel said, beaming as she entered the exam room.

CHAPTER FOURTEEN

"You're a hard man to track down, Wylie."

Wylie raised his gaze from the udders of the dairy cow he'd been inspecting and spotted Ronnie, standing at the gate. He was at an auction yard corral in Friar's Creek on Monday afternoon. Predictably, as soon as his attention shifted from bovine to matchmaker, the cow raised her rear hoof and stepped on his boot, shifting all her weight on him and making his toes sting.

"Not nice, girl." Wylie leaned his shoulder into her hip, muscling her off.

"I'm always nice." Ronnie smiled.

"Not you. I meant the... Oh, never mind." Wylie jotted a note about the heifer's udders on the auction yard inspection sheet. "What's up?"

"You aren't answering your phone," Ronnie chided.

"I left it in my truck." Wylie smirked, wondering how many voicemails Ronnie had left him. "The quickest way to finish livestock auction inspections is not to be interrupted while doing livestock auction inspections."

Which was part of the reason Wylie liked spending the afternoon at the auction yard. Unlike most people his age, he relished any time with his phone turned off or left behind. It gave Wylie an opportunity to think. Unfortunately, his thoughts today were mostly revolving around a woman with strawberry blond hair and dreams of faraway places.

The dairy cow ambled to the far side of the corral. Wylie followed, needing a look in her mouth.

"I made a date for you tonight," Ronnie announced with less fanfare than usual. A quick glance revealed her cheeks were flushed, her back arched, and her palm pressing on her pregnant belly.

"Haven't you had that baby yet? Are you having contractions?" He hurried to her side. "Should I remind you to relax and breathe? Do you need me to call Wade?"

Ronnie waved him off. "Wade is waiting in the truck. We have a doctor's appointment soon." She panted her way through a contraction. "But I wanted to assure you that I'm still going to find you true love."

"Don't you worry about me." Wylie turned his back on Ronnie and returned to the cow, taking a look in her ears without registering anything but thoughts of Hazel. "Please. Go have that baby."

"I can't. Not yet. People are depending on me."

Ronnie sounded earnest. "And I'm afraid you're falling for a dead end."

"Is that the reason you aren't backing off your matchmaking the way I asked you to?" Wylie took a look inside the cow's mouth, purposefully catching a whiff of her breath. All seemed well with her, unlike his love life. "I thought you liked Hazel."

"She doesn't meet any of the criteria on your list," Ronnie gently pointed out.

"And that's why you keep throwing me together with other women, even though I told you to put a pause on things?" Wylie should have turned to face her but he couldn't, the same way he couldn't face the reality of Hazel leaving. "Fletcher was never going to show up for that coffee date with Caitlyn, was he?"

"No." Ronnie's voice sounded strained. "Tonight, look for a woman carrying a red rose at seven thirty at Brown's Brewery."

"Ronnie? Honey, it's been more than five minutes." That was Wade's voice. He sped between the paddocks to reach his wife. "We're not having this baby in the auction yard."

"Agreed." Wylie turned toward Ronnie, trying to be gentle but firm. "My love life will be just fine while you have this baby."

"Wylie Newland!" Ronnie's voice rang out with authority. Her hands were fisted and her body rigid. "Finding love is like finding the right pair of boots. You have to try on a lot of different pairs to find what fits perfectly. And when one pair of boots you covet don't come in your size, you have to choose another."

Wylie set his jaw.

"Come on, honey." Wade put his arms around his wife and turned her away from Wylie. "I think it's time you go on maternity leave."

"I don't want to abandon Wylie in his hour of need," Ronnie sobbed, completely out of character. "Hazel's going to break his heart."

Wylie's heart panged, as if agreeing.

"Wylie's a grown man, honey." Wade slowly led his wife toward the exit. "If he doesn't know how to protect his heart by now, nothing you say is going to keep it from cracking."

HAZEL AWOKE WITH a start from her post-work catnap.

Something was burning.

Applause filled her ears, applause and canned laughter. Followed by the sound of voices, and then a gusty snore.

"Maisey..." Hazel rolled over on her bed, assuming that Maisey had tried to cook something again. "I told you I'd make dinner after I crashed."

Her brain had been fried after working all day and stressing about what the future may or may not hold, both personally and professionally. She was tense and on edge and feeling as if she hadn't recharged enough from her nap.

The burning smell grew stronger. Scarily stronger.

Fire!

Hazel bolted out of bed and rushed into the tiny kitchen.

Smoke was streaming out of the oven.

Maisey reclined on the couch, head back and snoring with Fluffy curled in her lap while an ancient sitcom played full-blast on TV.

Hazel turned off the oven, opened the oven door, and was inundated with black, billowing smoke. She used two pot holders to wave the smoke away.

The smoke alarm began an ear-piercing shriek that startled Maisey and Fluffy awake.

Hazel managed to remove the smoking pan from the oven, although she dropped it with a clatter on top of the stove.

"Hey, that's our dinner!" Maisey charged over, bleary-eyed and unsteady on her feet, followed at a much slower pace by Fluffy.

"*Our* dinner?" Hazel took a dish towel and waved it at the smoke alarm. "I can't even tell what that is." Everything in the pan was black and lumpy.

"I like a little char on my pork chop." Coughing, Maisey opened the small kitchen window.

"*A little char?*" Tired of shouting over the television, Hazel went over and turned off the TV.

She and Maisey had been getting along better but this… This was unacceptable. "You should set the timer if you only wanted a *little* char."

Fluffy plopped down near the staircase. Animals were usually stressed out by smoke alarms. The pink, hairless dog seemed unfazed.

Maisey took over dish-towel-waving duties. "The timer doesn't work."

"The timer doesn't work?" Hazel couldn't believe it. She went to the oven control panel, studying its outdated features but unable to diffuse her crankiness. "My grandmother used to have an oven like this. You just need to…" She rotated the timer knob. The orange timer hand didn't move.

"It doesn't work, genius." Maisey flapped the dish towel at Hazel.

"Just set the timer on your phone." The acrid smell of the ruined dinner was burning the back of Hazel's throat.

"This phone?" Maisey picked up the beige landline receiver.

"No." Hazel took it and placed it back in its cradle. "Your cell phone."

"You know I don't have a cell phone. I don't *need* a cell phone. I do just fine without all that newfangled technology." And the way Maisey raised her voice to a pained shout told Hazel this was a bridge she was willing to die on.

Hazel needed to smile, to joke and remind Maisey she used a tablet to email all the time. But still, Hazel couldn't seem to shake her prickly mood. So instead of tossing technology back in Maisey's face, she chose a different example.

"Miss Maisey, I have irrefutable evidence that contradicts your last statement about not needing tech." Hazel pointed at the still-smoking pork chop, which now looked like it was crumbling to ash. "Technology makes your life easier. In your case, it can keep you from burning the house down."

"I'm happy with the way things are," Maisey insisted, red-faced. "Just because you figured out how to work fancy electronics doesn't mean everyone wants to."

She's afraid.

Of something—technology, change, being irrelevant.

Whatever it was, Hazel's heart went out to the elderly woman. But she knew if she tried to be nice to Maisey at this point that she'd only be rebuffed. So, she put on some attitude, both in her body language and her tone. "Look, Miss Maisey. I'm going to walk into town. If you promise not to burn the place down before I return, I'll bring you back some gruel to go with your char."

"Don't do me any favors." But Maisey looked more like her stubborn self.

"Gruel it is." Grabbing her phone-wallet, and cowboy hat, Hazel hightailed it out of there.

A few minutes later, Hazel heard laughter from the outdoor tables at Brown's Brewery. Needing a little laughter, she headed that way. Once inside, the hostess pointed her in the direction of a tall table in the bar area that sat two. There was only one chair there now and she took it, setting her phone on the table.

Three large-screen televisions hanging from the ceiling were each playing different baseball games. The bar was sparsely filled with cowboys of all shapes and sizes. And...

Is that Wylie at the bar?

It was. His beer was half-finished and his dark head was bent over his cell phone.

Hazel considered joining him. But before she could, she was distracted.

"Hey, Doc." A cowboy she recognized from the Done Roamin' Ranch stopped at her table. He was holding two glasses of beer. "Thanks for giving Tornado Tom a medical note to miss another weekend of rodeo. I pulled fair duty this weekend. It was a real treat to be in town on a Saturday night."

"Glad I could help." Hazel smiled as the cowboy sat at a nearby table and gave another cowboy that extra beer.

"Hey, Dr. Hughes." It was Gustaf's owner, Joy. She wore a half apron over her blue jeans and held an order pad. She updated Hazel on her Labrador's ear infection before getting down to business. "What can I get you?"

Wylie joined Hazel at the small high table, dragging a chair over with him. He was wearing his going-out clothes and had combed that black hair into some semblance of order, at least the bits that were below his brown cowboy hat. "She'll have a cheeseburger plate, fried cheese, and a diet soda."

Joy glanced from Hazel to Wylie, then back to Hazel, brows raised.

"I'll give that a try. Sounds great." Hazel smiled at the waitress, then at Wylie. "But make it two orders. One to go."

"I'll put the takeaway order on delay." The waitress headed off.

Wylie leaned forward, sniffing. "Why do you smell like smoke? Did you burn incense in the office?"

"Do I smell like sandalwood?" Hazel rolled her eyes. "Just because I believe in natural supplements and acupuncture doesn't mean I want to burn sage everywhere."

"What is it I smell, then?" Wylie leaned in closer, aiming his nose toward her neck.

As if he's going to kiss me.

Hazel's heart pounded harder than when the smoke alarm went off earlier.

"You don't smell like sage," Wylie concluded, mischief in his green eyes as he sat back in his seat. "More like…grilled meat." His grin took its time coming. "I take it you're not a good cook."

Pride scuffled with an odd sense of loyalty toward her elderly roommate.

In the meantime, Wylie's grin faded. "Something's happened."

"Well..." Hazel decided to tell him about Maisey's dinner efforts, during which time, her diet soda arrived.

"I should upgrade those appliances," Wylie concluded when she was done ratting her roommate out. "And buy Maisey a cell phone. I think I've been avoiding changing anything upstairs because of the memories up there."

"I can relate." It had taken Hazel and her mother months before they felt like cleaning out Mike's bedroom at the house. But Wylie had included a cell phone for Maisey in his upgrade scheme and Hazel recalled their vet tech's pained shouts when she'd suggested much the same thing. "If you do buy Maisey a cell phone, you'll make both of our lives miserable. She's afraid of tech."

"Oh. Yeah. I'd forgotten." Wylie agreed but didn't look pleased. "I had it in the back of my mind that I'd upgrade the office when she retires."

"*If* she retires." Hazel remembered she'd forgotten to close her bedroom door and open her bedroom window. All her clothes were going to smell of charred pork chop.

"Hey, Ronnie and Wade had a little baby boy!" the cowboy who'd greeted Hazel announced, getting to his feet and raising his beer glass. "Let's toast to the arrival of Gary Lionel Keller!"

Hazel raised her diet soda while Wylie raised his beer. They clinked glasses.

Wylie took a sip of beer before checking his phone. "I got that notification, too."

"Did they say how big the baby was?" Hazel asked.

"Over nine pounds." Wylie turned the screen toward Hazel, revealing a chubby-cheeked newborn. "Mom and baby are doing fine." He set his phone down. "I saw them on their way to the doctor today. Both Wade and Ronnie looked ready to have that baby."

"Where did you see her?" Hazel wondered out loud. She knew that Wylie had had a busy schedule today.

"Over at the auction yard."

They talked shop for a few minutes, each updating the other on the patients of the day, sprinkling in anecdotes about Russ and Maisey. How domestic they sounded.

A woman entered the lobby carrying a single red rose. She was dressed to impress in a pink sundress, strappy white heels, and a fancy suede cowboy hat. Her blond hair hung in ringlets over her shoulders and her makeup was flawless. Her gaze searched the room, then came to land on Wylie.

"Oh, jeez," Wylie said, half under his breath. He popped off the chair and put on what seemed like a strained smile. "Hey…"

The woman stared at him, eyes widening, smile

broadening. Then she stared at Hazel, expression falling into a frown. And then, she dropped the red rose, turned heel, and ran.

A pit formed in Hazel's stomach. "Was she here for a date with you?"

Wylie faced Hazel, frowning. "It's not what you think."

"I think it is." The date at the fair a few days ago. And now this woman... Hazel reached deep for her air of good-humored detachment. And deeper... And deeper... She gripped the base of her seat. "I don't understand what's going on between us."

"You're leaving," Wylie said, taking his seat and keeping his voice lower than hers had been. "And Ronnie is trying to make sure you don't break my heart."

What about my heart?

Several patrons stared at them.

Hazel didn't care. "That's right. I *could* be leaving. But you...you and Ronnie... You're acting as if I'm already gone. Or you would be if you hadn't walked with me and Budge this morning." And held her hand while they got to know each other.

And then I confessed I wasn't ready to have kids. I might never...

Hazel's hands felt tingly.

What have I done?

But Hazel was afraid she knew.

I've fallen in love with Wylie.

Hazel studied the sharp angles of Wylie's face.

They didn't seem as sharp as they'd once seemed. And his eyes... She couldn't remember the last time they'd looked at her without warmth. And his hands... She'd been clasping hers in her lap earlier as a surrogate feeling to his fingers curled around her own.

"Here you go." Joy placed a plate with a cheeseburger and fries on the table, along with a plate with several fried cheese balls. "I'll bring out your to-go order in about fifteen minutes."

Fifteen minutes. That's how long Hazel had to sit here. With him. The man she'd fallen in love with.

The man who was still accepting dates from Ronnie to try and stop him from falling in love with me.

Just a few days ago, that had been...maybe not fine but understandable. But now... This...

"I can explain." And Wylie tried to. He really did.

But Hazel didn't listen closely because...she didn't like him having an explanation. An...an excuse. Whatever reason he gave...whatever obligation he felt toward showing up to meet a woman so she wouldn't feel stood up. Any of it... All of it...felt...disloyal.

But it's only disloyal if he loves me back.

They had, after all, avoided talking about their feelings since he'd kissed her the first time. How long ago was that? It felt like a lifetime but she knew it was only days.

Numbly, Hazel doctored her burger bun with generous amounts of ketchup and Tabasco, even though she'd lost her appetite.

"I can't exactly fault Ronnie," Wylie was saying. "I paid her to find me a life partner and today... Well, today, she pointed out how you've been adamant that you're not interested in staying in Clementine...with me."

"But that doesn't explain why..." Hazel took hold of her cheeseburger, squishing it until juices and condiments dripped onto her plate and her fingers were imprinted on the bun. She would *not* discuss her jealousy.

Find the humor, Hazel. Find your smile.

"I don't want you to take this the wrong way but...if I had a blind date with you, I wouldn't take a runner, the way that woman did. You don't look like a serial killer." There. Humor attempted. Her lips rose a fraction upward.

"Maybe she saw you with me and thought I was a player." The heat in Wylie's glittering green eyes matched the fire in his words. "Maybe she didn't like my smile. It happens. I'm not so fond of your smile right now."

"Right." Hazel set her cheeseburger down untouched, wiped her greasy fingers on a paper napkin, and waited for Wylie to say more. Because more of this angry Wylie might make her not think she was in love with him.

Someone gasped nearby—loud and dramatic.

Maisey marched up to their table, bringing with her the distinct aroma of charred pork chop. "I thought you were bringing food home." She grabbed a nearby chair almost before a woman vacated it, then dragged it over. "I heard the boss was in here waiting for a date. Was it with you?"

"Maisey, is that your famous *smoked* pork chops I smell?" Wylie deadpanned before Hazel could answer Maisey's question. He was caught off guard by his vet tech's presence and a bit annoyed at the interruption of his and Hazel's argument. Although he was no longer sure what they'd been arguing about.

"Tattletale," Maisey griped at Hazel with a fierce frown. But then the vet tech sniffed the neckline of her plain green T-shirt. "Nobody complained. The apartment didn't burn down."

"This time, anyway." For all Hazel was a big nighttime eater, she hadn't touched her food. "I came here for your gruel, Miss Maisey. It'll be here in a few more minutes. Did the smoke alarm stop? Or did you call the fire department?"

"I wouldn't have left Fluffy at home if it wasn't safe. All is quiet." Maisey sniffed her disdain.

Hazel grimaced.

Something had happened between the two women. The tension between them was as palpable as Hazel's first day at the clinic.

Maisey smirked at Hazel. "A woman like you is the reason country songs have so many sad verses."

"A woman like me?" Hazel laughed. And not mirthfully. "Well, if that's true, don't hate me when you can't stop singing along with the chorus."

Maisey's perennial frown looked like it might curl in a different direction—upward. "You have no shame."

"And you have no tact." Hazel slurped the last bit of diet soda through a straw. "Together, we're two halves that make a whole."

Uh-oh.

The table went silent for a beat too long.

"A little char," Hazel tossed at Maisey.

"Technology," Maisey tossed back.

And then both women started laughing.

Leaving Wylie feeling like the odd man out once more. "There will be no more cooking in the upstairs apartment until we get new appliances."

"Are you going to feed us every night?" Hazel's grin wasn't of the usual variety. It had harder angles and more snark than usual.

"You can live on cold cuts and white bread." Heaven knew that's what Wylie resorted to with his busy schedule.

"I prefer fast-food burgers." Hazel was still in attack mode.

"Frozen potpies," Maisey said dreamily, swiping another fry.

"Only if they're microwavable," Wylie insisted,

realizing the pair of them were getting along better than he and Hazel were. He set his jaw.

Their server appeared with Hazel's to-go order, which Maisey immediately took hold of.

"I'll have a large water," Maisey said.

"Water only comes in one size." Their waitress picked up Hazel's empty glass. "Another diet?"

Hazel nodded, tearing pieces of her hamburger bun into shreds.

Maisey unpacked her to-go bag food with the same steady rhythm as the erosion of Wylie's patience. "What were you talking about when I came in? The boss looked hangry."

"I think you're thinking of Hazel." Wylie stole a fried cheese ball from Hazel's plate. "She doesn't eat enough during the day to fuel her Zen-like outer shell."

"You sound just like her mother." Maisey blinked at Wylie.

Which gave Wylie pause. "When did you meet Hazel's mother?"

"We're good friends," Maisey said in a superior tone of voice.

And again, Wylie felt as if he was on the outside looking in.

HAZEL'S PHONE RANG, a welcome distraction when she'd lost her appetite over feelings she couldn't sort out involving Wylie. Not even sparring with

Maisey had brought it back. She glanced at the display. "It's Dr. Reed."

Wylie's expression didn't change but it hardened. Froze.

This is it. The end of us.

Hazel answered the phone.

Her mentor professor cut right to the chase. "Dr. Hughes, they've made a decision in Newmarket. If you're still amenable to making a change, they'd love to have you join their staff as a resident."

Hazel's heart felt as if it was being squeezed by the cold hand of heartbreak. And that crushing mixture of pain and regret stole every word in her vocabulary. But she had to say something. "I'm… flattered."

Flattered? Is that all I can manage to say?

It was. Because Hazel was looking into Wylie's suddenly sad green eyes.

He knows I'm leaving him.

And until that moment, Hazel hadn't really believed this opportunity would come. She'd been thinking about Clementine's friendly residents and Maisey's sharp humor and Wylie's gentle caress. She'd been thinking that this wasn't a bad place to build her life if she couldn't do what she and Mike had worked so hard for.

"They'll be calling you in the morning, Dr. Hughes," her mentor professor continued. "And if you're open to leaving, I'll need to call Dr. Newland and see if he's amenable to taking on a new resident."

Hazel's mouth felt dry.

Dr. Reed chuckled. "I must say. I envy you this opportunity. Our clinic here at the university is progressive but Newmarket... They're another level completely."

Wylie got up and left.

"What's wrong with him?" Maisey asked, turning to watch him go.

Outside, the sun was low in the sky, making the horizon a warm, purplish red.

Hazel opened her mouth to tell Dr. Reed she was accepting Newmarket's offer but no words came out. She couldn't remember seeing such colorful sunsets anywhere else. It was a horizon she'd remember all her life.

But it wasn't the horizon she was going to choose.

CHAPTER FIFTEEN

WYLIE FOUND HIMSELF at the maternity ward in the hospital, asking which room Wade and Ronnie Keller were in.

He needn't have asked. Laughter carried down the hallway, drawing him into its wake.

Hazel is leaving. I need a good laugh right now.

He entered the room filled with Done Roamin' Ranch cowboys and their significant others. There were balloons and banners. Teddy bears and bottles of unopened champagne. The women seemed to be exchanging birth stories while the men were slapping each other on the back while telling Wade how much his life would change.

Considering Wade's twelve-year-old daughter from his first marriage sat in the hospital bed next to Ronnie, cooing over her new baby brother, that seemed unnecessary.

"Look at this strapping lad." His foster father placed the baby into Wylie's arms. "That's Gary."

Gary. A no-nonsense name for a no-nonsense cowboy.

Wylie used to think of himself as no-nonsense. A nonromantic. But as he looked at Gary's cherubic cheeks, dark lashes, and puckering lips, a part of him melted.

I want this.

He'd wanted this with Hazel. Babies with purplish-gray eyes and strawberry blond hair. Sharp cookies that would fill his heart and arms with love. Family to come home to. Family to pass on his love of animals and science to. Family—

"Wylie?" Ronnie had wheeled her IV pole over to him. She wore a long, fuzzy pink bathrobe over a pair of bootie slippers. Her dark hair was in a neat braid. She looked more put-together than he felt, which seemed pretty amazing since she'd just pushed out a little human being since he'd seen her four or five hours ago.

"Congratulations," Wylie mumbled. "He's perfect."

"But you're not." Ronnie eased the baby into her arms, and then transferred him into Wade's. "Walk with me." She took hold of Wylie's arm, wheeling that IV pole with the other hand.

"Should you be walking?" Wylie glanced over his shoulder but no one in her hospital room seemed concerned.

"They want me to walk every hour or so." She headed toward the far end of the hallway, away from the nurses' station and the elevator. "Tell me what happened tonight."

And Wylie told her. Not about the woman who'd fled upon laying eyes on him. But about falling in love with Hazel and having the rug pulled out from under him.

"I knew I was right about the boots," Ronnie said absently, as they walked slowly back toward her room. "I heard around town that you and Hazel were falling for each other. I imagined I saw it when you two were together." She smiled up at him apologetically. "And I hoped you'd find a way to work things out but... I'm sorry. I'm too late."

"No need to apologize," Wylie said in a voice roughed by loss.

"And now, we need to think about what to do next."

"Next?" Wylie stared at his friend in disbelief. "This is nearly every veterinarian's dream. I have to say goodbye to Hazel and wish her well. And you need to take time off for maternity leave."

"Love doesn't just give up, Wylie." Ronnie drew him to a stop a few feet from her door.

Inside the room, the conversations were still exuberant, at odds with Wylie's mood.

"Why can't Hazel come back to you after her residency?" Ronnie asked.

"Because she'll be a rock star surgeon." Wylie shook his head. "She'll garner an incredible salary at the most exclusive veterinary surgery centers in the world. Coming back here would be a step down. And if she returns to a small practice, she told me it would be her mother's."

There were calls for Ronnie to rejoin the revelers.

Wade came to stand in the doorway, an unlit cigar in his mouth. "Time to rest, honey."

"In a minute." Ronnie's smile was tender. "Wylie, we'll talk later."

Wylie wasn't going to hold his breath.

"Hey, Mom." Hazel's smile felt brittle as her video call connected. She sat cross-legged on her bed with the door closed, although her window was open since it still smelled like burnt pork chops. "You'll never guess what happened."

"You've decided to come home to California and complete your residency here?" Mom was nothing if not predictable. "Your room is still available."

"No." Hazel explained about the opportunity in Newmarket. "This is my chance to learn from the best and honor Mike."

"I'm... I'm happy for you," Mom said slowly, with an obviously forced smile. "What does Miss Maisey have to say about that?"

Hazel's bedroom door was flung open.

Maisey walked in, followed by Fluffy. "Miss Maisey has only just been told. Is that why the boss was upset and walked out at dinner? Because you're bailing on us?"

"There's the answer to your question, Mom."

Hazel turned her phone to capture Maisey in all her affront.

"I can't say as I blame them for being upset when you agreed to work there for a year," Mom said, not without an edge to her words. "There might be something I can do but... Hi, Miss Maisey. I'm so sorry about this."

"I knew your mother would be on my side." Maisey sat down on the corner of Hazel's bed, then picked up Fluffy to put her in her lap. "Tell her not to leave, Deborah."

"I can't do that."

At her mother's words, Hazel turned the phone back to herself. "Mom?"

"This was your dream and Mike's, sweetie." Mom looked weary and alone. "And considering how rare dreams come true, you shouldn't let anyone or anything stand in your way."

"Not even love?" Hazel asked in a whisper, tears filling her eyes.

Maisey gasped, clutching Fluffy so tight that the little hairless Chihuahua growled.

"Not even love," Mom confirmed, looking just as teary. "But you knew that already, didn't you? You've always been so down-to-earth."

Hazel nodded. "More's the pity."

They talked for a few minutes more. All the while, Maisey became more and more agitated.

When Hazel finally hung up, Maisey blurted, "You didn't even bake the boss any cookies. I knew you two were becoming good friends. I thought it was because you were both doctors. But... How can you have fallen in love with him?"

"I don't know." Hazel's hands flailed helplessly. "We spent a lot of time walking together. And running into each other around town. And..." Her throat threatened to close, clogged as it was with tears. "Today, I just looked at him and I knew..."

"Before or after that call that made him stomp off?"

"Before."

Maisey nodded, staring out the window. "You've put us all in a pickle."

Hazel might have laughed at Maisey's inclusion of herself in the angst of the situation had she not been holding the pieces of her broken heart together by sheer force of will.

"Besides all the paperwork," Maisey began, "we started offering acupuncture. I ordered herbs and natural shampoos. Now I'm going to have to learn how to sell those things and the boss is going to have to learn how to stick those needles into the right places, although he probably won't be thanking you for it." Maisey set Fluffy down, got to her feet, and walked toward the door. "Thanks for nothing. I knew you were trouble from the moment you walked in."

"Likewise," Hazel murmured, although she was thinking about the moment she set eyes on Wylie.

THE NEXT MORNING, Hazel was just finishing up giving booster shots to a puppy when Maisey burst into the exam room.

"There's been a livestock accident at the fairgrounds." Maisey looked white. "You need to get over there right away with the mobile unit." She handed Hazel the keys.

"Okay." Hazel hurried into the lab to grab her backpack, stuffing her stethoscope into it. "Wasn't Wylie supposed to be judging livestock this morning?"

"He was. He is." Maisey seemed flustered. "Janie Crocket called and said they wanted you down there."

Hazel drove above the speed limit to the fairgrounds, then ran through the livestock gates with her backpack and the mobile unit's equipment bag.

Janie Crocket was waiting just inside the gate. "It's Hard Nose. He bolted from Tad and tried to leap out of the show arena. I think he broke his leg and..." The normally stoic Janie sobbed. "It'll break Tad's heart to put him down. But that's what we have to do, isn't it?"

"Not always. Take me to him." Hazel followed Janie to a shady spot on the far side of the empty show arena where Tad stood holding Hard Nose's lead rope.

The teen wiped at his cheeks when they approached. "I'm sorry."

"Nothing to be sorry about when accidents happen." Hazel put down her bags and moved closer to examine the bull's rear leg, which dangled at an awkward angle, possibly indicating a clean break since no bone protruded through his dark hide. "I think I can set this. But then he's going to need to be kept quiet and still in a stall for at least eight weeks, if not longer."

Tad buried his face in the bull's neck and started crying. "You're gonna be okay, buddy."

"A butcher from Friar's Creek offered to buy him," Janie explained quietly. "We're a bit fragile."

"I understand," Hazel said quietly, feeling just as brittle.

Hard Nose swung his head around to nuzzle Hazel's scrub top.

"Yes. I brought you treats." Hazel gave the bull an oat cube before rummaging around in her backpack for something to give him to stay calm while she worked. Even as her hands went on autopilot search, her mind was casting about for what she'd need to set the bull's leg. She'd seen some steel rods in the back of the mobile unit. She'd need that and plenty of sturdy tape, plus some kind of padding. Her eye caught on a spot of red beneath the bull's hoof. "Is that blood?"

"There's a sliver of bone protruding up high on his inner leg," Tad sniffed. "Is that bad?"

It was. But it was also treatable. For now, Hazel just wanted everyone to remain calm, including herself. "How did this happen?"

"We were competing. Hard Nose was doing great." Tad lifted his head. "He stood still when I asked him and ignored all the other contestants."

"He was a champ," Janie agreed, wiping a tear from her cheek. "Until he wasn't."

"The judge asked us to go around the ring a second time." Tad looked like he was going to dissolve into tears again. "We walked by someone with a bucket of popcorn close to the fence and..."

"He thought someone should share their popcorn?" Hazel guessed.

Tad nodded. "He bolted. And Doc Newland... He stepped in his way."

"The same way you did the other morning," Janie added.

Hazel stopped rummaging in her bag. She almost stopped breathing. Despite the heat... Despite the layers of clothing she wore... Hazel felt cold. "Wylie was in the ring?"

Where is Wylie?

Tad was nodding. Big, sweeping nods. "But Hard Nose just kept running."

"Ran right through him," Janie said, sniffing. "I heard the snap."

"What snap?" Hazel got to her feet, but she leaned on the bull for support because she didn't feel steady. Because Wylie...

"Bones," Tad whispered, and then he started crying again.

"They want us to put Hard Nose down, as if they

know him better than we do," Janie said in a low voice. "They're saying he's dangerous."

Snap, they said.

Dangerous, they said.

Wylie...

Hazel glanced around, not seeing the cowboy of her heart's desire. She had to swallow twice before she could ask, "Where's Wylie?"

"They took him away in an ambulance a few minutes before you got here." Janie slipped her arm around Tad's waist. "The fair director said we had to make a decision but... Hard Nose is..."

"He's family," Tad finished his mother's sentence. "And I knew you'd know what to do because..." He swallowed thickly. "...you're his doctor."

"That I am," Hazel said in a hoarse voice she didn't recognize.

"Here comes the death squad now." Janie gestured toward a group of approaching cowboys. "It's the fair committee."

"The fair committee..." Hazel noticed that behind all those cowboys there was a small, elderly cowgirl dressed in bright colors. She had a little poodle trotting at her side. Hazel turned to the Crockets. "Nobody's putting Hard Nose down."

And she meant it. Wylie would agree.

But it took a lot of convincing. A lot.

It probably didn't help that Wylie wasn't around to back Hazel up. Or that several committee members were worried about insurance premiums rising sharply because of the accident. They felt putting an end to Hard Nose would reassure the insurance company that the fair would make difficult decisions to prevent further incidents. And claims.

But finally, Hazel convinced the fair committee to allow her to set the bull's leg on-site. They had a squeeze chute for livestock procedures. And they had a crowd of folks who were curious about veterinary surgery. A crowd of folks willing to pay for admission to see Hazel work.

And that seemed to tip the odds in Hard Nose's favor.

"WE SHOULD BE at the hospital," Maisey said when she showed up to assist Hazel. "They're setting Wylie's leg in surgery." It must be bad. She'd called him Wylie, not boss or doc. "Broke in more than one place. He'll want to see us when he's out."

Hazel didn't share that sentiment. Wylie hadn't shown up for her morning walk with Budge. Maybe he was taking time to think, the way he had after their first kiss. Or maybe he didn't want to see Hazel ever again.

Hazel fixed Maisey with a hard stare. "Do you want him to wake up and ask us what happened to Hard Nose and…" She couldn't finish, could barely swallow. "You know he'd want us to do this. You know he would."

"He wouldn't want you to do it like this. They've

made this into a circus event." Maisey swung her finger around, pointing at their audience as if reprimanding them. But when she turned back to Hazel, she looked all business. "Have you done this surgery before?"

Hazel nodded. She didn't admit that it had been once and she'd performed it on a horse with a much smaller frame and in front of a much smaller audience and her mentor professor assisting her. No sense dampening the spirits of her vet tech when they were already dangerously low, even for her.

"Everything's going to be just fine." Tad stood at his bull's head. "Just fine." That had been his mantra for the past hour while Hazel had started an IV and administered a local anesthetic.

"Everything's going to be okay." Hazel took up Tad's optimism. Hard Nose... Wylie... Hazel would like to believe that. Hazel *had to* believe that. Or she was going to botch this procedure up completely.

"Whenever you're ready, Dr. Hughes." Maisey took her position at the equipment tray.

"Let's do this." Hazel took her time, cleaning out the wound where a shard of bone had pierced the bull's inner thigh. Thankfully, the bleeding had slowed to a slight ooze. But Hazel's hands shook. Her hands never shook.

Everything is going to be okay.
Not if she didn't calm down.
"What is she doing?" someone asked.

"I can't see," complained someone else.

"I thought she'd tell us what she was doing," another upset audience member griped.

Hazel straightened, staring at Maisey.

"What?" Maisey asked.

"We have an audience." Her audience was here to learn. Just as they had at university. "Someone get me a microphone. Hands-free."

Hazel's nerves settled. Her hands steadied. The world took on a familiar feel.

Hazel was going to make Wylie proud.

CHAPTER SIXTEEN

WYLIE WOKE UP to the murmur of voices and a lot of murky light, as if he were stranded down deep in a tunnel.

He shut his eyes, cold and confused.

"He's waking up." That was his foster father's voice.

A hand squeezed his. A calloused hand.

Not Hazel's hand.

Wylie struggled for a normal breath of air, one taken without grief or regret. He'd vowed the other night at Brown's Brewery to let Hazel go. Off to England. Off to make her dreams come true. To honor her brother's memory.

"Wake up, Wylie," Dad said quietly. "We're worried about you."

"Let him take his time." That was his foster mother's voice, always a rock for a large family of cowboys. "He knows we're waiting."

There was a lump in Wylie's throat. *Waiting.*

He had family waiting. Family who'd surround him in a hospital room to cheer him up because…

"I broke my leg," Wylie croaked, his throat raw from the tube they'd stuck down it while he was out. He opened his eyes. "Compound fracture."

He was in the surgery recovery room at the hospital with his foster parents at his side. Worry etched their pale features.

"You broke your leg," Mom repeated, nodding. Her short white hair had more curl to it since she'd gone through cancer treatment last year. But her eyes were still as gentle and understanding. "Must have hurt some."

Wylie nodded, remembering the smack when the runaway bull struck him and the incredible pain when Hard Nose had used his femur like a step-ladder to jump over the arena fence.

"You think you might have listened a time or two when I lectured about the dangers of standing in a bull's way," Dad said, going for humor the way Hazel might have. "It's not like you're a trained rodeo clown."

"I felt like one." Flung to the dirt and trampled on.

"Next time you go judging, we'll put a little face paint on you." Dad chuckled, but it was a stilted, awkward chuckle, as if he was as uncomfortable making jokes about Wylie's injury as he was sitting here helpless at his bedside.

"Might just try that," Wylie whispered, not wanting Dad to feel bad.

A nurse came by to take his vitals, pumping that

blood pressure cuff up high enough to make Wylie want to squirm. She peered at his face while the cuff drained slowly of air. "I'll get him something for the pain."

"I don't want knockout drugs," Wylie called after her. "I'm not feeling pain now."

"You might rethink that as time goes on," she called back. "I can tell it's wearing off."

"Everybody's been worried about you, son," Mom said softly, standing up and fussing with his hair. "You've got a waiting room full of visitors."

"Everybody?" *Hazel?* He wanted to ask.

"That vet you work with is performing surgery on the bull that got you," Dad said, as if reading Wylie's mind.

"He's got a broken leg, too," Mom added, giving up on Wylie's hair and content with smiling down on him. "Maisey went to help her."

"I heard she put up quite the fight to keep that bull from being put down." Dad still held on to Wylie's hand. "Folks in town were surprised given how friendly she always seems."

"She's stubborn," Wylie said, still in his froggy voice. "When am I getting out of here?"

When can I see Hazel?

"Not for a day or two." That was the nurse. He knew her but couldn't remember her name. "It wasn't a clean break. You've got pins."

Wylie recalled something being said to him

about that. But he'd been on painkillers and in a fog since they started him on an IV at the fairgrounds.

"I was serious about not wanting a lot of pain meds." He tried to scowl at the nurse but was afraid he looked more pathetic than intimidating, because she laughed.

"Doctors are always the worst patients." She tsked. "I used to think it was only human doctors but here you are, proving me wrong."

"Ha. Ha." Wylie wasn't giving up. "I meant what I said. I don't like brain fog."

"I'm just following doctor's orders." And it wasn't long after she injected something into Wylie's IV that his eyes closed again.

He heard someone say, "I love you." But he was certain it wasn't Hazel.

THE NEXT TIME Wylie awoke, it was nighttime.

He was in a hospital room with dim lighting and there was a woman in the chair beside him.

For a moment, he thought it was Hazel.

"Look at lucky me," Ronnie whispered, possibly because she had a baby in her arms that she didn't want to wake. She was still attached to an IV, the portable pole parked next to her. "I got the night shift since I knew I'd be awake with the baby anyway. And Sleeping Beauty has finally opened his eyes."

"I'd have opened my eyes a lot sooner if they'd have gone easy on the pain meds." Wylie looked toward the machine attached to his IV tube. "What did they put me on? Morphine? I need to turn down that dial." He reached for the equipment.

"*Dr.* Newland." A woman who looked like Maisey's clone in scrubs came to stand next to his bed, crossing her arms over her chest. "I heard you were going to be a problem."

He tried to shift himself into a sitting position and was immediately reminded of his broken leg, given the sharp pain his movement caused.

"Your patients might not have electric beds." The sour nurse placed the bed's remote control in his hand. "But they probably know better than to try and get up and walk around after surgery."

"Or adjust their pain meds," Ronnie said.

Traitor.

Wylie eased the bed into a near sitting position, swallowing groans the discomfort caused his leg. "When am I..." getting out of here "...going home?" To see Hazel. He was suddenly afraid she'd leave before he could apologize for walking out on her at Brown's Brewery.

"You'll be released as soon as you can safely get out of bed without rebreaking your leg or falling flat on your face." Oh, his nurse was indeed Maisey's sister from another mother. Her barbed bedside manner proved it. "For now, you've got a movement monitor on your bed. If you try and get out before the doctor says you can, a little warning bell goes off at my station." She tucked his linens tighter around him, discouraging movement. "Got it?"

"Do I have a choice?"

His nurse laughed as she walked away.

Wylie stared at Ronnie. "Are all the nurses in the hospital like this?"

"They're dears in the maternity ward." She stared down into Gary's slumbering face. "Hazel wanted you to know that Hard Nose's surgery was successful."

"She's not waiting…somewhere?" This was nearly as disappointing as her leaving because it meant—

"She and Maisey had a big day. Long surgery." Ronnie reached over to touch Wylie's shoulder. "And from what I hear, there was another emergency call after that. I'm sure she'll come visit tomorrow."

When Wylie woke up the next morning, Wade was in his bedside chair holding baby Gary.

"Shouldn't you guys be checked out of here already?" By Wylie's count, it had been at least two days.

"Ronnie developed a blood clot in her arm." Wade looked scared. "She's getting meds to dissolve it but we're here until it's completely gone."

The baby yawned, stretched, then seemed to fall back asleep. Wylie's nurse probably expected him to do the same.

No way.

"When are visiting hours?" The clock read half past seven. At this hour, Hazel and Budge should have completed their walk long ago.

Budge. What's going to happen to him if Hazel leaves?

It was expensive to transport animals across America. It had to be pricey to transport them overseas.

Maybe she'll stay...

Wylie rejected the thought almost immediately. He'd be lucky if Hazel returned to Clementine ever.

Wade rocked the baby from side to side. There were circles under his eyes and lines around his lips. "Maisey said she was going to come by this morning."

"Maisey's morning is closer to eight thirty or nine than seven." His vet tech wasn't a morning person. "What about Hazel?"

"Ronnie told me not to talk about her," Wade said, staring at Wylie and raising his brows.

"Did she leave town?" His heart rate monitor began to beep faster.

"She's not going to leave town until her replacement gets here and you're out of the hospital." Wade's gaze returned to his baby boy. "And that's probably more than Mommy wanted me to say to Uncle Wylie."

Wylie reached for the bed remote. But what

he really wanted, he couldn't see. "Where's my phone?"

"I think our parents took your things home with them—clothes, phone, car keys." Wade kept rocking. "Griff said he was going to buy a kilt for you to go home in. It's doubtful any of your jeans will fit over those pins."

Wylie gritted his teeth. "I'll wear a kilt if someone will just bring me my phone."

Wade scoffed, lowering his face to his baby's. "Funny Uncle Wylie. He thinks Hazel's going to answer his phone calls."

"If she doesn't..." Wylie didn't know how to finish that sentence. He worked his stiff lips into a smile that Hazel would be proud of. "She'll answer." He glanced around the room once more. "Don't I have a landline?"

"Nope."

Their parents entered, each carrying two bouquets of flowers. They were followed by Rose, who also carried two bouquets of flowers. And Maisey, similarly burdened.

"Who spent a fortune on flowers?" Wylie couldn't understand it.

"They're from all your single admirers." Maisey set a bag down on the foot of his bed, her severe expression a sight for sore eyes, especially at such an early hour. "I also brought a tin of fudge, another of sugar cookies, and a very large summer squash." She set the long, yellow gourd near Wylie's good leg.

"I'm not likely to eat the squash raw." Wylie gestured toward it. "Mom?"

"I'll cook it up and bring it back tonight," Mom promised.

While his parents fussed over the baby, Wylie gestured for Maisey to come closer. "How's Hard Nose?"

Maisey rolled her eyes. "That bull is loving all the attention he's getting. He's in a very small pen at the fair. Tad rarely leaves his side. And little kids have been bringing him all sorts of treats. Apples, oat cubes, bouquets of dandelions." She hefted the summer squash, perhaps considering bringing it to the bull.

"And the procedure? Tell me about it."

"She was good." Maisey set the gourd back on the bed. "She closed up the wound and made a Schroeder-Thomas splint. Took us nearly an hour to get it the right size. Had to call on some cowboys in the audience. And when the steel pole wouldn't bend easy, we got Simon Holstead to bring his welding equipment down to the fairgrounds. It was quite the show, especially when we moved him after the splint was set because Hazel worked her acupuncture magic on him, trying to ease the pain of him walking to a new stall."

Wylie would have liked to have seen that.

"We've had loads of calls for acupuncture,"

Maisey went on. "And not just for household pets. Folks want house calls. Got a message on our answering machine that someone's old alpaca needs a treatment. Can you imagine?"

Wylie couldn't. "Where's Ha—"

"Anyway, I've got to run. We're fully booked this morning. When you have a spare moment, you should look into getting your acupuncture certification. Looks like there's a need in town." And without further ado, Maisey hustled out of there.

Leaving Wylie just as lonely for Hazel's company as before.

CHAPTER SEVENTEEN

"He wants to see you," Maisey said for the umpteenth time that day.

"We've been busy, haven't we?" Hazel ascended the stairs to their shared apartment. "And he'll be out soon."

Perhaps when the resident she was trading places with arrived tomorrow.

"He wants to see *you*," Maisey repeated. "I didn't take you for a chicken."

Hazel had been about to flop onto her bed for a power nap. Instead, she turned to face Maisey. "Do you think this is easy for me?"

Fluffy walked over to Maisey and performed a shuddering stretch. She'd benefited from acupuncture.

"Nope." Maisey picked up her dog and headed back down the stairs. "But if you love him, you'll face him."

Hazel sat on the end of her bed, staring at her hands. And when that offered her no answers, she flopped over backward, staring at the ceiling.

There were no answers to be found there either.

"I love him and I'm leaving him. It's as simple as that." Her words echoed in her empty room.

Her phone rang, clanging to announce a video call. It was her mother, of course.

Hazel answered, still lying in defeat on the bed. "Mom, it's been a long day. Don't—"

"Sit up and behave yourself," Mom said in a voice Hazel couldn't recall her using in decades. "I've got Dr. Reed on the other line and I'm about to patch him in."

The video screen split.

Hazel sat up and greeted her mentor professor.

"I've been picking Dr. Reed's brain about our situation," Mom began.

"*Our* situation?" Hazel tried to smile as if her mother wasn't undercutting her somehow. "I'm sorry my mother's been meddling, Dr. Reed."

Mom shushed her. "I've already had a very productive conference with Dr. Reed. He agrees with what I'm about to say."

Dr. Reed straightened his black glasses, nodding.

Who was Hazel to argue?

"I'm all ears."

An hour later, Hazel entered Wylie's hospital room, uncertain of what she was going to say to him or what he'd answer. She'd showered and changed into her yellow sundress, leaving her hair free and uncovered to come see the man she'd fallen in love with.

His room smelled like a flower shop. Looked like one, too. A popular flower shop, given the room was full of visitors. Cowboys and cowgirls of all ages and sizes.

Hazel hesitated. She hadn't imagined an audience or one that didn't immediately make excuses upon seeing her so that she could have time alone with Wylie.

And Wylie...

His normally tan face seemed pale. Wires attached him to several monitors—blood oxygen, heart rate, IV. Wylie was sitting, the bed linens tucked in at his waist. His broken leg sat uncovered on pillows with metal pins sticking from his thigh. Someone had put a blue knit sock on his exposed foot and a hospital blanket over his shoulders.

He held a hand toward her.

"Are you here to say goodbye?" Ronnie asked. She was sitting in a chair, an IV pole of her own beside her.

Everyone seemed to stop talking and stare.

"I'm here..." Hazel's voice was clogged with emotion. She smiled and started over. "I'm here to talk to Wylie."

"Alone," he said, giving her the same measured smile she gave all of them. "Everyone out."

Just about everyone piped up with a loyal, "I'll stay."

"Out," Wylie said, using the hand he'd extended toward Hazel to sweep around the room. "All of you."

Folks said their goodbyes to Wylie, some telling them they'd be outside in the waiting room if he needed them. And then they started filing out, most of them people Hazel had come to know and was fond of.

Piper, raiser of pigmy piglets, and her mother, Allison.

Della-Mae and Izzy, who'd told her the car-struck Biff was thriving and napping with Laramie all the time.

Ronnie, holding a cherubic-looking baby with a dark thatch of hair. Wade following her, pushing her IV pole.

An older man with a white, wide-brimmed cowboy hat stopped to introduce himself. "I'm Frank Harrison. This is my wife, Mary."

"My parents," Wylie murmured.

Mary, an older cowgirl with a kind smile, patted Hazel on the shoulder. "You be gentle with our boy. He's not as tough as he looks."

"No one ever is," Hazel said, waiting until they left to approach Wylie's bedside. She gestured to the dozen or so bouquets. "You're a popular man. I was wondering why we hadn't received any more home-cooked goodies at the clinic. How are you?"

"I'm...*great*," he said, hurt in those bright green eyes as he reached for her hand. But his smile...

His smile was one she knew too well, having practiced it and wielded it numerous times over the years. It said he was okay but not to worry.

Hazel worried anyway. There was a lot riding on this conversation.

"This is goodbye, then?" Wylie said in a soft voice, fingers curling tighter around hers. "Get on with it. Best rip the bandage off quick, as my dad would say."

Hazel sank, half sitting on the mattress next to him. "Oh, Wylie."

He stared at her, refusing to say more.

And Hazel stared back, content to do so for the moment. She didn't see him in a hospital gown with a blanket around his shoulders and wires tangled across his chest. She saw him the way she had a few weeks ago, proud and strong, striding into the clinic as if he was a cowboy, tried and true, set to have things his way and being drawn up short by the woman standing in front of him.

Me.

"You felt it from the start, didn't you?" Hazel said in wonder. "The way I did. Like here was a person I wanted to be with." *My person.* "We've been dancing around the inevitable... Around what felt like concrete boundaries we couldn't cross."

"You don't know how to rip off a bandage, do you?" Wylie sounded pained.

Hazel settled more firmly on his bed. "My mother is selling her practice."

"She's retiring?" That seemed to have caught him by surprise.

"No. She's—"

"Going with you to practice in England." Wylie gave a resigned sigh. "I envy her that."

"No. She's—"

"Why are we talking about your mother?" Wylie blurted, jaw tense and thrust to one side.

"If I could get a word in edgewise, I'd tell you." Hazel laid her palm on Wylie's jaw. He hadn't shaved in days. The dark stubble was stiff, as unyielding as Wylie could be. Not for the first time, Hazel wondered what he was going to reply when she told him—

"Hazel." He covered her hand with his. "It took you two days to come see me."

"You have a busy practice," Hazel reminded him.

"Maisey didn't even email me to ask if you were treating patients right."

Hazel knew him well enough to know that wasn't what was bothering him. So, she kissed him, a brief buss on the lips. And then she sat back, pleased to see his smile was as easygoing as hers felt. "If you have anything else you want to complain about, get it off your chest before I start talking."

"The floor is yours," he said gruffly.

"My mother is going to sell her practice," Hazel

began but paused to see if he was going to interrupt her again.

Wylie raised his brows instead.

"She wants to move to Clementine."

"And retire?" Wylie's brow clouded.

Hazel gently laid a finger over his lips. "Let me finish."

He nodded, smiling broadly when she removed that finger from his tempting lips.

Hazel hesitated, unsure of how to proceed. "This is complicated."

"It's not," Wylie piped up once more. "I love you. You love me. You're going to England and I'll wait here to see what happens when you've finished your residency."

Hazel's grip on his hand loosened. "You'd follow me? You'd give up all this?" She gestured toward the flowers and then toward the door where there just might have been one nosy matchmaker hovering with her baby. "What kind of person would I be to take you away from your family? Or the community that's so important to you?"

"Maybe I should be quiet and let you talk." Because Wylie had no idea what was going on in that pretty head of Hazel's. The more they talked, the less certain he was of the direction she was headed.

Hazel nodded. "I'm going to try this again. I'm going to England." She laid a palm over her heart.

And then she did the oddest thing. She moved that same hand over his heart. "And so are you."

"Hobbling along behind you." He had mixed feelings about that.

"No," Hazel gently corrected, moving that hand up to cup his cheek. "Dr. Reed arranged for you to serve a residency with me."

"Wow…" Wylie couldn't believe it. "I used to dream about working in a place like that."

"I know." Hazel sat back, drawing his hand into her lap. "And according to Dr. Reed, you have the skill to back it up."

"And to do that with you…" It was a dream.

A noise outside in the hallway brought Wylie back to reality.

"But I can't leave my practice."

Hazel grinned. "That's where my mom comes in. And this part, I can't believe. She agreed to run your practice with Maisey while we complete our residencies."

"She's met Maisey, right?"

Hazel nodded. "Only on the phone and video chat but they've formed an odd kind of bond."

There was that sound again from out in the hallway.

Ronnie moved into view. She was jiggling the baby and smiling at Wylie.

"You do want to go…don't you?" Hazel's purplish-gray eyes clouded with doubt. "I love you, Wylie. And I want to spend as much time as possible with you. To create a foundation for love and a future."

"But…" And here, Wylie no longer felt as if this was a good dream. "What about afterward? What happens in Clementine? My family is important to me." Important enough that he didn't want to be tempted to further his training in surgery and then not return.

"Wylie…" Ronnie chastised from the hallway.

Hazel glanced over her shoulder. "It's fine, Ronnie." Then she turned back to face Wylie. "I want to come back here to practice with you. We can offer surgeries that are more complex…maybe convert that empty warehouse next door into a rehabilitation center for animals with more severe injuries."

"But…why? Why would you be willing to settle when you could have a stellar career?"

She lifted his hand, pressing a kiss to his knuckles. "I appreciate you worrying about me but it was never my dream to be the highest-paid veterinarian in the world. I want to learn and improve my skill set. But I want to see my patients grow old and thrive, as well as their owners. Working here has only solidified the importance of being a part of the community, the way I was growing up."

"Yes." Wylie breathed a sigh of relief, thinking of his father's outstanding surgery certificate. Thinking of how much he liked being connected to his clients. "That's it exactly."

"So you'll go with me?" Hazel beamed, belatedly gesturing to his broken leg. "As soon as your leg is good enough to go, that is. Mom's signed up for the jurisprudence exam to be able to practice here but her license won't come in overnight."

"Newmarket, England, here we come." Wylie opened his arms.

Hazel shifted sideways, lying next to him on the bed and filling his arms nicely. "Newmarket, England."

Wylie gathered her close, pressing a kiss on her forehead, hoping the nurse would ignore the increased rhythm of his heart monitor. "There's just one thing you forgot."

"What's that?" Hazel asked.

"Oh, I don't know," he teased, feeling lighter inside than he had in months. "Telling me you love me. Asking me to marry you. Promising we'll have babies someday."

Hazel lifted her head to look him in the eye, expression serious.

Too serious? She'd been uncertain about kids before.

"Dr. Wylie Newland..." Hazel drew a breath. "I love you. I've loved you since you stood before me smelling of horse sweat and prairie dirt. I want to marry you and have your babies...all in good time."

"That's good enough for me, love." Wylie brought her back down into his arms.

Out in the hallway, Ronnie giggled. "Way to go, Hazel."

"Ronnie, you can go now." Wylie raised his voice, also raising Hazel's chin so her lips were closer to his. "Your services are no longer required."

"What did I tell you, Wade?" Ronnie turned, disappearing from sight. "Another happy customer."

Wade's laughter echoed Wylie's mood—happy.

Happy days and the love ahead of them were all Wylie could think of as he kissed Hazel.

And he didn't stop kissing her until the nurse came to see why his heart monitor was beeping so fast.

EPILOGUE

One year later

"Mom, you've fluffed my skirt so many times that I expect it to float away like a balloon." Hazel turned to smile at her mother.

They stood in the church vestibule in Clementine waiting to hear the organ music to cue the bridal party's entry.

"I'm just happy we're having a church wedding with a traditional wedding dress." Mom got to her feet. She looked pretty in her lavender dress with her freshly highlighted hair pulled into a sophisticated swirl at the base of her neck.

"We half expected you to want to ride Budge down the wedding aisle." Maisey handed Mom a bridesmaid bouquet, keeping one for herself.

The two women and Hazel's older sister, Nina, were standing beside Hazel on the altar today. Her father waited on the other side of the door with Nina.

"They should have gotten married outdoors."

Mom fussed with the side of Hazel's white lace wedding gown. "It's a crush out there. And hot."

"That's what comes of not sending out formal wedding invitations." Maisey fiddled with the pearl comb holding Hazel's hair away from her face. "Everybody feels like they can show up."

"Good. Besides, Wylie has a large family," Hazel said in his defense. "He didn't want to exclude anyone."

Luckily, they were having a reception outside at the Done Roamin' Ranch.

They'd only returned to the States a week ago. But Wylie and Hazel were ready to start building their lives together.

"He excluded Fluffy," Maisey said gruffly.

"I told you to bring her to the reception." Hazel gave the ornery older woman a side hug. "She'll be a hit with all those kids on the dance floor. It'll be you and Rose wheeling dogs around in strollers." Along with all the babies and tots. Wylie's extended family seemed to be growing leaps and bounds.

"Oh, and Dr. Reed flew in," Mom said in a low tone.

"You don't have to be coy." Hazel hugged her mother next. "Maisey spilled the beans about you and Dr. Reed's long-distance romance." Her mentor professor had visited Clementine many times during Hazel and Wylie's time in England. Together, he and Mom had spruced up the clinic—new sign, new coat of paint, new technology (despite Maisey's protests).

Mom's cheeks blossomed an attractive pink. "We're good friends."

Maisey and Hazel laughed.

There was a lot of genuine laughter in Hazel's life lately. And it was because of the love she'd found with Wylie. He was the grounding she'd needed to soar. And she... Hazel liked to think she gave Wylie space to rest and have fun. They'd learned a tremendous amount in England. But they'd grown closer, too.

"It's time," Dad said, knocking on the door.

The organist began playing and her bridesmaids assembled. Mom and Maisey went through the door, joining Nina in a slow walk to the altar.

Dad held out his arm.

Hazel clutched her bouquet, ready to march down that aisle and see what wonderful surprises a future with Wylie would bring.

WYLIE STOOD AT the altar with Wade, Griff, and his foster father.

The organist was playing, and the guests were angling this way and that, trying to get a good look at the bridesmaids entering the church proper.

Maisey, who'd had her white hair done for the first time in his memory. She looked happier than he'd ever seen her before.

Hazel's mother Deborah, smiling at Dr. Reed as

she walked past his pew. She'd made a home for herself here in Clementine.

Nina, Hazel's older sister, a blonder, taller version of his fiancée, who carried herself with cool sophistication but was warm and loving to her family.

And then the organ music changed and the wedding march began.

Wade laid his hand on Wylie's shoulder and whispered, "This is it."

The wedding guests stood, some smiling Wylie's way before turning to look for his bride-to-be.

The empty space at the end of the aisle filled with a vision. *The vision.* Wylie's ideal soulmate—Hazel.

She was swathed in creamy white lace. Her strawberry blond hair was piled high on her head. She was beautiful. But she was always beautiful to him.

Their eyes met the way they had on the first day she'd stepped into his clinic. But this time, their smiles weren't guarded and polite. This time, their smiles were open, joyful, bursting with love.

And when Hazel reached the steps to the altar. When her father kissed her cheek and passed her hand to Wylie's. That's when a bit of Hazel's characteristic mischief returned to her gaze.

"We have a couple more last-minute wedding guests," Hazel told Wylie, nodding toward Russ.

The teenager stood at the side entrance in a blue suit that was too big for him.

Russ opened the door, revealing Budge, looking ten years younger than this time last year, Wylie noted, and Fluffy, who sat in a doll stroller with a lavender bow around her neck.

Their friends and family chuckled, none louder than Maisey.

"It's important to include family at events like these," Hazel said, love shining in her distinctive gray eyes. "The family you're born with and the family you find along the way."

"Human and otherwise." Wylie nodded.

Hazel would never have checked the boxes on the list Wylie had tried to give to Ronnie last year. She'd never be just a cowgirl, just a veterinarian, or just his wife. She'd never be *just* anything.

Other than the love of his life.

* * * * *

*For more romances in The Cowboy Academy miniseries from author Melinda Curtis and Harlequin Heartwarming,
visit www.Harlequin.com today!*

Harlequin Reader Service

Enjoyed your book?

Try the perfect subscription for Romance readers and get more great books like this delivered right to your door.

See why over 10+ million readers have tried Harlequin Reader Service.

Start with a Free Welcome Collection with free books and a gift—valued over $20.

Choose any series in print or ebook.
See website for details and order today:

TryReaderService.com/subscriptions